They bound Stork, spread-eagle, on the bottom bunk. Stuffing his mouth with a scrap of cloth, Aref squatted at his midsection and withdrew a razor-sharp stiletto.

J.C. began to sweat. Glancing at Aref's leering face, he nearly fainted. Obscene noises issued from a gaping red cavity where his tongue should have been. The stiletto flashed in the glare of the electric bulb as Stork groaned and opened his eyes.

Aref severed Stork's apron strings as if opening a gift. The heavy green fabric parted as he lightly ran the knife down past Stork's crotch.

Realizing that he was unarmed and unable to control Aref, J.C. pleaded with Stork, "Don't scream. Please, don't scream. I'll take the gag out so you can answer some questions, but promise not to scream."

Frantically nodding his head, Stork kept his eye on the knife.

Using the tip of the blade, Aref flicked out the gag and held it aloft.

"Where is it?" Raising himself up on his knees so that his face was near Stork's, J.C.'s voice was hoarse with fear, "Where's the Punjat's Ruby?"

ED MCBAIN'S MYSTERIES

JACK AND THE BEANSTALK   (17-083, $3.95)
Jack's dead, stabbed fourteen times. And thirty-six thousand's missing in cash. Matthew's questions are turning up some long-buried pasts, a second dead body, and some beautiful suspects. Like Sunny, Jack's sister, a surfer boy's fantasy, a delicious girl with some unsavory secrets.

BEAUTY AND THE BEAST   (17-134, $3.95)
She was spectacular—an unforgettable beauty with exquisite features. On Monday, the same woman appeared in Hope's law office to file a complaint. She had been badly beaten—a mass of purple bruises with one eye swollen completely shut. And she wanted her husband put away before something worse happened. Her body was discovered on Tuesday, bound with wire coat hangers and burned to a crisp. But her husband—big, and monstrously ugly—denies the charge.

A MISS DANFORTH MYSTERY
THE PUNJAT'S RUBY

MARIAN J. A.
JACKSON

PINNACLE BOOKS
WINDSOR PUBLISHING CORP.

PINNACLE BOOKS

are published by

Windsor Publishing Corp.
475 Park Avenue South
New York, NY 10016

First printing: April, 1990

Printed in the United States of America

To
J. T. R.

Detection is, or ought to be, an exact science, and should be treated in the same cold and unemotional manner. . . . to tinge it with romanticism . . . produces much the same effect as if you worked a love story or an elopement into the fifth proposition of Euclid.

Arthur Conan Doyle
The Sign of the Four

CAST OF CHARACTERS
(In Order of Appearance)

Abigail Patience Danforth	A young lady on the verge of her debut
Herbert Greenough Smith	Dr. Arthur Conan Doyle's editor
Dr. Arthur Conan Doyle	Author, and creator of Sherlock Holmes
Jacqueline	Abigail's lady's maid
Rodney Charles Danforth	Abigail's brother (second-born twin)
Kinkade	Mr. Danforth's valet
Lady Pepper	Abigail's hostess in London
Gilda Arrington	Houseguest at Hunterswell House
The Marchioness of Hunterswell	Lord Frederick's mother
Frederick Stuart Seymour, The Earl of Hunterswell	Abigail's suitor
Stork	Lord Frederick's valet
Maximilian Driscoll	Lord Frederick's friend
J.C.	Maximilian Driscoll's valet
Fergus Buchanan	Lord Frederick's friend
Maurice	Fergus Buchanan's valet
The Marquess of Hunterswell	Lord Frederick's father
Mark Twain	Most famous toastmaster in Europe
The Nawab Ahanti Khabir Abdulsamad	Burmese Prince

Aref	The Nawab's nephew
Andrew Benjamin Danforth	Abigail's father
Andrew Benjamin Danforth, Jr.	Abigail's brother (first born twin)
Maude Cunningham	Abigail's chaperon in New York
Molly O'Brien	Leader of Gramercy Park Irregulars
William Gillette	Star of the play, *Sherlock Holmes*
Various speaking parts and walk-ons	

ACKNOWLEDGMENTS

Without free access to the New York Public Library's newspapers, magazines, photographs, and books, I literally could not have written this book. Thank you for being there.

I am also immensely grateful to my agent Elizabeth Backman for all of her efforts in my behalf.

I would also like to thank Jon L. Lellenberg, editor of *The Quest for Sir Arthur Conan Doyle* (Southern Illinois University Press, 1987), for his invaluable assistance in making the scenes with Greenough Smith and Dr. Conan Doyle as realistic as possible, even though this book is entirely a work of fiction.

Preface

A straight line extends indefinitely far in each direction.

Euclid

When he could stop screaming, the tormented man began to babble.

With a slight smile to celebrate the knowledge that he had finally broken his enemy, the fat man adjusted his saffron robes to more comfortably accommodate his girth while he waited for the incoherent sobs to subside. Soon now, the Punjat Ruby would be his. Placing a clove in his cheek, he sighed as its pungent flavor soothed his excited nerves.

Prologue

If equals be subtracted from equals, the remainders are equals.

Euclid

"Then it is true, Mr. Greenough Smith. Sherlock Holmes is not merely dead, he never existed?" Abigail Danforth steeled herself against the answer she now knew to be inevitable. "Dr. Watson does not exist?"

"That, indeed, is the truth of the matter, Miss Danforth." Mr. Herbert Greenough Smith peered impassively through his rimless pince-nez at the young lady seated beside his large, cluttered desk at *The Strand Magazine*. "Sherlock Holmes was the creation of Dr. Arthur Conan Doyle, not Dr. Watson."

"How foolish of me." Time had not yet chiseled the youthful curve from Abigail's cheeks, which burned with embarrassment. Still, she held her head and a huge, stylishly befeathered hat, at that self-assured angle of a Gibson portrait. Although her nose did not tilt at the tip the way that artist would have drawn it, the clear line of her jaw could have come from his pen. Her hands were folded demurely in her lap and, peeking from the hem of the voluminous skirt of her fur-trimmed cloak, the toes of her boots exactly matched the shade of her skintight gloves. The wasp-waisted vogue suited her slender figure, but she was rather more radiant with health than was fashionable.

15

"You need not be embarrassed," Greenough Smith said with a small, dry smile that his trim moustache did nothing to conceal. "You are not the first, my dear Miss Danforth, and I daresay, you'll not be the last to be taken in by Dr. Conan Doyle's creations."

"And I daresay," Abigail's smile was rueful as she mimicked his English pronunciation before continuing in her natural American accent, "the neighbors on Baker Street had a good laugh watching me pace up and down for the most part of an hour, peering into doorways, trying to locate 221B, all the while my chaperon is fuming away." With a tilt of her head she indicated the gray-clad lady, her face a mask of disapproval, seated in a straight-backed chair by the bookcase opposite his desk.

Greenough Smith nodded expressionlessly in the chaperon's direction, but the good lady ignored him.

"However, more than simply embarrassed, I must admit the news saddens me." Abigail's dark eyes were somber as she continued, "I feel much the same as I did when I discovered that Father Christmas was not real."

Without deigning to comment, having heard many similar sentiments, Greenough Smith placed both hands on his desk, preparing to stand and call their interview to an end.

Catching his signal at once, the chaperon stood.

Seeming not to notice their impending dismissal, Abigail ignored his cue and remained seated. Clearing her throat with a dainty gesture of gloved fingertips to lips, she said, "I wonder, my dear Mr. Greenough Smith, if I might trouble you for an introduction to Dr. Conan Doyle."

"To what purpose?" Compelled by good manners to stand because of the chaperon, Greenough Smith stared down at Abigail. "Dr. Conan Doyle is a very busy gentleman, as you can well imagine." Realizing how overbearing he must sound, and appear, to the obviously well-born young lady as he towered over her, Smith softened his tone somewhat. "That is to say, why were you seeking out Dr. Watson? Are you in some difficulty?"

"O no, kind sir, I am in no danger." Abigail smiled winsomely as she gazed up at him from underneath the brim of her hat in her most captivating manner, resolutely keeping her seat. "Although the matter is of grave importance to me." By an almost imperceptible nod and raised eyebrow, she intimated that the chaperon who remained standing behind her was the reason for her next remark as she continued, "I would prefer, if I may, to keep the matter private."

Intrigued in spite of himself, Greenough Smith indicated with a somewhat impatient wave of his hand that the lady should take her seat as he resumed his. "That is quite impossible, my dear Miss Danforth," he said, his conspiratorial tone a futile attempt at excluding the chaperon as, tight-lipped and with an annoyed rustling of petticoats, she sat. "I would need to know the purpose behind your seeking an interview."

"I do not suppose he would see me because I am a devoted admirer of Sherlock Holmes—and Dr. Watson?"

Greenough Smith's barely perceptible frown and subtle shrug as he leaned back in his chair was as eloquent as any spoken refusal.

"Very well then." With a resigned glance at the wary and reserved editor, Abigail sighed. "When Mr. Holmes spoke of his entire life being one long effort to escape from the commonplaces of existence, I felt he spoke my own heart." Once again, the expression in her eyes grew somber as she gazed at her hands in her lap and continued, "An acute melancholy overwhelms me when I contemplate what is in store for me upon my return to New York—an endless circle of calls, dinner parties, and balls, all attended by the same people discussing all the same topics." Again, she sighed, more heavily this time. "And then my debut." She fell silent.

"And then marriage, of course?" Greenough Smith encouraged her to continue.

Abigail nodded wordlessly. She had told no one of her dream. If Dr. Watson and Sherlock Holmes were fiction, then she needs must share her secret with their creator, not this editor. Except for the social necessities, she did not care for dissembling and was trying to think of something to say to convince him to grant her an interview without revealing her true reason when Greenough Smith spoke.

Mistaking her silence for that most highly prized of feminine virtues, modesty, his tone was knowing as he said, "And so you wish to occupy yourself and try your hand at writing?"

"Oh my dear Mr. Greenough Smith." With a shy smile, she fluttered her lashes bashfully. "How did you ever guess?" Delighted that he was so wide of the mark, and relieved that she'd not had to make up the lie herself, she continued, "How terribly clever you are."

Greenough Smith confessed his pleasure at the compliment with a slight twitch of his lips.

Having taken note of Greenough Smith's genteel Englishman's demeanor, Abigail surmised that he might be more amenable to assisting a member of the nobility than a mere commoner, and a foreigner at that. Therefore, as she swiftly embellished upon his guess, she let it slip, blushing prettily, that her dilemma involved none other than one of the most desirable bachelors in England, Frederick, Lord Hunterswell, who would be pursuing her to New York to petition her father for her hand. While neglecting to mention that she'd not yet made up her mind about marrying the future marquess, she made it clear that she'd be ever so grateful for whatever assistance he could extend to a potential marchioness.

And thus Greenough Smith was beguiled into arranging an appointment for Miss Abigail Patience Danforth to meet Dr. A. Conan Doyle, the master storyteller.

Abigail was not, by nature, timid, but as the train sped through that uncommonly mild December day in 1899 toward Hindhead, Surrey, and her appointment with Dr. A. Conan Doyle at Undershaw, his home, the qualms that had kept her awake most of the night, returned.

She knew beyond doubt what her father's response would be were she to so much as mention her dream to him. First, a red-faced display of temper accompanied by shouting, followed by days—or weeks, depending upon how injured he deemed himself to be—of stern silence to insure that she would never again broach the subject. Forever after, she would be spied upon by servants who'd be paid a little extra to supply him with proof that she was not daring to disobey him. And obey him, she must. Or marry, and obey a husband.

What if Dr. Conan Doyle responded in like manner? What if—for her own good, of course—he were to write to her father and tell him her secret? Should he commit such a perfidious deed, it would seal her fate.

Staring out of the window of the speeding train, she chafed at the presence of her new maid, Jacqueline. In an effort to have an ally in the household when she returned home, she had hired the young Frenchwoman without her father's formal approval. By pretending that their errand was a last-minute shopping trip, with Jacqueline as chaperon Abigail had been able to escape the watchful eye of her hostess, Lady Pepper. She'd sworn Jacqueline to secrecy about their true destination without mentioning the reason for their journey, but with Jacqueline as witness, it was now impossible to return to London before her interview with Conan Doyle without suffering an intolerable loss of face.

All too soon they were at the station, and it was by sheer force of will that Abigail relinquished her doubts to the pleasures of the jingling harness and smartly trotting pair as Holden, Conan Doyle's chauffeur, drove them through the beautiful, rolling countryside toward Undershaw. But as the landau began its descent into the long drive through a veritable forest of trees and bushes toward the forecourt of the sprawling, two-storied brick edifice crowned by red-tiled gables, her feeling of dread returned in full force. Her heart sank as they entered the great receiving hall with its stained-glass windows emblazoning the Doyle family's heraldic shields, and she finally realized the root cause of her fears. She was an imposter. She had gained this meeting under false pretenses. No matter that Greenough Smith had misguessed her purpose, how was she going to get past the lie to the truth without Conan Doyle's dismissing her out of hand?

She immediately discarded the idea of brazening her way through by pretending a passion for writing. Although a voracious reader, she scarcely had patience to put ink to paper to issue invitations, or to pen the innumerable requisite bread-and-butter notes. She was perpetually behind in her correspondence with her father and brothers, and hadn't the slightest desire to keep a diary, much less write a novel. Almost numb with panic as Jacqueline was ushered off to the nether regions of the house, Abigail was escorted into the drawing room to await her host.

The spacious, wood-paneled room was encircled by a high, fitted shelf displaying artifacts from faraway places as diverse as the Arctic, Egypt, Switzerland, and several that seemed to have come from America. She was surprised to note that while the graciously furnished, light-filled room was no doubt intended to be formal, errant rugby and cricket balls had escaped their proper place in the household to rest beside a group of chairs and underneath a side table. In her father's house, such untidiness would be just cause for a supperless bedtime. Wondering what Conan Doyle's reaction was going to be when he saw them, she was strolling toward an alcove on the far side of the room where a coal fire was burning briskly in a deep-set fireplace, which was flanked by wing chairs, when the door swung wide. She whirled around.

A robust man as large as her father strode toward her, hand outstretched. "So sorry to have kept you waiting, Miss Danforth!" he said heartily. His energy filled the room.

But size was Conan Doyle's only resemblance to her father. Dressed casually for the country, his tweeds, with matching waistcoat and conservative cravat, bespoke a desire for comfort rather than devotion to the latest fashion. His generous hair looked as though he might have recently run a hand through it, a gesture her father would never make. Abigail had no doubt that his large moustache, with tips waxed to scythelike perfection, concealed a smile, the expression in his eyes was so friendly.

"Dr. Conan Doyle." She managed a tremulous smile. Hoping that he could not detect the trembling of her hand, she barely caught herself before curtsying like a child greeting her elders. With a formal nod, she relied upon the enormous brim of her elaborate hat to cast doubt upon her years. "How terribly kind of you to see me."

She had carefully chosen her plain suit of cinnamon gabardine to enhance the seriousness of her errand, its only adornment being a scrollwork of braid on the large lapels, which repeated itself down the center and around the hem of the stylishly wide skirt. A cameo broach nestling in the lace at her throat and pearls dangling from her ears were her only jewelry, and, as was her habit for morning calls, her glove and boot leather matched. Having surrendered her muff with her cloak in the receiving hall, only her reticule and fan hung from her wrist.

Releasing her hand, Conan Doyle indicated that she should continue to the fireside and that he would follow. He had received the clipping from *The Times* that Greenough Smith had sent, announcing that Abigail was to be among the guests who'd be dining with the marquess and marchioness at Hunterswell House this Saturday, with no less a personage than His Royal Highness, the Prince of Wales, as guest of honor. Europe's most celebrated toastmaster, Mark Twain, was to be in attendance as well, as was his Highness, the Nawab Ahanti Khabir Abdulsamad. Heady company. And yet she seemed flustered at meeting *him,* a mere writer, albeit a successful, if not to say, famous, one. In light of her lofty connections, he was flattered by her charmingly feminine agitation. Annoyance at his editor's foisting a dilettante heiress upon him, especially since he'd neglected to post a sample of her writing along with the column of gossip, abated somewhat.

Waiting until she was settled in one of the wing chairs by the fire before seating himself in the chair opposite, he set about putting Abigail at her ease by getting her to talk about herself, hoping to be rid of her before tea. "America is one of my favorite countries," he said sincerely. "May I ask

21

what took you away from such an exciting home as New York?''

''My mother died when I was born, and father has not remarried,'' Abigail replied with a small smile to indicate that she was quite used to the loss. ''Father despaired of raising me to proper ladyhood in the same household with my older twin brothers. Needing them nearby for business, he sent me to stay with Lord and Lady Pepper while I continued my education in Europe.''

Duly noting her lack of self-pity and concise manner of speaking, he continued, ''My estimable editor tells me you want to be a writer.'' Although expecting a brief answer, he leaned back in his chair as if getting comfortable to listen indefinitely. ''And what, my dear girl, have you written?''

Abigail liked him at once, which only served to heighten her remorse at being an imposter. Stalling for time, she said, ''No one could ever write anything to equal your stories of Sherlock Holmes.''

Irritated anew that she'd chosen his tiresome detective to praise out of all the characters he had created, he struck the soft arm of the chair with his palm as he exclaimed, ''Oh, a pox upon Holmes!'' Frowning, he added, ''I killed him over six years ago, and as far as I am concerned, he is dead forever.''

''But, sir—'' She unfurled her fan and fluttered it nervously. ''I am given to understand that William Gillette is enjoying great success in New York in your new play, *Sherlock Holmes.*''

''That play is more Gillette's invention than mine,'' he said gruffly. ''I have no intention of ever writing about Holmes again.''

Astonished by the vehemence of his reaction, Abigail hastened to add, ''Oh, sir, I pray you, do not feel thus.'' She leaned forward eagerly. ''Sherlock Holmes is my inspiration!''

''That is a capital mistake, my dear Miss Danforth,'' he said with a reproving shake of his head and an admonishing finger. ''You must write about what you know.''

''Ah, but, Dr. Conan Doyle, I fear I have misled you.''

She stilled her fan. "I have no desire to write about a detective."

"You confuse me, Miss Danforth." Mentally composing a severe note to Greenough Smith regarding his screening methods, he added patiently, "What is it exactly that you *do* want to write about?"

"Actually, sir." She cleared her throat with a delicate gesture of gloved fingertips to lips. "I have no desire to write about anything."

He stiffened. "Have you sought me out just to pester me into resurrecting Holmes?" All warmth drained from his manner. "I warn you, Miss Danforth," his tone grew ominous, "I have had my fill of abuse from ladies who write letters only to call me a brute for having dispatched him."

"Oh, no, sir!" She looked directly into his eyes. "But I must beseech you to tell no one of our interview." Her voice lost its tremulous quality.

"Surely, Miss Danforth, you did not come all the way here to play conundrums. What is it you wish to say to me?"

Her gaze did not waver. "First you must promise."

Thoroughly annoyed, longing to dismiss her and return to his study forthwith, but too chivalrous to do so, he crossed his heart impatiently. "I swear I shall tell no one."

With a relieved sigh, she nodded to acknowledge his promise, which set her earrings to dancing beneath her enormous hat. "Well, then." She stood quickly, her posture regal.

Conan Doyle was on his feet in an instant.

Skirts arustle, she paced to the center of the room and turned to face him before she declared, "It is my heart's desire to devote the rest of my life to that infant science of detection."

Stunned, his eyes widened. Conan Doyle was speechless. The fire crackled and snapped.

Abigail continued rapidly, her voice firm. "But please understand, I have no ambition to imitate Holmes's method, or his life." With a sweep of her furled fan, she indicated the souvenirs that encircled the room. "Like you, sir, I have

23

a thirst for travel. I could not bear to stay cooped up in rooms on Baker Street. Nor could I inject myself with drugs." She shuddered. "And thank heavens, musical talent has little to do with the art of detection." Her grin was wicked as she walked back toward him. "I'd be quite hopeless at playing the violin. I'm barely passable on the piano, which is *de rigueur* if I am to turn into the lady my father intends."

The passionate young woman with dark, sparkling eyes who stood before him was so different from the timorous girl who'd been sitting by the fire that he could scarcely believe his senses. While he had to admit to not a little authorial pride in that she'd actually sought out Dr. Watson, believing Holmes's adventures to be real, he was appalled that his irritating fictional character had had such an independent life that he had inflamed her imagination with such untoward results. "And what about your father?" He ran a hand through his hair. "What would he say?"

"He would disown me." Her eyes grew solemn as she continued, her voice subdued. "I am due my mother's inheritance upon my debut." She shrugged matter-of-factly. "Father would no doubt disinherit me into the bargain."

"Well then, my dear young lady, does that not settle it?" Spying the errant cricket ball, he took a few quick steps and stooped easily to retrieve it. Much to Abigail's delight, not only did he absentmindedly place it beside the candy dish on a side table—a capital offense in her father's house—but he made no reference whatever to the inconsiderate carelessness of children as he rejoined her at the fireplace.

"Not quite, sir." Taking courage from his apparent good nature, and his not having laughed at her outright, she said, "I am determined to become the world's first female consulting detective."

Taken aback by her resolve, he frowned. "But you have everything, my dear." He spread his hands wide to indicate the outside world as well as to express his consternation. "Everything!" he exclaimed. "Why on earth would you risk losing it all?"

She perched daintily on the edge of the chair. "I am not

insensitive to the advantages of being a rich man's daughter," she said with a wry smile. "Or a titled man's wife." Her glance was piercing as she watched the perplexed writer as he eased himself into the chair opposite. "I have been trained to be charming, and I've been groomed, rather like a horse, to capture a title for my father's pride." She leaned forward earnestly. "Am I selfish to want more from life than to be empty-headed, extravagantly adorned, and worn on a man's arm to broadcast his wealth?" She turned her gaze toward the fire to conceal the intense longing in her eyes. "I do so hunger for a life of my own."

His gaze was wary. "You are not one of those suffragettes, are you?"

"I do not understand you, sir," she said with an expression of hauteur. "What does unraveling a mystery to bring the guilty to justice have to do with the vote?"

She was proving to be slippery to argue with and, unsure of the best way to dissuade her from pursuing her perilous course, it was with some exasperation that he said, "If you are so determined to storm the bastions of the male's preserve, then why not a legitimate profession? Why not become a lawyer?" He waved his hand airily. "Or a doctor."

"Oh come now, Dr. Conan Doyle." She unfurled her fan with a harsh snap. "Pray do not mock me." She drew herself tall. "A doctor?" Her fan sliced the air like the wings of an angry bird. "What hospital would have me were I to find a school that would?"

"It is not my intention to mock you, Miss Danforth." His expression was sincere, his voice soothing. "Albeit they are few in number, woman are being allowed into the medical profession—"

"If I may be frank, sir," Abigail interrupted, her fan eloquent testimony to her distaste, "the truth is, unwashed, diseased, and most certainly unclothed, bodies hold no attraction for me. And as for law, even if a university were to accept me, nowhere in the world is there a law firm that would hire me."

"Ah, but you could have a private practice!"

Abigail shook her head as vigorously as she dared without

unseating her hat. "I mean no disrespect, sir, but the practice of law is dry and dull. Its machinations all take place after the criminal is caught. I want to partake in the hunt, the discovery and capture of the felon, not his prosecution." Closing the fan, she rested it on top of the reticule on her lap. "Don't you see?" She leaned forward eagerly. "For the infant science of detection, I need only find a companion as felicitous as Dr. Watson to accompany me, and chronicle my adventures." Sitting tall again, she added triumphantly, "That way I need not intrude myself upon the male's natural preserves."

Alarmed by her unwavering enthusiasm for his irksome detective, and certain that the pampered and sheltered girl hadn't the slightest notion of the piteous fate in store for an abandoned and destitute woman, he cast about for another tack to dissuade her from her obsession. "But Miss Danforth," he said earnestly, "any other member of your fair sex would consider being a marchioness occupation enough."

"Oh, but so dreadfully boring!" she exclaimed. "Being caretaker for some preposterously huge, drafty old museum to hand over intact to the next generation, while hostage to squabbling servants who may or may not have dinner ready for the confined circle of people you may entertain—"

"Come, come, Miss Danforth," Conan Doyle frowned as he interrupted. "Household duties notwithstanding, you are to dine with the Prince of Wales! What more could you aspire to? Why, people are going to ask you to tell them about that night for the rest of your life, even if you never see His Royal Highness again."

"And after the first telling, I should be bored to distraction!" She rolled her eyes heavenward. "Furthermore, sir, although, once again, I mean no disrespect, sitting in the presence of someone I may not speak to until he has spoken first, fails to excite me overmuch. Makes one feel much like a servant must." With a mischievous grin, she continued, "Ah, but I was thrilled to learn that the marquess is going to present the Prince with the Punjat's Ruby as a belated

26

birthday gift.'' Her eyes were alight with excitement. ''I am eager to hear the details of its lurid history.''

With a resigned sigh, he drew his watch from his waist-coat pocket. As he consulted it, he said wearily, ''I fail to understand why you have taken such trouble to see me.''

''You created the profession, sir.'' She spoke quickly, be-fore he could declare an end to the interview. ''I had hoped that you could advise me.''

''Advise you how, Miss Danforth? I sit upstairs in a room and write.'' He waved his hand in the general direction of his study. ''Except for what I read, I personally know noth-ing about being a detective.'' His gaze slipped into the past. ''When I was at Edinburgh University, I had a most re-markable mentor who was blessed with fantastic powers of observation and deduction. Dr. Joseph Bell was my model for Holmes.''

''Do you think it possible that I might—''

''As you well know, Miss Danforth,'' he held up his hand to forestall her question, ''your future is entirely up to your father.''

''You will not tell him of our interview?'' she asked anx-iously.

Offended, he drew back. ''I gave my word!''

Relieved, she stood, with a delicate tug at the front of her jacket to restore its flawless line, smiled shyly as she said, ''I don't suppose you would consider giving me an intro-duction to Mr. Gillette in New York?''

He shook his head as he stood. ''Pray do not ask me to be a party to your folly, Miss Danforth.''

''Just one word of encouragement?'' she asked coquet-tishly as they strolled toward the door.

''I assure you, I hold feminine strength of character and ability in the highest regard. And I must admit you possess audacity enough and more. And persistence. However, your morbid thirst for adventure is apt to lead you into danger, quite unnecessarily considering your station in life. I'd say the odds are overwhelmingly against you.''

Although she held her head high, her voice was subdued as she asked, ''Then there is no hope for me?''

Bracing himself against the female's ultimate weapon of tears, his voice was not unsympathetic as he said, "The life that stretches before you is one of luxury and ease. It would be foolhardy in the extreme for you to risk it just to satisfy an overwrought imagination, inspired by a not altogether admirable creature of fantasy." Placing his hand on the door handle, his voice was gruff as he added firmly, "While I admire your pluck and enthusiasm, I may not—nay—I *must* not, in all conscience, encourage you, Miss Danforth."

He need not have worried about her weeping. Abigail saved her tears until she was quite alone.

Chapter One

A line is breadthless length.
Euclid

"Oh, fanny feathers!" Abigail exclaimed, staring out of her bedroom window in Lady Pepper's London townhouse the next morning. "Where can my brother be?" Impatient, yet careful not to crush wrinkles into the voluminous skirts of her morning costume, she gathered handfuls of the blue-striped fabric and rearranged it to fall more precisely. "If I could walk about in trousers instead of hundredweights of cloth, I'd never be late!"

But it was not the weight of her dress that fueled Abigail's frustration. Nor was it her brother's tardiness. When bedtime had finally arrived the night before, after a lonely bout of tears of disappointment, she had remained awake long into the night. In the end, Conan Doyle's refusal to advise or encourage her had merely served to strengthen her resolve to pursue a career in detection. After all, was not the path to solving a mystery strewn with obstacles? She'd be a poor detective indeed were she to allow herself to become discouraged over every little setback. All she really needed was to find someone to chronicle her adventures. And her freedom. No sooner had she reached that conclusion when, like a giant shadow cast by the nightstand candle, the issue of marriage loomed before her.

Although Lord Hunterswell was by no means her first

serious suitor, with his wealth and title he was certainly more likely to please her father than the others had. And it would seem that he was serious. This very day she was to meet his parents. Then he was to travel to New York to meet her father. Yet she'd scarcely had more than a few hours' conversation with him, not one word of it alone. Their superficial gossip about weather had not given her the slightest clue whether he would be the kind of husband who would want her by his side every moment, or whether he'd allow her to lead a private life. Nor had he actually asked her for her hand, which while not terribly romantic, she supposed was the practical, if not the only, course of action, since her consent would be meaningless without their parents' approval. All of which served to trap her very neatly. These might be modern times with a new century beginning, and while she was determined not to be coerced into an alliance like that poor Duchess of Marlborough, should she discover that she did not wish to marry Lord Hunterswell, her lack of desire to have him as a husband would be worth little, perhaps nothing, once her father had made up his mind. Her destiny. Yet she'd be the last to be consulted. So much for a life of independence and adventure.

And then there was the indignity of having her brother come to London to escort her back to New York, as though she were some half-witted child who could not find her way alone across a room. It was almost more than she could bear. "Oh, where can Rodney be!" She exclaimed again, turning to confront Jacqueline.

"Je ne sais pas, Mlle. Danforth."

"Pray, speak in English, Jacqueline," Abigail cleared her throat before continuing. "We will soon be in America, where no one speaks French." Leaving her vigil at the window, she crossed the room to the dressing table. "Fetch me my hat, please." Sighing, she sat before the mirror.

"Yes, Miss." Jacqueline whirled away, apron strings flying like the tail of a kite.

"I shall leave Rodney behind if he's not on time for the marquess's carriage," Abigail said emphatically. "He can come in the dray with you and Kinkade for all I care."

Turning to watch Jacqueline hurry to the stack of trunks on the far side of the semicanopied bed, she sighed once again. She was more than pleased with her new maid, and enormously pleased with herself for having dared to hire her before consulting her father. But her own opinion counted for naught unless Kinkade approved. Her father valued Kinkade's opinion and would dismiss Jacqueline out of hand, should he not like her. "You must not let Kinkade's pugnacious physiognomy frighten you." Abigail was careful to remove any tone of reproach from her voice, lest Jacqueline misunderstand and, thinking it directed at her, become flustered and make a poor impression. "He has been father's valet for as long as I can remember. I am surprised that father permitted him to come with Rodney, he depends upon him so."

Abigail faced the mirror and was admiring the modish style with which Jacqueline had dressed her hair as her maid returned. "I warrant he has orders to watch after my brother." She grimaced at her reflection. "And me as well."

Since Abigail had been talking quite freely to her, Jacqueline decided she might risk a question as she reverently adjusted the curved brim of the plumed hat on her mistress's pompadour. "Please, Miss, you are thrilling to meet the Prince of Wales?" she ventured.

Delight with Jacqueline's boldness in speaking without being spoken to—which would stand her in good stead when dealing with Kinkade—Abigail smiled, and decided not to correct her grammar. "If the truth be told, Jacqueline, I am more thrilled about seeing the Punjat's Ruby."

"Beg pardon, Miss?"

Determined not to speak French so that Jacqueline would more quickly learn English, but at a loss to explain so complicated an object as the Punjat's Ruby in terms that her maid would understand, Abigail ignored the question, as she had many others when time, or her patience, grew short. Instead, concentrating upon drawing on her skintight gloves, she asked, "Am I all packed for these next three days at Hunterswell House?"

"Yes, Miss." More concerned with her vocabulary than

her ability to pack, Jacqueline closed her eyes and began to recite, "Three morning outfits, the blue linen costume for the bicycle with ribbons for the hat and neck bows for the riding of two times, three tea gowns, and four dinner dresses, one to spare. The gold-threaded satin with the topaz necklace and the earrings is to dine with the Prince. Two riding habits, one for the hunt. Two short cloaks, one is the squirrel, one fur-trimmed merely, and one long cloth coat." Opening her eyes, Jacqueline added, "I do not package your full-length furs. I think it will not be so cold to need them."

"I quite agree." Abigail gestured for her to continue.

"Two tweed walking suits and sturdy boots. Shoes, one case for the gloves, jewels in the box, and fans. And many understandings and necessaries and hats and parasols. And the second best gray wool traveling gown to wear to the boat."

Abigail's underslips rustled as she stood and nodded her approval. "Your English has improved immeasurably these past few weeks. Your accent is atrocious, of course. But, there again, so is mine to the English ear. I daresay I shall be accused of sounding British when I get home."

"Thank you, Miss." Although Jacqueline did not understand all that she said, it was clear from Abigail's tone that her mistress was pleased, and she blushed with pleasure. "May I say, Miss, his lordship is sure to lose his heart."

Blushing in turn, Abigail did not acknowledge the compliment. "If Rodney is in a fume when he discovers that Lady Pepper and I have left him behind, do not let him bully you."

"Yes, Miss."

"I do so wish that Benjamin had recovered sufficiently to make the voyage to fetch me instead of Rodney. You will be astonished when you meet him that he and Rodney are twins."

"Miss?"

Abigail turned to face the mirror again, her gaze thoughtful. "Benjamin is the firstborn, the original, if you will." Her moonstone earrings swayed daintily as she touched the lace at her throat and made infinitesimal adjustments to her richly embroidered bodice. "Perhaps if Rodney were not so jealous, father and he might get along better."

Jacqueline nodded as if she had understood Abigail perfectly.

Abigail held out her hand.

Jacqueline knew at once what her mistress wanted and handed her the parasol of shot silk with a small curtsy.

"Yet it must be difficult to be the second son by only minutes." Beckoning with the parasol for the small mink muff on the nightstand, Abigail added, "And I talk too much. Do let my remarks be my secret, like yesterday's journey."

"Yes, Miss," Jacqueline presented the muff with a curtsy.

"Pray, do not bob up and down like that all the time." Abigail frowned. "I am not royalty." She gazed at Jacqueline solemnly. "Under no circumstances are you to tell anyone, not Kinkade—not anyone—about our visit to Dr. Conan Doyle."

"Oh, no, Miss," Jacqueline said earnestly. "I understand the secret. A runaway horse cannot pull me with it."

Turning aside to conceal her amusement, "It is wild horses, Jacqueline. Wild horses that—" Interrupted by a soft tapping at the door, she turned to the footman standing in the doorway.

Addressing the space above Abigail's head, he intoned, "The marquess's coach awaits Miss Danforth's pleasure."

"You may tell Lady Pepper that I shall be down at once." Abigail's posture was regal as she paused in front of the mirror for a final glance. "Now even if Kinkade stays behind to wait for Rodney, I want you to hurry out as planned. I will need you."

"Yes, Miss." Jacqueline beamed as her mistress swept from the room and blinked with surprise when Abigail immediately reappeared.

"Another secret," Abigail whispered. "I do not worry as much about pleasing Earl Hunterswell as I do about meeting his formidable mother, the marchioness."

As Abigail disappeared for the last time, Jacqueline

hugged herself with pleasure at her good fortune for having found such a kind mistress. Forgetting that she'd had no breakfast, she surveyed the littered room. She enjoyed restoring order from chaos, and limitless energy had honed her petite figure into childlike proportions. Half an hour had passed, she was humming merrily, had nearly completed packing, and was bent over, almost in, a trunk when she heard running footsteps in the hall and a piercing wail, "AAAbbeeeeee!"

Jacqueline jumped, dropping an undergarment on the floor as the trunk lid slammed shut.

"Abigail?" Rodney beat on the door frame with the heavy silver head of his cane. "Where is Abigail?"

"Mon Dieu, Monsieur!" she stammered, too paralyzed with fright to say anything else.

"Well! Where is she? Have you packed her in one of those trunks?" He shook his cane at her as he strode into the room.

When Jacqueline continued to stare at him in wide-eyed silence, he spoke more loudly, "You cannot mean to tell me—if you are able to speak—that she left without me?"

Jacqueline nodded mutely.

Tossing his hat onto the dressing table, Rodney slumped into the chair. *"Mon Dieu,* indeed!" That jolly well tears it for me." With large brown eyes and well-proportioned features, had his expression not been so petulant as he peered into the mirror to criticize his perfectly knotted four-in-hand, he might have been handsome. But an unseen weight rounded his broad shoulders and spoiled the excellent cut of his morning coat. "I can hear Father now," he muttered, folding both hands on top of his cane. His voice grew deeper. "Gave you the slip, again, did she? Can't even keep up with a stupid girl, eh? Bah!" He pounded the cane into the carpet and swung around abruptly to face Jacqueline. "Whatever are you doing?"

Taking advantage of Rodney's discourse with the mirror, she had bent down to retrieve the undergarment, but it had eluded her in the many layers of her skirts. Raising herself to answer him, it was still underfoot. Her face was aflame.

"Miss Danforth does not mean to slip you, sir," she spoke as clearly as she could when pressed to speak quickly. "You can come with Kinkade and me."

"Me?" He stood. "Travel with servants?"

Jacqueline nodded wordlessly.

"Don't be absurd!" He strode toward her. "Living in Europe these past few years has driven my sister off her onion if she thinks I'd ride with servants!" Towering over her, he commanded. "Talk to me now that we know you can speak. What are you hiding?"

"Nothing, sir." Toeing the undergarment under the bed, she backed away, placing her trembling hand on top of the trunk. "I make the packing for Miss Danforth."

"You and my sister were gone most of yesterday." He glowered at her. "Where were you?"

"Shopping, *Monsieur.*" Jacqueline's blush intensified with the fib.

"Ah, but you had no packages when you returned." Having noticed her discomfort, Rodney pressed for the cause, on the off-chance she was trying to hide something.

Too frightened to embellish the lie with the possibility of their having used a delivery service, Jacqueline could but stare at him.

Swinging his cane, he caught the end behind his back and glared down at her like an officer inspecting a raw recruit. "Just exactly where did you go shopping?"

"Oh, *Monsieur, s'il vous plait,* it is the secret."

"Even from her brother?"

"I promise not to tell."

"So my sister is visiting a secret lover, eh?" Rodney said ominously, raising an eyebrow.

"No, no *Monsieur!* Do not speak slander!"

"I shall have to tell our father something." Rodney's smile pulled the corner of his mouth down. "Perhaps if I knew the truth, I could decide whether to tell him or not."

Jacqueline stared at the carpet, her mouth a grim line of silence.

"If you leave me to guess at the worst, girl, I shall tell him that Abigail has a lover who is after her money."

"Oh, no, *Monsieur!*"

"It all depends on you."

Jacqueline shrank back against the trunk.

Rodney moved closer and, placing the silver head of his cane under her chin, forced her to look him in the eyes. "There is no need for Abigail to find out." His voice enveloped her like smoke, "If you tell me everything, then it can be *our* secret that I know."

"Oh, *Monsieur!* You promise? You do not tell Miss Danforth?"

"A bargain is a bargain."

Pulling away, Jacqueline held his gaze, "Miss Danforth goes to Surrey."

"Where?"

"To Hindeshead, Surrey, sir."

"Why!"

"To see Dr. Conan Doyle, *Monsieur.*"

"The writer?" He frowned. "But why?"

"Je ne sais pas, Monsieur."

Rodney could scarcely believe his good fortune at so soon discovering his perfect sister in an indiscretion. That she'd lied to keep it a secret surely meant that it was a matter serious enough to incur their father's wrath. Unable to conceal his glee, he lifted Jacqueline in the air and spun her full circle. Depositing her at the foot of the bed, he held her by the shoulders and said, "It is agreed! You understand? As you value your job, do not tell my sister what you have told me. This is our secret." He kissed her soundly on the forehead.

Her face shone with happiness, "Oh, *Merci, Monsieur. Merci! Merci!*"

From the open doorway, Kinkade coughed. When neither of them responded, he coughed again, more loudly.

"Ah, there you are at last, Kinkade." Rodney released Jacqueline and strode toward the dressing table. "Fetch me a hansom. Be sure it is well horsed. I am in a hurry."

"Yes, sir. At once, Master Rodney," Kinkade said. "If I may spare a moment to tell Miss Bordeaux that the butler is on his way upstairs to supervise the disposition of Miss Danforth's luggage.''

"Yes, yes, well, you've told her, haven't you?'' Rodney retrieved his hat from the dressing table and placed it, just so, on his sandy hair. ''Now begone! Jacqueline is ready for the butler, aren't you, my dear?''

Jacqueline had fled to retrieve the undergarment the instant Rodney had released her. Upon tightening the last strap, she looked up to assure Kinkade that the luggage was ready. He was gone.

Rodney shook his cane at her from the doorway, ''Remember! It is our secret!''

The footman had left with the last box and Jacqueline was checking the drawers of the dressing table again when she noticed that her cap was askew and her hair in messy tendrils. ''What must the servants have thought of me,'' she moaned in French. Cheeks scarlet with embarrassment, she quickly restored her hair to its usual neatness.

''Miss Bordeaux!''

Jacqueline whirled around, her hand on her heart. *''Mon Dieu, Monsieur* Kinkade! What a fright!''

''Primping is for the ladies of the house.''

''Oui, but I—''

''You especially do not primp in front of your master's grand mirrors. There is looking glass enough in the servants' quarters.''

''But I—''

''I'll thank you not to talk back to me.'' Broken in a childhood accident, Kinkade's misshapen nose endowed his voice with resonance and lent a pugilistic aspect to his appearance that his peaceful nature did not deserve. His lips were thin with distaste. ''I will be frank with you, Miss Bordeaux. I do not approve of what I saw.''

''Monsieur?'' Jacqueline smiled her most charming. ''Forgive the arranging of the hair—''

''You need not pretend to mistake my meaning!'' he exclaimed. ''For a strumpet to pretend she's an honest lady's maid and lure the young master of the house is an all too common occurrence. I must warn you that your plot will not succeed in the Danforth household."

"I am not the strumpet!" Jacqueline was horrified.

"I saw you kissing Master Rodney," he replied stiffly. "I will not argue with the likes of you. Now go get your mantle. We have much to do."

Unable to summon the English to explain her dilemma, Jacqueline silently trailed him down the back staircase. Considering the bad odor she was in, she did not risk asking for something to eat to assuage her hunger.

Freed from the mire of London's traffic, the two high-spirited, matched grays needed no urging from the driver to quicken their pace. Sensing a return to the stable, they sped the marquess's brougham toward Hunterswell House. Sitting across from Lady Pepper, Abigail decided, with some surprise, that she was going to miss her hostess. The dear soul was as plump as a partridge and as flighty. A lifetime of squeezing into corsets had rendered her permanently breathless. She was vaguely aware that tea came from China or perhaps India, but how it got from her pantry, brewed for teatime, was a mystery. It had never occurred to her to wonder, nor had she any need to, there would always be servants to call upon to replenish the teapot. Much of the world outside her closed circle was equally mysterious. Just the sort of woman Abigail was afraid of becoming. But she had a generous heart. And she knew what she needed to know.

With much earnestness, Lady Pepper was trying to impart some of her knowledge of the nuances in the use of the fan to the snippet of a girl who sat beside her. Miss Gilda Arrington was a much younger, slimmer, version of Lady Pepper. Without the kindness.

"You have a natural grace with the fan, Miss Arrington." Lady Pepper swiftly faced Abigail and smiled. "As do you, of course, my dear." She turned back to Miss Arrington. "It will develop into a flair with practice. You must practice."

"Yes, m'Lady," Miss Arrington sighed, her glance rueful. "It is just that I am weary of practice."

"Weariness is woman's natural condition." Lady Pepper came perilously close to being impatient. "Now, the Prince of Wales particularly enjoys a graceful hand with the fan—"

Miss Arrington needed to hear no more, and willingly, nay eagerly, followed Lady Pepper's drills in the movements to prepare, unfurl, discharge, ground, and recover her fan.

Watching Miss Arrington, for the first time Abigail appreciated Disraeli's remark that women were armed with fans as men with swords, and sometimes did more executions with them. Miss Arrington had certainly spent enough time behind a fan flirting with that friend of Lord Hunterswell's, Mr. Buchanan. Fairly seduced him, too, from the gleam in his eye as his glance would follow her when she'd flounce away. Abigail had not cared for the way Miss Arrington had toyed with Mr. Buchanan's affections. Now that gossip had it that she'd caught the eye of the Prince, the girl had become impossibly arrogant. Her pouting mouth, which had seemed alluring while flirting with Mr. Buchanan, had become greedy. Or so it seemed to Abigail.

"I do believe you are ready for a trial with Wales." Lady Pepper beamed at her protégé. "And see how quickly a little practice has made the time pass? We are here."

Clouds churned across the dirty sky. Bleak, leftover light outlined the ponderous bulk of meandering stone that was Hunterswell House.

Even as the coachman brought the carriage to a stop, liveried footmen rushed forward to hand the ladies down as though they were fragile crystal.

Dwarfed by the cavernous doorway, the butler greeted them somberly. Guiding them through the vaulted inner hall past the smoking room, he said, "The marchioness will receive Miss Danforth in her sitting room at once. The marchioness will receive Lady Pepper and Miss Arrington at luncheon." As they mounted the marble staircase, he gestured toward the first landing. "Mrs. Budge will show your Ladyship and Miss Arrington to your rooms."

So still that she could have been mistaken for one of the suits of armor standing guard in the countless nooks, Mrs. Budge awaited their arrival. With a formal nod, she indicated that Lady Pepper and Miss Arrington should precede her up the left side of the staircase. Keys, the badge of her exalted station as housekeeper, jangled at her waist as she followed in Lady Pepper's wake.

Having paused to bid Lady Pepper farewell, Abigail was obliged to hurry to catch up with the butler and was breathless when she reached the top of the stairs. Standing beside a newel post that supported a green marble urn taller than he, he was looking at his watch as though he might have been timing her ascent. With some amusement, she wondered if she were about to be scolded for an unseemly rush, or tardiness.

Snapping the watch shut, he replaced it in his vest pocket. "The marchioness will be most pleased that you have arrived in time to meet the—ah—children."

He was off again, to remain three paces ahead of her. In her rush to keep up, she nearly slipped, and her heart sank at the thought that someday she might be mistress of this absurdly large house with its yawning, dimly lit corridors and their endless miles of floors. By the time they finally stopped in front of a pair of ornate doors, Abigail was unsure of her bearings. "Are we facing south?" she asked.

A slight hesitation before knocking bespoke the butler's astonishment. The tortuous walk from the main staircase to the marchioness's chambers seldom failed to disorient the most frequent visitor. "Yes, Miss." His voice was as cool as the hallway. "The marchioness prefers the south wing for its view of the lake."

The doors swung wide and, above the sudden cacophony of incessantly barking dogs, Abigail's full name echoed in several different masculine voices.

A female voice that a Sgt. Major would have envied, cried, "For the sake of Jove, shut up! I can see her! And for Jove's sake, shut those doors! If one of my babies is lost, I shall have you all sacked!''

Frantically scratching the highly polished floor, scores of manicured nails scrambled to gain traction. A swarm of barking, wheezing pugs, all waving their behinds so that their corkscrew tails could wag, tumbled over each other. Some had napery tied at their necks, others had lost theirs in the competition to reach Abigail first.

''Fagan, Bumble, Vilkins, and Oliver are in the lead!'' The marchioness's voice easily pierced the uproar. ''Sowerbelly, wake up! Unwin! Limbkins, move your rump!''

''Is m'Lady fond of Dickens?'' Abigail shouted over the din. Two of the pugs began a tug of war with the hem of her skirt, hindering her progress toward the marchioness, reclining on her chaise near a fire.

Deep lines gouged semicircles underneath the marchioness's enormous green eyes and descended to further define her voluptuous mouth. Her voice scaled the heights again. ''Oh, my, me, my, no, no, no,'' she laughed. ''My tiresome, holier-than-*any*body sister pesters me constantly for money for her wretched orphans. I torment her in return by feeding my little darlings better than her homeless waifs.'' She clapped her hands, ''Manners, children! Manners! You there!'' she pointed at the liveried menservants. ''Who gave the children permission to leave the table? Naughty! Naughty! Return them at once!'' Her voice plummeted as she looked directly at Abigail. ''You like to read?''

Powdered wigs askew, servants struggled to snap golden leashes on the wriggling gold chain harnesses worn by the pugs whose names were spelled out in diamonds on gold disks. Satin-pillowed, cane baskets were anchored to armchairs so that, when seated, the dogs' damask-napkined chests would be at table height. The men had difficulty restoring the missing napery as the dogs had gotten a whiff of the roast pheasant being carved at a buffet.

Drawing closer to the chaise, Abigail was amazed to discover that it was a tiny woman, no larger than Jacqueline, who possessed the large voice. Admiring the aplomb with which the servants performed their duties, she replied, "Yes, ma'am. I like to read."

"Pity," the marchioness said, examining Abigail through her lorgnette. "Well, at least you're pretty. Turn around, girl."

Abigail obeyed.

"And well dressed. Hmmmmm. Flattering hat. Looks expensive. My son had best watch out for Bertie. If you stayed in London, you could vie for Public Beauty."

"Thank you, m'Lady," Abigail replied, thoroughly annoyed with herself for blushing.

"You can see for yourself that the future marquess of Hunterswell has no need for a dollar princess."

"Yes, m'Lady."

The marchioness gestured toward the busy table. "Breeding then feeding, I always say." She stood abruptly, "Do you ride?"

"Yes, m'Lady."

"Good! That is something. Let us go then before it rains."

Abigail hesitated, "But my clothes, m'Lady. My riding habit has not yet arrived."

"Come, come, girl," the marchioness beckoned. "I have an outfit for you." Passing alongside the table, she whispered at Abigail's ear as though she did not want the dogs to listen, "Hear my little darlings swallowing all that air?" She chuckled. "The results will be, alas, predictable."

Entering an enormous anteroom that was entirely devoted to the storage of clothes, the marchioness summoned her lady's maid who joined them in the dressing room bearing a riding habit. An obviously new apprentice carried the usual understandings.

Abigail noticed that her skirt was divided, but the maid seemed to consider it normal, so she made no comment. She had once heard of a notorious Frenchwoman who rode astride in split skirts, but had never known of an Englishwoman behaving so scandalously.

After a few deft adjustments by the maid, the costume fit Abigail perfectly. Voluminous fabric disguised the division

42

in the skirt when she walked. There had been no need to re-dress her hair to wear the feathered riding hat. It was not until she had fallen several paces behind the marchioness while descending the south wing staircase, that she fancied she saw that the marchioness's skirts were also divided.

Suddenly furious, Abigail no longer heard the marchioness's incessant chatter. It was unwomanly and courting injury to ride astride. Her hostess should have given her an opportunity to politely decline. Instead, the impossible woman had lent her a costume as though she would not only condone her disreputable act, but also be willing to partake in it. By the time they reached the gloomy ground-floor vestibule, Abigail felt trapped between her offended sensibilities and the inflexible code that forbade her to so much as consider criticizing her noble hostess.

In the cobblestoned courtyard, snorting with high spirits, three magnificent English thoroughbreds were held by their grooms. Two were cross-saddled. One, sidesaddled.

"I have a confession to make," the marchioness said, sounding not in the least abashed. "The first time I was in India as a girl about your age, with my wretched sister I was taught to ride astride by the fall-off bareback method. Want to learn?"

Abigail disliked being dared. It made her feel like a child again, maneuvered into mischief by her brothers.

Ignoring Abigail's silence, the marchioness patted her mount affectionately. "With the proper saddle, it shouldn't take you as long or be as painful as it was for me. By the by, my sister fainted when I presented her with that costume you're wearing. She had refused to even try to learn to ride astride after witnessing my first spill. At least you donned it without comment, though I must say you have been quiet since." She laughed. "Don't suppose I have given you much opportunity to speak, eh?"

As suddenly as it had come, Abigail's anger vanished, erased by a glimpse of her own hypocrisy. What a perfect Mrs. Grundy she was, judging the marchioness. Just yesterday hadn't she revealed her desire to become a consulting detective?

43

"Come, come, girl!" the marchioness's voice intruded. "What shall it be?"

"Yes, m'Lady." Abigail restrained a giggle. "I shall be honored if m'Lady would teach me to ride astride."

"Enough talk, now. Mount up!"

Abigail had been riding since before she could walk and had excellent hands. Her mount was superbly trained. Within a half hour of following the marchioness's barked instructions, she felt confident in her extraordinary seat.

The marchioness controlled her own horse as though she had taken possession of its mind. As soon as she noticed that subtle shift in Abigail's attitude that bespoke her readiness, she shouted, "To the lake!"

Abigail let loose with the rebel yell, which she'd learned from a cousin who'd fought in The War, and pursued the marchioness. They raced past acres of massive trees in the park and skirted the swan-dotted lake.

The marchioness could not maintain her lead. Reining her horse in to a walk, she signaled Abigail to slow down and join her so that they could continue side by side on the shore of the lake. "How do you like it? Riding astride?" she asked.

"I am forever in your debt, m'Lady." Abigail was breathless with delight. "When I remember to keep my toes higher than my heels, I feel like a centaur."

"Even though it is wicked? Or *because* it is wicked?" The marchioness laughed. "You see?" She continued before Abigail could speak. "You can do any thing if you have enough money. You may find your limbs a trifle sore tomorrow. The best remedy is a hot soak and a short ride. Does Crosspatches suit you?"

"Yes, m'Lady. He is a splendid fellow, indeed."

"I shall inform the stable that you may call for him anytime you choose: One of the grooms is always ready to accompany you, if I am not available."

"M'Lady is most generous."

"Did you know that my son is journeying to New York just to be near you?"

Caught unawares by the marchioness's direct manner, Abigail dissembled, "No, ma'am."

"This is the first time in his thirty-two years that I have known him to be so smitten. Girls, or their ambitious parents, have always pursued him. And not so subtly, I might add. The marquess had to bail him out of a breach of contract suit two years ago. Cost a pretty penny, but that was all the girl had really wanted. Money. Being very rich and titled, makes one vulnerable to that sort of thing, but there again, I would not know how to get along without a lot of money," she sighed. "Everything needs paying for."

"Even people?"

"Especially people."

Abigail ventured to contradict her. "Naturally one pays for servants, m'Lady, but surely not all people. Not the Prince of Wales?"

"Especially Bertie!" the marchioness exclaimed, with her raucous laugh. "One needs a great deal of money to run in his crowd, child. For the clothes alone! Why, the marquess paid a king's ransom to the Nawab Abdulsamad for the Punjat's Ruby for his birthday present."

"I am most eager to see it, m'Lady."

"And who knows what poor Poopsie had to pay Mark Twain to persuade him to entertain us with its history!"

"How jolly it will be to see him again!" Abigail smiled. "Some of my fondest memories are of trips to the Clemens's wondrous home in Hartford. Yet, during my entire stay in Europe, our paths have not crossed."

"Well, this ruby, my girl, presented by the most famous toastmaster in Europe, cost a fortune. All to try and entertain His Majesty for one evening."

"It should be a thrilling evening, m'Lady."

"Oh, my, me, my, I do hope so," the marchioness sighed heavily and reined in her mount. When he was perfectly still, she removed a small, emerald-studded box from the folds of her riding habit. "I wanted to have this private chat with you before the other guests arrived. And away from the gossiping servants."

Abigail brought Crosspatches to a halt beside her. "Is that cocaine, m'Lady?"

"Why, yes." She held the box toward Abigail. "Would you like some?"

"Oh, no." Abigail recoiled. "Thank you." She concealed her disgust with a smile. "It is just that I've read about someone who injects himself with it. He says it makes the boredom bearable."

"Needles? Ugh!" Holding one nostril closed, she inhaled the white powder from a tiny compartment in the box. "Much more civilized to snort." She replaced the box. "But he is quite right about the boredom." She nudged her horse into a slow walk. "And do you think you could love my son, Miss Danforth?"

The boldness of the question took Abigail aback and she wished Crosspatches would bolt, but refused to shame him by pretending he had. During all of her ponderings about marriage the night before, she had never considered the possibility of falling in love. Hoping that her voice held none of the turmoil she felt, she replied bashfully, "I do not know, m'Lady."

"Surely you cannot be interested in those new companions of my son's, Mr. Buchanan or Driscoll? They might have saved my boy's life, but neither has a title or fortune." She raked Abigail with a penetrating glance. "That didn't seem to bother that Miss Arrington, however, until the Prince took notice of her, eh?"

Abigail was saved from further comment by a groom galloping toward them. The marquess wished to see the marchioness urgently.

"You need not end your ride just yet," the marchioness said dreamily. "When you are ready, the groom will escort you to my private entrance. A footman will await your arrival to see you to your rooms."

Turning her horse to leave, the marchioness spoke to the groom, "See to it that Miss Danforth has Crosspatches and an escort anytime she pleases."

Relieved that her ordeal was over and satisfied that she'd acquitted herself properly, Abigail vowed not to get caught alone again with the marchioness. She shook herself and Crosspatches pranced in response. Lured by the immense expanse of grounds stretching before her, she touched him lightly with her crop and urged him into his incredibly swift gallop. Not so grandly mounted, the groom contented himself with keeping them in sight.

Nearing the park, she spotted a hansom emerging from the trees on its final approach to the formal entrance. "Rodney!" she cried, though she knew he could not possibly hear her. Spirits soaring, she spurred Crosspatches to intercept him. Whooping like a red Indian, brandishing her riding crop like a tomahawk, she circled the nonplussed cabby. Drawing abreast of the window, she shouted, "See what I can do!"

Rodney's top hat was at a dangerous tilt and his mouth worked like a wounded fish.

She rode off toward the south courtyard with the hansom careering after.

Before the cabby could clatter to a complete stop, Rodney tore himself out of the hansom and stalked toward Abigail, shaking his cane. "Abigail Patience Danforth! You shameless, empty-headed girl!" he shrieked. "Climb down off that horse this minute!"

The groom who had tried to escort her held Crosspatches while another groom and a stablehand rushed forward to help her dismount.

Abigail was radiant, "But, Rodney, I've just had the most marvelous ride. For the first time—"

"How dare you!" he sputtered. "You could have permanently injured yourself. Then who would marry you? I came halfway around the world to make sure you got home safely. First you run away from me in London. And now this! What would Father say if he found out that you rode astride? He'd have my hide! Can't you think of anyone but yourself?"

Knowing full well the difficulties that Rodney had with their father, she was instantly contrite. "Oh, Rodney, I am sorry. How thoughtless of me." All joy drained from her face. "I would not willingly cause trouble for you."

"Then why didn't you wait for me?"

"I do apologize, Rodney. But you knew what time the marquess's carriage was due. I couldn't keep Lady Pepper waiting."

All of the servants, who had been avidly listening without appearing to, suddenly came to attention. Those who had no duties in the courtyard vanished. The driver removed his hat. Approaching astride her prancing thoroughbred, the marchioness was an awesome sight.

Rodney groaned, desperately hoping that she had not overheard him.

"What is going on here! Who is this!" she demanded in her Sgt. Major's voice.

"My brother, m'Lady," Abigail responded, biting the inside of her cheek to stifle her amusement at Rodney's discomfort. "Rodney Charles Danforth."

"Oh, my, you can't help family can you?" The marchioness circled Rodney slowly as he, hat in hand, spun around to keep her in view. "It would appear that your brother is as obnoxious as my sister." Pointing her crop at Rodney, her voice was scathing, "What do you think you are doing in that tradesman's vehicle in my private courtyard?"

Mouth agape, Rodney stared at her. When Abigail realized he was unable to speak, she said, "He followed me here, your Ladyship. It's—"

"So you enjoy berating your sister, do you?" The marchioness paid not the slightest attention to Abigail's intercession, nor did she await an answer from Rodney. "This cannot possibly be construed as a proper introduction, young man."

"Forgive me, your Ladyship," Rodney pleaded, fearing banishment to London.

"Get to the entrance hall where you belong so the servants will know what to do with you. At once!"

Mortified, Rodney turned to go. As he passed Abigail, his mouth was tight so that only she could hear him say, "I'll get you for this."

Chapter Two

A point is that which has no parts.
                                        Euclid

Frederick Stuart Seymour, the Earl of Hunterswell, was not a tall man, but he was as lean and supple as a bullwhip. Although his head was seldom uncovered by helmet, hat, or cap, the sun had so often touched his fair hair that it was bleached the color of dry sand. Ravaged by the smallpox that had killed his older brother and had almost claimed him, his face was pitted with scars that no amount of tanning could conceal. Nor could beard or moustache prosper. He had inherited the prominent nose of his paternal ancestors, and although it had escaped scarring, it was sunscorched many different shades. Contrasted by his deep tan, the green of his eyes seemed paler than his mother's. His craggy features, the scars, and a profile that resembled a desolate shoreline all served to render him irredeemably shy, and irresistible to women.

Crashing through snake-laden brush in the howdah of an elephant, or reeling across the desert on the saddle of a panicked camel was all in a day's good sport. He would have scoffed at any suggestion that fear tinged the thrills he sought in the hunt or a dangerous chase, but the thought of executing a path through the morass of protocol in the drawing room filled him with dread.

He knew the whole of his sprawling home intimately and

49

was as equally at ease in many a faraway city. But as he stood at his bedchamber windows watching Abigail race Crosspatches toward the south courtyard, his emotions erupted into uncharted territory. He'd never before met such an extraordinary, adventuresome girl.

"Stork?" he called to his valet. "Where is Miss Danforth staying?"

Stork joined him, whisk broom in hand. "Next to Lord and Lady Pepper, m'Lord. In the Green Bedchamber."

"Rides as well as mother." Frederick's voice filled with pride. "How jolly it would be if she liked the hunt."

"Yes, m'Lord." Pretending not to notice his master's agitation, Stork gave a final, unnecessary whisking to Frederick's superbly tailored jacket.

"What high spirits she has." Frederick's smile transformed his face. "That must be her brother climbing out of the hansom. What splendid fun!"

Stork watched from the window also, as Frederick muttered, "Now what do you suppose mother is up to?"

Unable to hear the commotion, he was puzzled by Rodney's departure toward the formal entrance instead of using the south side with his sister. Suddenly inspired, he said casually, "Before I receive her brother in the Blue Drawing Room, perhaps I could intercept Miss Danforth at Tapestry Hall." He started toward the door. "It is the logical route from the south courtyard."

Stork's expression was noncommittal. "M'Lord will be seeing Miss Danforth at luncheon."

"Yes, but not alone." Frederick called over his shoulder, "Tell Mr. Driscoll that I shall join him and Mr. Buchanan in the Blue Drawing Room instead of his bedchambers."

"Yes, m'Lord." Glancing after his master as he hurried down the corridor, Stork left on his errand.

His heart racing as though he were stalking a kill, Frederick was nearing his destination when it struck him that he might have need to worry about the Prince's taking a liking to Miss Danforth. Perhaps it would be better if she did not partake in the hunt on the morrow. But then she might despise him if she learned that he'd denied her the opportunity every woman in the kingdom longed for. Yet where would he be if she preferred the company of Wales? Or the blond, handsome Maximilian Driscoll for that matter? Or the lanky Scotsman, Fergus Buchanan? His quandary was disconcerting and, paying scant attention to his whereabouts, he turned the last corner into the Hall of Tapestries.

Nearing the middle of the cavernous room from the opposite direction, rapidly closing the distance between them, Abigail was striding purposefully ahead of a footman.

Frederick was dumbstruck. The color in her cheeks still high from her encounter with Rodney, her beauty, up close, took his breath away. "Oh, why, Miss Danforth," he stammered, failing miserably at imitating surprise. "Uh. There you are!"

Surprised to see him so unexpectedly, Abigail immediately wished for her fan. The marchioness's piercing question about love had jumbled her feelings about him, and she had no desire to reveal her turmoil. But as she drew closer, Abigail could not miss seeing how truly bashful he was. Her heart went out to him as she slowed to a stop and said, tactfully, "I have been admiring your house, your Lordship. These tapestries are magnificent." Taking care not to mention the musty odor that permeated the air, she gestured toward the one hanging nearest them. "Each one must have a fascinating story of its own. Not merely the tapestry itself, but also how it came into your ancestors' possession." Although she had intended primarily to supply him with a subject of discourse, her interest was genuine.

Gratitude for the conversational lifeline showed in his voice. "Thank you, Miss Danforth. Some of them date back to the twelfth century. I shall be more than happy to tell you about them all—with your brother or Lady Pepper in attendance, of course."

The peruked and powdered footman discreetly melted into the background, taking care to remain within earshot.

Knowing that he should not tarry and risk besmirching her reputation, Frederick abruptly changed the subject to the reason he'd run to meet her. "I say, Miss Danforth, I witnessed your ambush of the hansom from my window."

51

"Did you?" Abigail froze. Horribly embarrassed, she wondered if he had also overheard Rodney scolding her as if she were an imbecilic child.

With a tinge of awe in his voice, he continued, "You rode as though you were unafraid of injury."

Mistaking his tone for one of chastisement, Abigail blushed with sudden fury. She'd had quite enough of being fussed at for behavior she well knew was improper, even though it had been his mother who had enticed her. "Pray excuse me, your Lordship." Her voice was ice. "I need dress for luncheon." She swept past him, jaw set firmly lest she cry out that any injury she might have sustained which rendered her unmarriageable would be none of his concern.

Frederick was devastated. He had just paid Abigail the highest possible tribute to her courage. Yet rather than please her, he had somehow managed to give offense. Not knowing what else to do, he snapped his fingers to summon the footman. His heart in shreds, he watched her retreating back until she disappeared around a corner, then he struck off toward Maximilian's rooms.

If, indeed, misery acquaints a man with strange bedfellows, then greed can be said to bind them together. Much advanced in the world from their piteous condition when they'd first met in Rangoon, four men gathered by the fire in Maximilian Driscoll's bedchambers.

Warming his backside, it was Maximilian Driscoll who addressed the others standing in front of him. "Fergus here tells me Miss Arrington is threatening to tattle to the Prince." Heavily muscled, but privy to Lord Hunterswell's tailor, Max was flawlessly dressed. The blond of his curly hair seemed mismatched with the dark of his full, neatly clipped beard.

Fergus Buchanan's lanky frame was also perfectly outfitted for lunch, courtesy of Lord Frederick. "We can't let her tell the Prince about our connection with the Punjat's Ruby." Masking his feelings of jealous rage with his much-practiced air of nonchalance, he settled himself into the set-tee. "But what are we going to do about her?"

The other two men, J.C. and Maurice, wore the standard garb of valets. Wide-eyed, they glanced at one another and shrugged.

Matching Fergus's casual demeanor, Max joined him on the settee. "I say she's got to go."

"What do you mean—got to go?" Maurice asked as he assumed Max's vacated position at the huge mantel and J.C. joined him.

Max and Fergus stared at their pseudoservants without speaking.

The significance of their silence slowly dawned on Maurice. He gasped. "Murder?"

Jaw slack, J.C. shook his head in disbelief.

"We can make it look like an accident." Max nodded toward Fergus. "You two don't have to get involved at all."

"She's not overly graceful on a bicycle." Anger twisted Fergus's mouth. "We've come too far to let a stupid girl undo it all with a careless remark."

"You *do* mean murder!" J.C. exclaimed, his voice rising. "Are you daft?"

Hand to lips, Max cautioned J.C. to speak more softly.

"You heard Stork!" J.C. shouted. "Lord Hunterswell ain't comin' here!"

"Shhhh!" Maurice said. "Better to play it safe."

J.C. complied sarcastically by whispering, "How'd she find out anything, anyhow?" He shook his fist at Fergus. "You tell her?"

"She guessed." Fergus said, examining his nails.

"And you're going to kill her for guessing?" J.C. shouted.

"What does it matter if it's just a guess?" Fergus shrugged. "She'd still put the Prince on our trail after we steal it, if we don't pay her off."

"I want no part of it." J.C. turned to Maurice, "It was all well and good for us to act your valets to get into that swell hotel in Rangoon to pull this Punjat's Ruby scam, but I want no part of murder!''

"You won't have to have anything to do with it," Max's voice was its most persuasive. "Fergus and I will take care of everything."

"Like hell!" Maurice glared at the two men at their ease on the settee. "Like you two took care of J.C. and me? You live like dukes in these fancy rooms. We sleep in the attic and eat below the salt in the servants' quarters!"

"You accusing us of cheating?" Fergus's temper flared at last. "It was you who drew the short straws!" Fist clenched, he tensed to rise.

Max grasped Fergus's arm to calm him. "How did we know we'd hit it so lucky, boys?" His voice was soothing.

With great effort, Fergus calmed himself. "Just a few more days," he coaxed. "We'll be safe in America."

"I never signed on to go to America either," Maurice muttered.

"But we won't be able to stay in Europe." Fergus had completely regained his composure. He stood and sauntered toward Maurice.

"And after tomorrow, we can say we've hunted with the Prince of Wales," Max continued from the settee. "Our reputations will be made!"

"Your reputations! You're the ones playing at being gentlemen!" Maurice thumped himself on the chest. "What about us? We'll still just be servants!"

"Aw, come on, old boy," Fergus reached out to put his arm around Maurice. "You're me best pal. You know half of what's mine is—"

Before he could complete his sentence, the bedchamber door flew open and a most agitated Lord Hunterswell rushed in.

Stunned, Fergus snatched his arm away from Maurice.

J.C. and Maurice nearly tripped and fell as they stumbled over each other in their haste to leave. Once outside, J.C. lingered near the door to listen while Maurice watched the corridor.

Max sprang from the settee and hurried toward Lord

Hunterswell, a ready explanation forming on his lips for what he might have overheard.

Regarding servants much like furniture, Frederick had not noticed J.C. and Maurice's presence. Nor had he taken the slightest interest in their hectic departure.

Max forced amusement into his voice, "We weren't expecting you, your Lordship."

Knees weak, Fergus returned to the settee and, for once, had no need to pretend to be relaxed as he nearly collapsed upon it with relief. "We were about to leave to meet you in the Blue Room."

"This couldn't wait." Frederick paced in front of the fireplace. "I had to see you—"

"What is the matter?" Max joined Fergus on the settee.

"You saved my life once." Frederick stopped his pacing to face them. "Now you must help me make it worth living."

"Such melodrama, your Lordship." Max's smile was wide enough to reveal slightly uneven teeth, giving his bearded face an expression of ingenuous honesty.

"Do not jest," Frederick said ominously. "I fear something terrible is happening to me."

Max held his breath, prepared for the worst. "Whatever can you mean, Your Lordship."

"I believe I might be falling in love."

Fergus choked on a laugh of sheer relief.

Max concealed a smile behind his hand as he asked, "What is so terrible about that?"

"It is hopeless." Frederick began his pacing anew. "I am accustomed to running away from women. How do I reverse myself and pursue one?" He stopped to face them again. "I have already, just now, made a mess of it." He waved his hand in the direction of Tapestry Hall. "Miss Danforth ran from me as though the very sight of me was despicable. I have no idea what I said to inspire such an effect." He spread his hands and searched the ceiling for an answer. "I thought I was paying her a compliment."

"Women are, by nature, devious creatures, your Lordship," Fergus said.

"Miss Danforth is the exception." Frederick's tone brooked no disagreement. "Never have I met a girl so straightforward. That is why I find her so captivating."

Fergus and Max exchanged glances as Frederick sat dejectedly in a chair opposite them and continued. "My parents lost my older brother, their natural heir, to the smallpox. As the survivor, in my entire life I have never wanted anything that was not given to me before I asked. Now, I do not know how to go about getting what I want for myself." He glanced at them bashfully. "I appeal to you for help."

Max's voice was soothing, "Of course, we will help." He glanced at Fergus who shook his head in agreement. "You need not even ask."

Frederick stared at the carpet. "You have probably guessed that I, too, was quite ill as a child."

Max and Fergus nodded wordlessly, while Frederick continued, "Even while recuperating, I had to spend most of my time in solitude because of the quarantine. Afterwards not too many people dared to associate with me. The quarantine stuck. And to be fair, I suppose the doctors were afraid I'd catch something else if I were exposed to other people." He sighed. "Hunting in the fresh air is supposed to be healthy. I have hunted a great deal. Lonely business, with only servants about. Until you came along." Leaning forward, he spoke earnestly, "You both are so jolly with people." His smile was grim. "I never know what to say."

"Now I don't know what to say, your Lordship." Max smiled. "I'm in your debt. I'd have been in real difficulties with my creditors without your intercession."

"And replacing my stolen wardrobe—" Fergus fingered the lapel of his jacket.

"That's only money!" Frederick protested.

Max shrugged. "Who knows how much longer it will take for grandfather's estate to be settled?"

"I'll not hear another word about money, you two. Your friendship has no price."

"You must admit, your Lordship, paying for us and our valets to accompany you to America is most generous."

"Nonsense! You cannot travel without servants," Frederick said. "And now you know that I had an ulterior motive in asking you to join me," he sighed. "I had not intended to be so frank with you."

"What can we do?" Max asked.

"In spite of your dubious fortune, Fergus, I can not help but notice that Miss Arrington is attracted to you." Frederick stood, took a few steps, and turned to face him. "Perhaps you could show me how to capture the affections of a maiden?"

Not by the flicker of an eyelash did Fergus betray that he was planning that young lady's demise when he stretched, then stood also. Adjusting his tie needlessly, he said, "Perhaps if you were to pretend that Miss Danforth is a tiger?" He paused and ventured a smile.

Frederick nodded.

"Yes." Max stood. "The first thing we must do is to put you at your ease."

Frederick pulled his watch from its pocket. Upon seeing the time, he started for the door. "I have kept Mr. Danforth waiting."

J.C. bolted from his listening post and dashed toward the backstairs with Maurice close behind.

"Her brother? Wait a moment, your Lordship," Max said. "I have an idea."

"What is it, Max?" Frederick stopped. "Be quick."

"Would you say that Miss Danforth would listen to the council of her brother?" Max caught up to him.

"I suppose so. They seemed to be having a jolly time with their chase just a while ago."

"Why not enlist her brother's aid to plead your case?"

Frederick's broad smile returned as he stared at Max in open admiration. "Of course," he said. "Now why didn't I think of that? Capital idea!"

"Then let us not keep the man waiting," Fergus said as he held the door open for Max and Frederick to precede him.

* * *

Invariably titillated by opulence, Rodney's humor was completely restored by the splendor of the Blue Drawing Room. High overhead, countless brilliant crystals cascaded from three immense chandeliers, each suspended from a separate centerwork in the extravagantly gilded, bas-relief ceiling. Lavishly embroidered Prussian blue velvet festooned massive, gilt-embellished valances at the tops of the tremendous windows and descended to frame them to the floor.

Tables abounded. Carved and inlaid in every imaginable style, they lined the picture-glutted walls. Flanked by antique chairs, they also stood on the muted shades of Aubusson carpets that were strewn about like so many throw rugs on the highly polished oak floors. Every surface was encumbered with innumerable baubles, some beautiful, many hideous, all costly. Monumental vases held fresh-cut hothouse flowers in abundance.

Having relinquished his overcoat, however, Rodney discovered that to venture too far from the huge marble fireplace was to court chilblains. He had just returned to the hearth from a foray into the chill to more closely examine some of the treasures and was warming his hands, when a footman swung the door wide and three gentlemen strode toward him. A man with curly blond hair and a mismatched brown beard was slightly in front of a tall lanky gentleman. Ahead of both of them strode a smaller, darkly tanned man with sun-burned hair.

Reaching the fireplace, Frederick grasped Rodney's hand, saying, "You must be Miss Danforth's brother." After introducing Max and Fergus, he continued, "Sorry we've kept you waiting. We were overlong with the ponies this morning. Threw our whole schedule awry. Do you play?"

"Play what?"

"Why, polo, of course."

"No, I don't," Rodney replied defensively, feeling at a disadvantage. "It's my brother, Benjamin, who's the sportsman in our family. But he's been ill. Too ill to come for our sister, so I came in his place."

"That is too bad," Frederick said. Then concerned that

58

he'd be misunderstood, he explained, "Not too bad that you're here, old boy. Too bad your brother is ill." He glanced beseechingly at Max and Fergus.

Fergus groaned inwardly.

Max motioned with his hand to indicate the couches and chairs arranged near the fire.

Still distracted by the ostentation surrounding him, Rodney noticed nothing awry, and sat in the chair Frederick indicated.

"Ah, yes," Frederick said. "Might as well be comfortable while we wait for the others." But when they were comfortably settled, he could think of nothing further to say.

Max cleared his throat and was about to break the lengthening silence, when Rodney said, "This is the handsomest room I've ever seen outside a museum."

Frederick visibly relaxed. "Then you should see the Porcelain Room," he said expansively, grateful to be on safe ground, discussing something that could not possibly offend. "The fourth marquess collected many masterpieces from the Yuan period."

"I'd very much enjoy seeing them," Rodney said eagerly. "My father is an avid collector, especially of jade. He started the collection himself and he's determined to make it the best in America."

Vastly relieved to have so swiftly found a common ground upon which to meet Miss Danforth's brother, Frederick continued, "Bicycling is planned after lunch." Suddenly worried, he asked, "You do cycle, don't you?"

"Of course," Rodney replied huffily.

"Perhaps afterwards," Frederick continued earnestly, "there'll be time to inspect a portion of the modest Hunterswell collection. Before tea. And perhaps your sister will join us?"

The plaintive note in Frederick's voice as he included Abigail did not escape Rodney, and, in a flash, he knew how he could sabotage her. But before he could respond, the doors swung wide.

"Father!" Frederick jumped to his feet.

Max, Fergus, and Rodney all stood, but remained by the fire while Frederick crossed the room to greet the marquess.

Father and son were about the same height, but a recently acquired paunch enhanced the dignity of the older man. His beard, trimmed in the style of Vandyke, and his thinning hair were the color of old polished sterling. High upon his generous nose, gold-rimmed glasses enlarged his gray eyes to an expression of perpetual astonishment. Even though his bejeweled hand trembled on Frederick's sleeve, he was clearly master of his household.

"Good to see you as always, boys." The marquess extended his hand graciously. Max and Fergus in turn bowed slightly and grasped his fingertips.

Rodney imitated their greeting.

"And where is your charming sister?" The marquess's eyes were mischievous behind his glasses. "I have heard so much about her I am all aquiver to meet her," he teased, exaggerating his natural tremor. Not expecting a response, he turned to Max and Fergus, winking broadly, "Women! Always late!" He signalled for a footman. "Good thing, too. Gives us a chance to enjoy some sherry."

After they had toasted the Queen, the marquess raised his glass in salute to Max and Fergus. "And thank you, gentlemen, once again, for having such a sharp eye. You shot that panther in the nick of time." He turned to Rodney. "These young men saved my son's life. Did you know that?" Without waiting for Rodney to reply, he launched into the story with great relish.

With a swift glance at one another, Max and Fergus then stared modestly into the fire as if wishing they were somewhere else, until, at last, the marquess reached the end of the tale he so clearly enjoyed.

"I'm just pleased that we happened along," Max said on cue, when the marquess finished.

"Anyone would have done the same," Fergus shrugged.

"Ah, but if it hadn't been for you chaps," Frederick said, "we'd never have met the Nawab Abdulsamad."

"Quite right, my boy," the marquess chimed in. "You'd be searching for him still." He raised his glass high to salute both Max and Fergus. "Without you, we'd never have captured the Punjat's Ruby for Wales."

"What is the Punjat's Ruby?" Rodney asked.

"Now, let's not spoil a fine evening's entertainment, shall we?" the marquess said, not unkindly. "Mr. Mark Twain is going to tell us all about the ruby after dinner tonight."

"I am looking forward to meeting Mr. Clemens," Max said. "When is he arriving?"

"Sometime before tea," the marquess said. "I expect that he and the Nawab will have some details—"

Before he finished his sentence, a footman opened the door and announced, "Lord Pepper has arrived, your Lordship."

The marquess remained seated as he called to his old friend, "Hallo, Lord Pepper. Come join us by this lovely fire. We're awaiting the company of the ladies."

Three stories underneath the Blue Drawing Room, Stork stood in the doorway of Mrs. Budge's tiny office. Sliding his right foot up behind his left calf, he wriggled his stiff ankle. This reminder of his youthful service as batman to the Regimental Colonel of the Royal Fusiliers would always be with him. He had been ignominiously stepped on by a horse, which had shattered both his right foot and his career. It had taken the whole of his twentieth year to defy the surgeons and walk again, but not without a limp. The unremitting ache had long since etched lines beneath his kind blue eyes and on the sides of his mouth.

As a child of six, Frederick had taken one look at the tall and terribly thin man with his stooped posture and one-legged stance, and promptly christened him Stork. He had been called nothing else for more than twenty-five years, and it was unlikely that anyone but he could remember his real name. Stork was not displeased.

The ache was worse today as it always was when the weather turned damp. He hardly felt like acting the arbiter he had been summoned to be.

The butler's voice was more pinched than usual as he

said, "Come in and close the door, Stork. I don't want the lower servants to overhear." Seated with Mrs. Budge at the cloth-covered table, he gestured for Stork to join them as he continued, "You know how they tattle."

Stork could hear the jangle of Mrs. Budge's keys as she fingered them impatiently. Her face was a study in indignation. Stork knew trouble was afoot when the teapot was missing. When he'd seated himself, the butler spoke as though he were restraining his temper at great cost. "State your case, Mrs. Budge."

"I tell you, Stork, it ain't fittin'." Stork's worst suspicions were confirmed as her carefully suppressed cockney accent burst forth, "I won't 'ave it in me 'ouse!" She glared at Stork in defiance.

Putting both of his hands on the table, knuckles down, the butler rose from his chair to lean across the table. "And I tell you that you don't know what the future holds!" He sat back down and spoke more softly, as though ashamed of having lost his composure. "You had better play your cards so that either way—"

Stork held up his hands. "Wait a minute, you two. Hold on. What are you talking about? Whose future? Isn't today enough to take care of? The Prince of Wales is coming!"

"That's just me point!" Jaw set, Mrs. Budge nodded her head emphatically.

"And that is exactly my point!" the butler glared at her.

If he had not been so exasperated, Stork might have laughed. "If you both have taken the same point, what is your argument?"

Mrs. Budge twisted her mouth and mumbled at the table. "It's that Frenchie, that's what."

"Speak up, please, Mrs. Budge," Stork said patiently. "I can't hear you."

She raised her head and squared her shoulders. Her white starched cap could have been a coronet, "It's that Miss Bordeaux, it is. And that Mr. Kinkade who's coming, that's what."

"I don't understand," Stork replied. "They serve Mr. and Miss Danforth, who are guests. What is the problem?"

The butler nudged Stork as he shook his finger at the housekeeper. "Mrs. Budge is so shortsighted that she can't see that his Lordship and Miss Danforth—" Shrugging, he finished lamely, "Well, that some day—"

"Hah! Now he's the one what won't spit it out!" Mrs. Budge was gleeful, her accent under control. "Well, right now, right this minute, Miss Danforth is a commoner." She thrust the watch that dangled from a chain around her neck at them. "And so's her brother. And I ain't entertaining no commoner's servants in my parlor. Not alongside them as is serving His Royal Majesty, the Prince of Wales. It ain't right!"

The butler leaned toward her again, "If Lord Hunterswell marries Miss Danforth, someday she will be the marchioness. If that comes to pass, you better hope Miss Bordeaux does not have a long memory!"

"Hmmmmpf! You are skylarking. Right now," she pointed at her watch, "they belong in servant's hall."

"But you entertain J.C. and Maurice," Stork said. "Mr. Driscoll and Mr. Buchanan are commoners."

"That's different, that is!" Mrs. Budge looked at both men as though they were simpletons. "They saved the young master's life!"

"And where will Lord and Lady Pepper's staff take tea?" Stork glanced significantly at the butler, as he questioned Mrs. Budge.

Staring at Stork as though he'd gone daft, Mrs. Budge said, "Where they always have! With the house steward and me. Lord Pepper's an earl!"

"I'd be willing to stake a guinea that Miss Bordeaux takes her meals with the upper servants in Lord Pepper's house." Stork winked at the butler. "Turnabout is fair play."

"But that's only an earl's house," she snapped back scornfully, unaware of any contradiction. "They don't even have a housekeeper like me, they don't."

Stork stood to leave. "And so you want me to decide where Bordeaux and Kinkade will take meals?"

The butler waved him back to his seat, "Well, not exactly. You see—"

Mrs. Budge interrupted, "Just you sit down," she said imperiously. "And then there's that Nawab fella coming, too. What kinda title is that?"

"He's a Burmese Prince. A Hindu." Stork held out a bony hand to forestall Mrs. Budge's comments as he returned to his chair. "I'll remind you that our beloved Queen is Empress of India. The Nawab is one of Her Majesty's subjects, same as any duke."

Mrs. Budge conceded his point with a slight nod.

"And besides," Stork continued, "you won't be having any difficulties with his servants. He only travels with one."

"See!" the butler said as if he'd just won a large wager. "I told you so!"

"Well, I never!" Mrs. Budge gasped.

"And I know for a fact," Stork continued, "that the Nawab don't go anywhere without Aref being three steps behind him. Eating and sleeping."

"Sleeping?" Mrs. Budge was astonished. "You ain't trying to tell me his man sleeps with him in the same room?"

Stifling a smile, Stork nodded his head solemnly.

"What is this house coming to!" Mrs. Budge's distress was genuine. "Heathens what sleep with their masters! Americans! Another crazy Frenchie to put up with besides that chef!"

"And you won't be needing a footman at table for His Highness Abdulsamad, neither," Stork addressed the butler, " 'cause little Aref not only serves him, he stands right behind him tasting and drinking everything before the Nawab gets a drop."

"You don't say!" Mrs. Budge's eyes were wide. "Whatever for?"

"Palace intrigue," Stork replied, in as matter-of-fact a tone as he could manage. "The Nawab is afraid of being poisoned. I watched them doing it in Rangoon. Lord Hunterswell told me that Aref is the Nawab's taster even in public restaurants. Can't see why he'd be any different here."

"Poison! In the marquess's house! Why I never!" Mrs. Budge stood. "You'd better get somebody else to tell the

Chef. And Cook, too, for that matter, that somebody's tasting their food for poison. I'll not be the one to tell 'em. Why, if either one of 'em quit, the marchioness'd have me head on the block.''

With a scraping of chairs on the stone floor, both men had stood when Mrs. Budge rose. The butler held her chair for her to be seated again. "Now don't go getting all upset again, Mrs. Budge," he said furtively. "What they don't know won't harm them. Right?" He sat beside her. "I mean, why do they have to be told at all?"

"The marchioness would be so insulted!" Mrs. Budge exclaimed. "Her table *poisoned!*"

"Her Ladyship won't even notice." Stork remained standing, automatically lifting his aching ankle to exercise it. "Aref is quite discreet."

"Appears like we won't be having any problems about where to serve Aref, Mrs. Budge," the butler chuckled. "If he never leaves the Nawab's side, he won't be taking tea with us."

"I don't know why we bothered to get your opinion at all, Stork." She looked at his gaunt figure disparagingly. "Why should you care? You go galavanting with Lord Hunterswell all over the place. It's me what is left behind to keep up the standards here."

"Then, please, Mrs. Budge, don't forget that I am soon leaving for New York with his Lordship. How well I am treated there may depend on how well you treat Kinkade and Bordeaux here. And besides," he sat again to plead with her, "Americans aren't like us. They don't have royalty. All they need to have to be treated like kings is a lot of money."

"That's more of me point!" she sighed. "Bordeaux and Kinkade, they won't know the difference either. But you can be sure that them as serves the Princess will. And it's us as has to live here."

Stork stood again, preparing to leave, his patience at last worn thin. "You asked me down here for my opinion. Well, my opinion is that you should treat Bordeaux and Kinkade with the same courtesy that you would extend to Lord and

Lady Pepper's servants. They need not be treated as grandly as His Royal Highness's servants are, of course. But I don't think they deserve being thrown into the lower servants' hall either.''

''I suppose next you'll be tellin' me to escort Miss Bordeaux to her quarters personally.'' She glared at Stork resentfully. ''Well, she'll get a tweenie or maybe an underhouse parlormaid, if I can spare her.''

The butler cleared his throat, ''Well, what about it Stork?'' he stood also. ''Isn't your real reason that you expect Lord Frederick to marry Miss Danforth?''

Mrs. Budge did not wait for Stork's response as she stood and walked to the sideboard where she faced them, arms folded, ''And they'll make a royal mess of things, too. Not knowing how to behave in a noble house. Mark my words!''

Stork kept his voice quiet as he said, ''Miss Danforth has finished her ride with the marchioness. Have you ordered her bath?''

Mrs. Budge straightened herself to her full height, ''Her room is ready. Her fire is lit, and that's that until her maid gets here with further instructions. Maybe Miss Danforth don't bathe for lunch. How'm I to know about Americans?''

''But Miss Bordeaux ain't here yet to order her bath,'' Stork said, impatience growing in his voice.

''Don't you push me no more, Stork. I know me job. And I ain't anticipating for no commoner. I don't care who she might become. Only the real article gets anticipating service in this house.''

''Well, what about it, Stork?'' the butler asked. ''Will the earl marry Miss Danforth?''

Stork allowed himself a guarded smile, ''Swear you won't tell?''

Both Mrs. Budge and the butler silently put hand to heart and raised the other heavenward while drawing closer to Stork.

''Just between us,'' Stork whispered. ''I think it just depends on her.''

''Hmmmpf!'' Keys ajangle, Mrs. Budge strode to the

door. She opened it and motioned for the two men to leave. As they passed her, she growled, "And you'd best believe it, if it don't happen, it's gonna be me as has the long memory!"

As her door slammed behind them, Stork asked, "Do you have time for a cuppa?"

Consulting his watch, the butler said, "Oh, blast, no. Sure could use one. That took longer than I thought it would. Before the dray arrives with all that luggage and those people, I've got to check the footmen's hose for luncheon." He started toward the narrow stone stairway to the kitchen. "The marchioness has a stinking fit if anyone is caught with a snag, but after feeding those—ah—children of hers, there's hardly an unscarred leg among them."

Stork limped after him, "From what I'm hearing about the Prince's birthday present from the marquess, you'd best have some of the more trustworthy of your footmen on duty. The lads will be having a lot of temptation put before them."

The butler stopped and turned his head. "You wouldn't be trying to tell me how to run my job?" He glared at Stork, his formal manner once more in place. Satisfied that Stork meant no criticism, he said, starting up the stairs, "You need not warn me. Only those who have been in the family over ten years are on duty tonight."

"I've been thinking," Stork said quickly before he lost the butler's attention altogether, "would it be possible for me to go with Kinkade's escort to his quarters. As Mrs. Budge says, he won't know the difference. I could maybe talk to him, judge what kind of man he is, how it'll be for me in New York."

Not bothering to look back, the butler shook his head, no. While slowing his speed up the stairs, he said over his shoulder, "You know well enough that showing guest servants to their quarters is what I reserve for training new underfootmen so's they'll learn the house. Thanks to those blasted Boers, I've got three new ones. I've already assigned, let me see—Timothy—as escort." He stopped. When Stork caught up with him, he whispered, "Timothy ain't all that bright, but he's got a good calf." He smiled ruefully, "Her Ladyship likes them tall, good-looking, and with a well-turned leg. Can't always find them with the proper looks and smart, too. 'Fraid it would give Timothy airs to see a man of your station doing usher duty," he shook his head again. Before Stork could protest, he continued, "You'll have your chance to chat a bit at tea."

When they reached the windowed landing overlooking the servant's entrance, the butler peered out of the leaded-glass panes at the courtyard. "Oh, double blast!" he exclaimed. "They're here already!"

"It's them, all right," Stork said. "I recognize that plain blonde girl. She's Lady Pepper's maid. And there's Lord Pepper's man. That tiny dark girl must be Miss Bordeaux. Why, she's hardly as big as the marchioness."

"That Kinkade fellow of your looks more like a prize-fighter than a gentleman's gentleman."

"So he does," Stork agreed. "What's that he's holding?" He tried looking through another pane for a better view. "What's he doing?"

"He's got a camera, blast it all!" the butler said, annoyed. "How can I enforce discipline if he's taking pictures of the staff. They've got duties!" Without bidding Stork good-bye, he stalked off for the courtyard.

Gazing at the scene below, Stork muttered to himself, "Lucky thing little Frenchie's not staying behind to get her picture taken. What a sour face!"

Pausing briefly at the servant's entrance to Hunterswell House, Jacqueline watched Kinkade's charm in action as he cajoled the other servants into posing for his Kodak. Compared to his frosty manner toward her during the trip, she was dismayed to observe just how gay he could be.

Trouble was, she deserved it. A traitor to her mistress. Her predicament had only one honorable solution. Fear lanced her hunger pangs, drying her mouth and destroying her appetite. Surprised at how swiftly the specter of destitution could threaten, she wasted no time mourning her demolished future.

While trying to figure out the most propitious moment to tell Miss Danforth of her treachery, she scarcely noticed the number of flights of dingy, narrow stairs she climbed. Nor did she pay the least attention to the tweenie who was guiding her to her shared quarters under the rafters.

Unaware that Jacqueline could not understand a word of her heavily accented English, the tweenie interpreted her silence as a sympathetic ear and, thrilled that she had such a good listener, was enjoying a fine grumble.

"Ooooh!" the tweenie exclaimed, upon reaching the tiny cubicle at last. Eyes wide with fright, she unceremoniously dropped Jacqueline's cardboard box of belongings onto the bare floor. "Betsy'll fair catch it if Miz B. finds 'em pallets ain't made. She's me friend, Miss. I gotta find 'er. I'll be back to fetch ya quick as you can blink!"

Too distracted to notice the meanness of her lodgings, Jacqueline hung her mantle and bonnet on a peg. Swiftly removing a fresh apron from the box, she wished for an iron to smooth out the fold marks. A ring of ice clung to the inside of the pitcher when she poured water into the bowl. Shivering, she forced herself to rinse her hands and splash her face.

She had no idea why her escort had left in such a flurry. There was no opportunity to become concerned about her return, for she had no sooner dried her hands on her cotton underskirt—there being no towel available—than there was a great commotion in the doorway. As alike as two daisies, the girls beamed at her. "Bless ya, luv," Betsy said. "Ya saved me ears a boxing from old Miz Fudge Pudge, ya did."

Jacqueline smiled in return, not knowing what else to do.

"See?" the tweenie tickled Betsy in the ribs. "She ain't snotty like Lady Pepper's lady. She'd a had yer head, with her pallet not being ready. Didn't I tell ya? She gets a extra blanket, she does."

Unaware that she'd just guaranteed Abigail the finest service the great house had to offer, Jacqueline followed her talkative tweenie on the long, tortuous route to the Green Bedchamber. Knowing that she was about to be dismissed, she only hoped that she'd be allowed to remain long enough to dress her mistress for meeting the Prince of Wales. There was some tricky ruching at the back of the heavy satin gown that she did not trust to fingers less nimble than her own.

Abigail's annoyance with her brother and Lord Hunterswell had melted in the warmth of a bath before the fire. Engrossed in her own thoughts during the tedious process of dressing, she was grateful for Jacqueline's silence. Only when her toilette was complete and she was admiring herself in the mirror and her maid's usual compliments were not forthcoming did she look at Jacqueline and actually see her.

"Why, Jacqueline, whatever is the matter?"

"Oh, Miss Danforth, I do not know how to tell you."

"Come, come, Jacqueline. Your English is good enough to tell me anything."

"The problem is not the English, if you please, Miss. The reason is treason."

"Whatever do you mean?"

"You are so beautiful, Miss Danforth. Everything I ever desire for the mistress. And I have much pleasure in serving you. And now," she sighed. *"Finis!"*

"Why must it come to an end?" Abigail was flabbergasted. "Has someone offered you a better position?"

"No. Oh, never. But after what I must tell you, the sack will be mine."

"Enough riddles! I must not be late for luncheon, and it is probably a ten-minute hike to the Blue Room. Tell me."

"You know the secret you told me to no matter the wild horse I must keep?"

"That I visited Dr. Conan Doyle?"

Jacqueline nodded, tears welling in her eyes.

Realizing just how distraught Jacqueline was, Abigail asked gently, "Whom did you tell?"

Controlling her tears, Jacqueline managed to choke out, "Master Rodney comes into your bedroom. He says he will tell your father that you have a lover after your money. Now we have a secret against you."

"Say that again. What is the secret?"

Taking a handkerchief from her apron pocket, Jacqueline blew her nose. "He does not want you to know he knows your secret." She shook her head sadly, watching Abigail walk slowly to the window. She sighed heavily, "I cannot live in the worry that he will tell you my treason. I am afraid of what else can he make me do, so he won't tell you. Better I tell you myself and have the sack."

"I see." Abigail stared out at the expanse of sculptured terraces, trying to fathom Rodney's behavior. Could he be planning to blackmail Jacqueline into dallying with him? With a sigh, she turned to her maid. "You really believed that I would dismiss you, yet you confessed anyway?"

"*Oui, Mlle.*"

"English!"

"Yes, Miss." She bobbed automatically.

"Are you certain that this is not some ploy, so that you can get out of going to New York?" Abigail searched her face, "You haven't gotten cold feet, have you?"

"Miss?" Jacqueline frowned. "My feet are warm."

"Oh, never mind." Abigail checked her hair again in the mirror.

"Please, Miss, may I stay until you sail?"

"Don't be tiresome, Jacqueline. I am not going to dismiss you."

"No?" Jacqueline was incredulous.

"What do you take me for?" Abigail began to feel insulted. "You think I cannot recognize courage when I see it?"

"Oh, Miss Danforth!" Jacqueline blushed.

"Now don't start sniveling! Hand me my shawl and fan. The last luncheon gong has sounded. I must run."

Seated at the enormous dining table, Abigail felt divided, much as the moon might be by the sun halving its surface. A fire screen behind her chair deflected the heat from the fireplace, but her left side was blistering while her right froze. To her left, so near the fire that even with a fire screen

71

she marveled that he did not burst into flames, sat Lord Hunterswell, unperturbed by the heat. She was much impressed with his stoicism. Regretting her breach of manners by having left him so abruptly, she had favored him with several warm smiles, a clear indication that she had forgiven him and was ready to converse.

On Frederick's left, Lady Pepper tried not to watch her husband too jealously as he played court to the marchioness at the foot of the table, while, next to her, Rodney emptied a glass of wine meant for toasting the Queen. A footman hastily refilled it.

Directly across from Abigail, on the marquess's honored right, Miss Arrington flirted with Fergus, who was all attention next to her. Max vied with Lord Pepper for the marchioness's attention.

To Abigail's right, the marquess reigned at the head of the table. Although his hair was gray and his hand trembled while toasting the Queen, his voice commanded their attention as he raised his glass, again, to salute Max and Fergus. "Thank you, gentlemen."

Miss Arrington graced Fergus with an admiring glance, while the two men, again, seemed properly abashed by the toast.

Abigail sampled the fish and hoped for better luck with the meat course.

As one of the footmen removed her plate, Miss Arrington peered at Abigail across the lavishly appointed table. "Tonight we will meet the Prince of Wales," she said, with a sly glance at Fergus. "Ain't you excited?"

Appalled by Miss Arrington's naked attempt to make Mr. Driscoll jealous, Abigail searched for words.

Frederick held his breath, astonished by how much Abigail's answer meant to him.

Before Abigail could respond, emboldened by the wine, Rodney interrupted in a voice loud enough for all to hear, "I am not sure my little sister will be all that impressed, Miss Arrington." His tone was sarcastic. "After all, she has been allowed to meet some colorful people all on her own."

"Whatever do you mean!" Lady Pepper turned to him

indignantly. "Are you implying that we did not watch after your sister? She was chaperoned every minute!" She leaned forward to address Abigail, "What have you done, child?"

Grateful for Jacqueline's warning, Abigail spoke before Rodney could, "My brother is probably referring to my visit to Dr. Conan Doyle at his home in Surrey."

Shocked into silence by his sister's easy confession, Rodney watched Frederick carefully.

Lady Pepper was about to shriek and faint, but caught a glimpse of the marchioness's calm demeanor and contented herself with an agitated fanning.

"But why, my child?" The marchioness asked. "Surely Lady Pepper would have had him to dinner had she known you wished to meet him?"

Recovering from his surprise, Frederick discovered that Abigail's adventure made her all the more appealing.

Suddenly, Abigail realized that if she were to have any chance whatever to realize her dream, she could no longer keep it a secret. "Dear Lady Pepper," she spoke before Rodney could interrupt again, "it is my deepest desire to become a consulting detective like the one Dr. Conan Doyle writes about."

"Wait until I tell father." Rodney put his wine glass down. "You may no longer be his daughter!"

"We'll see." Abigail held her head high. Not at all sure how she'd implement her words, she added, "I intend to tell him the moment we disembark."

Lady Pepper fanned herself frantically.

"How extraordinary!" Frederick's admiration for Abigail's spunk knew no bounds.

Abigail addressed the marchioness. "Do you remember my mentioning someone I'd read about this morning while we were riding?"

"The one who injects himself?"

"Yes," Abigail responded. "Dr. Conan Doyle wrote that Sherlock Holmes's entire life is devoted to one long effort to escape from the commonplace of existence."

"An admirable pursuit," the marchioness responded with a sleepy glance at Rodney.

Silently appearing at the marquess's side, the butler cleared his throat, extending the small silver tray holding crested notepaper toward his master.

"Not now!" Intent on Abigail, the marquess glanced at him, annoyed.

"Beg pardon, your Lordship," the butler insisted. "With your permission, the message is from His Royal Highness, the Prince of Wales."

Nonchalantly waving his knife at him, the marquess said, "Ah, well then. Read it. Read it!"

Abigail fell silent.

Opening the note, the butler read, "Our right and trusty and entirely beloved cousin—"

"Not that drivel, for God's sake, man," the marquess said around a bite of mutton chop. "Get to the message."

Scanning the heavy vellum document, the butler said, "Beg pardon, m'Lord, the Prince of Wales must cancel dinner this evening."

"What?" The marquess held out his hand. "Give me that!" Snatching it from the proffered salver, he read the note, the heavy stationery trembling in his hands. "Faughh!" he exclaimed, flinging the note toward his son. "It's true!"

"Oh, my poor Poopsie!"

Miss Arrington was stunned and looked near tears.

With their plans in shambles, Fergus glanced at Max, his expression bleak.

Lady Pepper wailed, "My new gown—"

Relieved that the Prince had been so smoothly eliminated as a possible rival, Frederick was guilt-stricken at his selfishness. "Are you terribly disappointed, Miss Danforth?"

"I confess I am more disappointed at the prospect of not seeing Mr. Clemens and the Punjat's Ruby," Abigail said, surprised, and grateful, that her announcement was being forgotten in the crisis.

"But what am I to do?" the marquess asked as his sherbet was served. "I cannot reach His Highness, the Nawab Abdulsamad, and tell him not to come."

"And Mr. Twain, too, Poopsie!" the marchioness said.

"He is not going to be so easy to engage again, if we cancel at the last minute."

"Why must you cancel the presentation?" Max asked.

"What's that you say, son?" the marchioness leaned toward Max, the better to hear him.

Raising his voice so that all could hear, Max replied, "Why not have the Prince here, in absentia? You could reserve a seat for him, and Alexandra, too, of course, and carry on as though they were present."

"Yes," Fergus added. "Later, the marquess can give it to him, but without all the folderol."

"By Jove, it might work!" The marchioness beamed at them as she dipped her fingertips into her finger bowl. "How about it, Poopsie?"

"But how can we go ahead?" the marquess said. "The Punjat's Ruby is for Bertie. Its whole history is being retold for his benefit."

"I don't know, Max," Frederick joined in. "I want to see Wales's reaction when he first sees it."

"But you'll be gone to America for weeks!" the marchioness cried, drying her hands. "I simply will not wait any longer to see that ruby." She began drawing on her gloves. "Either that Abdulla fella shows it to me the moment he arrives, or we carry on with the party."

"But mother," Frederick protested, frowning at Max, "won't the Nawab and Mr. Twain miss the presence of His Royal Highness?"

"Come to think of it, son," the marquess replied. "The Nawab will be glad enough to get his money. I have refused to pay him but half until it is actually in my possession."

"And I am certain that Mr. Twain will be so charmed to see Miss Danforth again that he won't mind missing His Majesty," Max said, smiling at Abigail.

"Thank you, Mr. Driscoll." Abigail smiled demurely in return.

Desperately sorry that he'd opposed Max's idea for a moment, Frederick watched Abigail adoringly.

"Then it is settled!" Alert for her signal, the footmen assisted the marchioness and her guests with their chairs.

Standing, she said, "Now everyone change for cycling. We will meet on the front terrace."

Upstaged by Abigail's confession, Rodney's disappointment was bitter and deep. He planned on taking a long draught from the flask in his room before reappearing for cycling.

As planned, J.C. left Maurice when they reached belowstairs and began a stealthy search for Stork. Locating him in Budge's office, he was left with the problem of where to intercept him, alone. From the sounds of the voices issuing from the office, he figured Stork would be wanting a cuppa when finished, so he stationed himself in a cul-de-sac outside the house steward's parlor and waited.

He nearly missed his rendezvous when his favorite parlormaid chanced by and paused to flirt. With his black hair parted in the exact middle and his sideburns clipped precisely at the tips of his earlobes, he cut a romantic figure. She'd been gone but a moment when he heard Stork's distinctive footsteps.

"Pssst! Stork!" he stage-whispered.

"Who's there?" Stork's question was peevish. He heartily disliked games. "Oh, it's you!" his voice filled with disgust.

"You don't need to take that tone with me," J.C. said unctuously.

"What do you want!"

J.C.'s grin was sly, "I just wanted to remind you about tomorrow."

"I don't need reminding!" Stork snarled at him.

"Now don't carry on like that, old pal. After all I done for you?"

Glancing about furtively to see if their interchange had been observed, Stork fled.

Chapter Three

A straight line can be drawn from any point to any
other point.

Euclid

Miss Gilda Arrington was thoroughly upset. Flouncing
down the stairs behind the footman in her modish cycling
costume, ribbons aflutter from her hat of straw, she tried to
size up her situation, but it was difficult to think clearly with
her plans in shreds. The Prince was not coming. Her big
chance gone. And no other in the immediate offing.

Yet if she could but catch his fancy, she'd be set for life.
When their affair ended, and she was realist enough to know
that it would eventually end, she had intended to persuade
him to set her up in a hat shop. Every woman in England
was eager to hear tidbits about His Royal Highness, and
her success would have been assured. But she needed more
time in his presence than a glance or two at the opera and
a few words at a reception to attract him. And soon. With
all the competition for his attention, he'd forget about her,
if she didn't see him again soon.

Then there was Fergus. If truth be told, she should not
have begun a flirtation with him in the first place. The
source of his money was doubtful. He'd soon be leaving for
America for a stay of uncertain length. Yet, when he'd returned from Burma with Lord Hunterswell, there'd been
an air of mystery about him, quite beyond her limited ex-

perience, which had intrigued her beyond her powers to resist. It had been a tactical error to tease Fergus about the Prince. She should have been much more certain of attaining Wales's affection before trying to make Fergus jealous. His eyes had taken on an expression that had frightened her when she'd touched upon the subject of the Punjat's Ruby. She knew something was afoot. But what? And what good would it do to know *now,* if she didn't have the Prince to tell it to? She had flirted with Fergus at lunch to test his response. Underneath his apparent forgiveness, his eyes had flashed that danger signal again.

Reaching the outdoors, she calmed herself. Might as well enjoy the day. Fergus would be gone soon enough. Perhaps she could entice a promise from him to return to her when his visit was done. Even if she failed, the flirtation would be good practice for Wales. Pouting prettily, she strolled toward the group assembled at the bicycles.

Having kept an eye on the door for her appearance, Fergus spotted Miss Arrington at once, and broke away from the group to meet her. Smiling, one hand on its handlebars, the other on its high-set seat, he wheeled a cycle tall enough for his lanky frame toward her.

Hesitating before Mrs. Budge's parlor door, Jacqueline listened to the reassuring sounds of laughter, but her heart sank when she identified Kinkade's voice. Too famished to deny herself lunch for fear of what he might say, she knocked timidly and stepped into the room. A most attractive man, his black hair parted in the center in the latest fashion with perfectly clipped sideburns, immediately rose from his place at the crowded table and came toward her.

"You must be Miss Bordeaux," he said, extending his hand in greeting. "My name is J.C. Won't you join us?" He held out a chair for her.

Half-rising from his chair in greeting, Maurice was impressed anew with his companion's unflagging interest in women.

The other menservants rose also, reseating themselves when she took the proffered chair.

Jacqueline smiled shyly at J.C. *"Merci, Monsieur."* The round, highly polished table was laden with much crockery, but food was sparse. She selected a thin chicken sandwich. Cook was in attendance.

The atmosphere was friendly enough with a cosy fire and the familiar smells of beeswax and starch. As Mrs. Budge poured tea, Kinkade said in stentorian tones for all to hear, "You need not waste your time being polite with the likes of her, J.C., she's only interested in the gentlemen of a household. She's not likely to favor a mere gentleman's gentleman." He laughed at his play on words.

Everyone laughed awkwardly. J.C. looked at her, genuinely intrigued.

Jacqueline bit into the sandwich hungrily, only to find it disappointing, without taste. She refused to respond. While the conversation continued around her, she ate without comment, wondering how she could redeem herself in Kinkade's eyes. And what was Master Rodney going to do to her when he discovered her treachery? As she took a sip of the weak tea, it occurred to her that had Miss Danforth dismissed her, life might have been a good deal simpler. She, along with everyone else in the room, looked up when the door swung wide and Stork entered.

Stork's smile twisted into a grimace when he spotted J.C. and Maurice. He left abruptly, slamming the door behind him.

Abigail had tarried overlong with Jacqueline, and her crisp linen cycling costume fairly crackled as she raced down the corridor, footman in tow. As they approached the last corner before the staircase, she could hear the butler's nasal voice. Hoping he was escorting Mark Twain, which would give her an opportunity to speak with him alone, she slowed her pace and composed herself.

As the butler appeared around the corner, in his wake followed a man whose shoulders, chest, and stomach were so large, he seemed precariously balanced on legs too slender and feet too small for support. Indeed, Abigail thought, he seemed in imminent danger of toppling over.

"Miss Danforth," the butler said. "May I present his Highness, the Nawab Ahanti Khabir Abdulsamad."

Although he wore a turban, which had a gigantic fire opal surrounded by diamonds in the center, the Nawab was otherwise dressed in the latest Western mode. He extended a disproportionately tiny hand in greeting. "You are even more beautiful than Lord Hunterswell has led me to believe," he said graciously. "And Lord Hunterswell's praise was the highest, I hasten to assure you, in case my poor remarks do him an injustice."

Considering his size, his voice was surprisingly light and, although she had no idea what she had expected, his diction, perfect. She thought she detected the haunting fragrance of cloves as she made a shallow, all-purpose curtsy while murmuring, "Thank you, your Highness. You are most kind."

The Nawab gestured toward the white-clad youth behind him and said, "And this is my nephew, Aref."

She blinked. Aref's high cheekbones, delicately shaped nose, and a complexion the color of butterscotch created an effect of beauty rather than manly handsomeness. He bowed gravely.

"Aref understands everything you say perfectly, Miss Danforth," the Nawab said. "Regrettably, he is unable to speak. He is mute."

"Hello, Aref." Her smile froze. Aref's slender wrists were shackled to the velvet-draped box he was holding. His chains were lightweight and golden, but he was nonetheless bound. Realizing that he was probably attached to the Punjat's Ruby, she groaned at her own naivete in having thought that it might somehow disappear, just so she could begin a career of detection by recovering it.

"I look forward to chatting with you at tea, Miss Danforth," the Nawab said as he motioned for the butler to move on. "Come, Aref, you have time to bathe me before we meet this lovely lady again."

Abigail knew she should hurry on her way, but she could

not refrain from staring after the Nawab, marveling at how lightly he carried his great bulk, with the exotic Aref seeming to float behind him. Nor could she resist speculating upon how they had come to possess the ruby. Or wondering how they must feel about parting with it. And precisely how had Messrs. Driscoll and Buchanan helped in finding the Nawab? A princely sum indeed must be changing hands. With a grimace and a shake of her head, she dismissed her thoughts. The ruby was being so closely guarded that any chance of its being stolen was clearly impossible. In haste, she turned to resume her journey to the cyclists and almost crashed into the footman escorting Mark Twain.

After a moment's confusion, Twain said, "Why Abigail Danforth, is that you?" He held his arms wide with obvious delight. "I heard tell you'd be here."

After a fond embrace, he stepped back. "What a sight you are for these hungry eyes," he sighed. "But I reckon any pretty girl with chestnut hair's gonna remind me of my Susy."

Abigail's memories of Twain's daughter were vague, but pleasurable, and her dark eyes were sad as she said, solemnly, "I was grieved to hear of her death."

"It was all so horribly quick." His unruly hair was turning white. Bereavement had deposited lines around his mouth that his bristling moustache could not conceal.

"How's Miss Livy?" she asked.

"Oh, just tolerable."

"We heard about how things got pretty bad for you financially. Father said he knew that you'd ask him if you needed anything."

"Naw . . . got enough of my friends in the soup—or machinery—on that one. The man just plain chouselled me—"

Intent upon her own difficulties, and eager to have his opinion, Abigail interrupted, "Oh, I am so happy to have this moment alone with you. Much has happened, and I need your advice."

The footmen stationed themselves within earshot as Twain said, "Well, honey bunch, there's nothing I like better than giving advice, so long as you know you need not take it.''

Abigail took a deep breath and looked at him earnestly. ''Promise you won't laugh?''

Hand to his heart, he gazed with mock solemnity at the ceiling.

Before she could lose her courage, she said quickly, ''This last spring, I was fortunate enough to come upon a most exciting story, *A Study in Scarlet,* wherein Dr. Watson chronicled the adventures of a most remarkable man, Sherlock Holmes. Perhaps you've read it?''

''Clever.'' Twain nodded his head. ''Yes, go on.''

''Well, naturally, after that, I read everything about Holmes that I could find. Each story was more thrilling than the last. Mr. Holmes seemed to live a life of unparalleled adventure.'' Chin high, her voice firm, she continued. ''I decided that I want to become a detective, too.'' She watched him closely.

His mouth tight against smiling at her youthful enthusiasm, not her desire, Twain indicated that she should continue.

In the interest of saving time, she decided that Twain need not know of her error in thinking Holmes real as she said, ''I'll not go into the details of how I arranged it, but I managed to visit Dr. Conan Doyle at his home, Undershaw, to seek his advice.''

''And what did he say, my child?'' Although he refrained from smiling, his eyes twinkled with delight at her audacity.

''I daresay he discouraged me because he is not overly fond of Holmes himself. He absolutely refuses to write any more stories about him.''

''And you want my opinion?''

She nodded eagerly.

Twain paused for a moment, gazing down the corridor. Finally he turned to her. ''The twentieth century is a stranger to me, Miss Abigail. I wish it well.'' He patted her hand. ''Who can tell what it will hold for you?''

''Then you don't think it is impossible?''

Without responding to her question directly, he said,

"Not too long ago, I had a book published, which might be of interest to you, by the title of *Pudd'nhead Wilson*. I used a newfangled idea that will some day, I wager, come into general use as a device for trapping criminals."

"Isn't that the story about the switched boys?"

"Yep, but more important for you is a device better than footprints in the snow—which don't do you much good in the summertime—or ashes from a cigarette put together."

"Fingerprints!"

"Yep. And I'll bet Conan Doyle hasn't read it 'cause in only one of Holmes's cases has he ever so much as made a glancing reference to a thumbprint."

Abigail was speechless with excitement at his casual acceptance.

He shook a finger at her, "And you might tell him for me, that I'm a little miffed at being so ignored."

"Yes, sir."

"And there's something else. Did you know that Will Gillette is starring in a play called *Sherlock Holmes*, in New York?"

"Yes," she said with a pout. "Dr. Conan Doyle refused to give me an introduction to him."

"Did he now?" Twain tucked his thumb into his vest pocket as he grinned. "Well, it just so happens that I got Willie his first acting job back when his folks were dead set against his becoming an actor. Happy to say my little joke backfired." He paused before asking, "What ship are you sailing on, and when?"

"The *St. Louis*. She leaves Southampton Monday morning."

"There'll be a letter of introduction to Willie waiting for you in your cabin. And I'll try 'n' scrounge a copy of *Pudd'nhead Wilson* for you, too."

"I don't know how to thank you," Abigail hugged him. The footmen stirred, ready to resume their duties, as Abigail asked, "Were you told that the Prince of Wales is not coming?"

"Yep, my escort here gave me the glad tidings." Smiling, he indicated the tall, expressionless man beside him.

"I'm sorry to miss His Highness again, but the show will go on. The Nawab wants to collect his loot. Though why they picked on me to tell the tale, I'll never know. There's nary a drop of humor in it, it's that bloodthirsty."

"You are only the most famous master of ceremonies in all of Europe, that's why," she said with a shiver of anticipation.

He beamed. "And with a few more engagements that pay as well as this one, I too shall be going home."

A broad smile perfectly masked Fergus's anger as he wheeled the bicycle toward Miss Arrington. For him, life was simple. White. Or black. You were for him or against him. And woe be it to you, if you were against him. He often, and loudly, had decried the passing of the duel as swift vengeance for an insult. Not that he'd deign to duel with a female.

Bitch! How dare she tantalize him? Promise favors she had no intention of bestowing. Beguile him into hinting of his plans for the Punjat's Ruby in order to impress her? She'd been impressed all right. So impressed, she'd threatened to embellish on what he'd told her in confidence, just to get the ear of the Prince. Ambitious doxy! No better than her sisters of the night who sold themselves for a farthing.

His plan was simple. Charm her into riding a cycle too unwieldy to manage, so that he'd have to hold her steady. While Max diverted the attention of the others, he'd lure her far enough away from the main body of cyclers so that his movements would be interpreted as helping her, if anyone did happen to be watching. What could be more natural than for a girl to go cycling off with an attentive beau to assist her? A sharp twist on the handlebars and a shove should do it. If the fall did not kill her outright, he would finish her off with the stone in his pocket before anyone came close enough to witness.

His plan was working.

Miss Arrington's confidence in her powers to seduce had returned during Fergus's obvious efforts to please her by cavorting on the bicycle, amusing the others, cajoling her into riding it so he'd have the excuse to help her. Clearly he wanted to be alone with her. Persuading him to return to her was going to be easier than she had thought. Even though her toe barely touched the pedal when it was on the down-sweep, she was only too eager to allow Fergus and a footman to assist her atop the cycle.

She had cycled many times before, but the bikes had been smaller, easier to manage. She could not seem to gain her balance on this one. When they had started out, Fergus had trotted by her side to steady her. But now that they had taken a different path, away from the others, he had fallen behind. Only occasionally would he give her a push to keep up her momentum. She did not realize that he'd been keeping her off balance with every shove. It was all she could do to control the handlebars. Wondering why he didn't draw beside her to talk, now that they were alone, she risked a quick glance over her shoulder. She gasped in shock at the enraged expression on his face. Swiftly facing forward, she mustered all her strength to force down the pedal. The cycle wobbled. She could gain no speed. Desperate, she looked around for help. There was no one. She glanced back again, hoping that she'd been wrong about the look on Fergus's face. He was closer. His expression even more clear. And murderous.

Way behind him, much too faraway to hear a shout for help, two people on a bicycle for two had turned onto the path.

Gasping with panic, she faced forward again. Again, she tried to pedal faster.

Fergus drew beside her with ease.

"Bitch!" he shouted in her ear. "Whore!" Wrenching the handlebars to the side, he gave the bicycle a final, vicious shove. He hoped the fall wouldn't kill her. He wanted the pleasure of smashing her silly skull himself.

Shrieking in terror, she pitched forward.

Grateful that the rain had held off, Lord Hunterswell had lingered behind where the bicycles were stationed to wait for Abigail. He had hoped to have a word with her brother, but Rodney had not appeared. Presumably the man did not care for cycling, and had an American's rudimentary manners that permitted him to do what he pleased rather than join in and add his part to the planned entertainments, like Fergus had with his tricks on the bike. Frederick had begun to fear that Abigail was cut from the same cloth when, at long last, she appeared, irresistibly attired, with the proper apologies for being late.

Still enthralled by her encounter with Mark Twain, when Frederick suggested that they ride in tandem, Abigail acquiesced and, with footmen holding it steady, climbed onto the back seat of the double-cycle while Frederick commanded the front. After a push-off by the footmen, it took her but a moment to match his rhythm and soon they were speeding along the paved path. Calling to her over his shoulder, Frederick suggested that they follow after Miss Arrington and Mr. Buchanan. Miss Arrington had been so wobbly, they probably weren't too far beyond the turn, while goodness knew where the others had gotten to by now.

No sooner had they maneuvered their cycle around the corner than they heard Miss Arrington's scream in the distance. Abigail looked up in time to see her land on the pavement with a terrible force. She winced, so totally losing the pedaling rhythm with Frederick that she sat with limbs outstretched so that he could pedal more rapidly and guide the cycle. Thus occupied, Lord Frederick did not see Fergus raise his arm as if to strike her as he bent over Miss Arrington. Abigail did.

"Stop!" Abigail shouted.

Lord Frederick instantly slowed his frantic pedaling.

"Not you, Lord Frederick!" Abigail shouted. "Hurry! He's trying to kill her!"

"What?" Frederick looked over his shoulder at Abigail.

"No! No!" One hand on the handlebar, Abigail motioned with the other for him to turn around. "Look!" She pointed in the direction of the accident. "Hurry!"

By the time Abigail and Frederick reached the fallen bicycle, Fergus was seated beside Miss Arrington's sprawled figure. Ever so tenderly, he had gathered her into his arms and, rocking her inert body, he was keening with grief.

Leaving Lord Frederick to set the bike stand and shout for help, Abigail rushed to Fergus's side and, kneeling, examined Miss Arrington. "You should not have picked her up," she scolded. "You could be making her injuries worse."

"Who are you to tell me what to do?" Fergus kept his voice low so that Frederick could not hear.

The menace in his tone made Abigail hesitate but a moment. Hat lost upon impact, Miss Arrington's head was bleeding from a wound hidden in her hair and it needed staunching. Although he held her fondly enough, Fergus was just staring at her, whining, watching the blood ooze. Abigail pulled a handkerchief from a pocket and held it to as much of the wound as she could see. Only then did she believe that Miss Arrington might truly be dead. Eyes closed, she was so very still, her face drained of all color. The palms of both gloves were ripped and her bloody hands testified to the impact of her landing.

"You did kill her!" Abigail exclaimed.

Fergus's eyes narrowed. How much had this bitch actually seen? He said nothing. Holding his breath, he waited for Lord Hunterswell's reaction when he came to stand over them.

"Miss Danforth!" Frederick was appalled by her accusation. Relieved beyond measure, Fergus took a chance. "It is true, Lord Frederick," he sobbed. "I killed her."

"Nonsense, man." Frederick kneeled to comfort him. "It was an accident. A tragic, horrible accident."

"But she is dead." Fergus could scarcely speak, he was so overwrought. "And I did it."

"No, she isn't," Abigail's smile was ironic. "The blood from her wound is still pulsing. I can feel it. Hold this!" Grabbing Frederick's hand, she placed it on the soggy handkerchief so that she could bend close and listen for Miss Arrington's breathing.

Frederick pulled out a clean handkerchief and placed it

over the blood-soaked one. His admiration for Abigail knew no bounds. Any other girl of his acquaintance would have fainted long before now.

Again, Fergus held his breath.

"She is breathing!" Abigail sat up to look directly at Fergus. "You did not kill her after all!"

"Oh, thank God!" Fergus exclaimed, clutching Miss Arrington closer, dislodging Frederick's hand. "Thank God!"

Distracted in his efforts to keep Miss Arrington's wound covered, Frederick's voice grew impatient. "Miss Arrington has taken a nasty spill, Miss Danforth. A regrettable occurrence, to be sure, but a murder attempt?" He turned to Fergus. "Hold still, old boy, will you?" He looked at Abigail. "Can't you see that Mr. Buchanan is distraught?"

"Do not be distressed with Miss Danforth, m'Lord." Fergus's tone was patronizing. "Any girl who wants to become a detective must have an overly suspicious mind."

Abigail was furious. Implanted upon her brain was the image of Fergus's arm raised to strike Miss Arrington as she lay helpless on the ground. She stood. In trying to brush herself off, she succeeded in bloodying everything her soaked gloves touched. Sighing, she peeled them off. The girl was not dead. As the others drew near, commenting upon her ghastly appearance, she held her peace. When Miss Arrington came to, she would ask her what really had happened. Offended that Lord Hunterswell had not taken her word, but had protected his friend, she kept him at a distance as footmen wrapped the unconscious Miss Arrington in blankets and carried her to the house. A doctor had already been summoned. Miss Arrington's condition had been pronounced uncertain by the doctor, with some danger of brain fever developing from the severity of the blow her head had endured. She should remain in bed with someone in constant attendance in case she woke up. Her condition had not changed by dinnertime.

Miss Arrington's absence from dinner was explained by an indignant marchioness as a stupid accident by a girl too inept to hold her seat on a bicycle even while assisted by a beau.

88

Throughout the evening, Fergus maintained a subdued demeanor.

While Abigail had found luncheon cold and dull, dinner had been both exquisitely presented and delicious. True, the larks had been a trifle dry and tasted overmuch of rosemary, but clearly there had been a master chef, probably French, in charge of the kitchen. Of the wines, the Chateau Lafite '93 had been especially fine.

The Nawab had proved to be a clever raconteur and he and Twain had kept the table amused. Fascinated by his beauty, Abigail had watched Aref's movements closely and it was with a shiver of foreboding that she realized he was tasting the Nawab's food. No one else seemed to notice.

The other guests, some thirty in all, had not been told of the Prince's cancellation and there were many diamond tiaras among the titled ladies who might not have so taxed themselves with headaches had they known. While the men were enjoying their cigars and port at table, they had retired to the magnificent Gilt Drawing Room for coffee.

Lavishly carved armless chairs in curved rows faced a slim-limbed inlaid table. Two high-backed arm chairs were front and center, tasseled cords reserving the seats. Looking like a statue, except for the drop of sweat trickling down his right temple from the heat of his wig, a liveried footman stood guard over the velvet-draped box on the table.

In full fig with their decorations and white-tied evening dress, the men rejoined the ladies in due course. While everyone maneuvered for the imaginary best seat from which to view the table, Twain took Abigail aside. Even with his disheveled hair, he was elegant, looking as though he'd been enjoying himself.

Kissing her gloved fingertips, he held her hand. "I must say my farewell, now, honey. I have a carriage waiting and will leave the moment I have finished." He nodded in the direction of the Nawab who, opal aglint from his turban, was enchanting an elderly dowager with Aref a respectful pace behind. "His Highness will answer all the questions about how it came to be in his possession and such."

"I wish you could stay." Unfurling her fan, she shielded

their conversation with it. "I know I saw Mr. Buchanan raising his arm to strike Miss Arrington. Lord Hunterswell is furious with me because I accused him. So is the marchioness, who thinks Miss Arrington merely awkward."

"My dear," Twain said hastily, preoccupied with his impending dissertation. "You must not let your desire to emulate Sherlock Holmes make you suspicious of every little accident." Blowing a kiss at her cheek, he released her hand and joined the marquess.

Tiny diamonds set off the gold-encircled smoky topaz at Abigail's ears and throat, enhancing her low-cut, gold-threaded satin gown, with its huge, fashionable leg-of-mutton sleeves. Knowing she looked her best, she was determined not to let her disappointment at Twain's dismissal of her suspicions spoil her appearance, thus her manner was friendly as she took her place in the front row between Lord Hunterswell and Max.

Enraptured anew by her appearance the moment he'd seen her before dinner, Frederick had instantly forgiven her for suspecting his friend.

Still subdued, Fergus sat next to the exquisitely gowned and expensively perfumed marchioness.

Dismissing the perspiring footman, the marquess adjusted his spectacles to better read his notes and tapped on the table for attention. Knowing full well why they were foregathered, his glittering audience composed themselves with uncommon alacrity. Relishing his moment in the spotlight, the marquess took his time introducing one of the few men in the world who needed no introduction.

As the marquess took his place next to his wife, Twain bowed in response to the muffled applause of kid-gloved hands. Greeting the absent royalty and those present, he began, "I reckon everybody here knows that the finest rubies come from Burma."

An appreciative murmur rippled through the audience.

"Well, the whereabouts of this fabulous treasure may be common knowledge now," he drawled, "but how it was first discovered is shrouded in obscurity. A royal edict of the year 1597 contains the first known, official reference to those ruby fields of Mogok. The story you're about to hear is probably as close to the truth as we'll get. I have here," he slowly removed the velvet cloth and tapped the sides of the gold-trimmed teak box, "some evidence that substantiates the more conspicuous—ah—details."

He waited until the speculative titters quieted before continuing, "Now, according to legend, the king of Pergu maintained a park, called Liparo, where he kept lions and tigers and other beasts of prey. Many Burmese sovereigns kept fierce animals to be hunted, much like you English keep deer and game.

"Although possessing an unreliable temper when grown, with great patience a tiger cub could be tamed." He smiled. "Not without some danger to its attendants. Amply fed, the royal pet would roam the palace. With its claws burnished with gold, and a gem-encrusted collar, it would be displayed near the throne on occasions requiring pomp and ceremony. I do not need to tell you," he glanced at his rapt listeners from underneath his shaggy brows, "that the untamed great cats were often pitted against one another. Huge fortunes were wagered upon the outcome.

"But what you may not know is," he lowered his voice, "the fierce cats of Liparo were also frequently employed to amuse the court as executioners of criminals or slaves. Much like the Romans throwing Christians to the lions, Burmese princes were fond of the spectacle of a tiger or panther attacking and eating its terror-stricken victim.

There were gasps, fan flutterings, and not a few horrified titters from the audience.

"I apologize if I have distressed the ladies." He glanced at the marchioness who nodded impatiently, urging him to continue. "I merely wished to emphasize the urgent necessity of constantly replenishing the supply of wild animals at Liparo. This particular king reserved the actual capture of these wild beasts for his favorite sons as a test of manhood.

"Anxious to prove himself to the king, one of his sons, a *punjat,* hired an augur who told him of a rare pride of albino leopards. His quest for the phantom cats eventually led him into the trackless Mogok Valley in the Shan Province.

91

There, he came upon a band of robbers who'd been exiled as punishment for their crimes. Their leader, seeking to pay for the punjat's protection, led him to a remarkable find." Twain paused, cupping his hand and holding it up, as if examining its contents. "Imagine if you will, the punjat's excitement as he held the blood red specimen of a giant ruby mothered in white marble."

The marchioness fanned herself violently as he continued, "Executing the robbers to ensure secrecy, the punjat began the long trek back to Pergu. After several nights in the forest, he came upon the fabled white leopard in her lair. His triumph was complete. But only one of her cubs was to grow as white as she, and only the white cub survived the remaining journey.

"The king was so pleased with his son that he awarded him both the ruby and the white cub. He then began his treacherous negotiations with the Shan princes, using the tortuous paths of diplomacy to trade a worthless tract of land for the immeasurably rich treasure of Mogok.

"As most of you present know," he said with lifted eyebrow and a smile, "rubies never occur as large crystals. Specimens of more than five carats are very rare, and those of ten or more are exceptions. As time passed, the king began to realize that the stone he had awarded his son had been too generous a gift. Even after having been cut and faceted, it was a monster the size of a walnut."

The marchioness's gasp was audible. Max and Fergus exchanged glances as Abigail fanned herself gracefully.

"Desiring this incredible gem for his treasury," Twain continued, "the king decided to stage a robbery, at no little risk to the health of his son. But this particular son had broken all tradition and had trained the phantom cub himself. Gentle and playful, the cat was considered so harmless that it slept curled at his feet. Yet when the thieves broke into his bedchamber to steal the great ruby, the leopard sprang upon them and dispatched them—without a sound. Thus, without alarming the palace guards, the punjat was able to escape with the jewel and the cat. Joined by his loyal friends, he prospered mightily in the Hungawng Valley in the North. He attributed his prosperity to the luck brought by possessing the white cat. You may be certain that he, in turn, sent his many sons on expeditions to find another. All were fruitless.

"Now this punjat," thumb in vest pocket, Twain began to pace, "like most Burmese, had been raised in the religion of Hinayana Buddhism. However, as he came to believe in the miraculous powers of his cat, he was converted to a sect of Hindoo that revered the leopard. None could be harmed. They were sacred. Over the years, his love of his pet had transformed into reverence. He despaired of replacing his aging idol alive. Convinced that, with the appropriate ceremonies and incantations, the great cat's spirit could be persuaded to inhabit a replica, he devoted his considerable fortune to discovering a suitably grand manner in which to immortalize him.

"An old man by now, the punjat wished above all else to achieve *moksah*, or *mukti*, which is the liberation of the spirit from suffering, and the freedom from the compulsion of rebirth." Twain paused. His smile was wry. "Having attained worldly fortune and power in this life, he didn't figure on being born again to a lower station. He believed with his whole heart that he would be able to achieve this *moksah* by worshipping the statue, after his pet was dead.

"Situated within his kingdom, 'round Tawmaw and along the precipitous slopes of the Uru River, resided the most prolific of jadeite mines." Both the marchioness's and Lady Pepper's fans were suddenly stilled. "Much of the punjat's wealth had been amassed by trafficking in the jewel of heaven. He made it known throughout his kingdom that he desired a rare specimen of pure, translucent white jadeite, untinged by pink or green. Meantime, he procured a young master of carving.

"Long before the perfect piece of jade was found, the artisan practiced carving the design the punjat desired. Using priceless samples of jade, each model would take months of painstaking labor in deepest secrecy. Each was smashed upon completion.

"In time, the flawless specimen of jadeite was found for

him to carve. Perfection was achieved. The punjat was content. At last he had his miniature leopard, the head of which is said to be an exact replica of his beloved cat.

"The artisan's reward for his life's work was to be executed along with his assistants and family."

When his audience quieted, Twain continued, "After all, having created a masterpiece of such beauty and mystery, the punjat wished to ensure that it would never be duplicated." He cleared his throat, "It is said that their deaths were merciful, by the sword.

"What the punjat ordered, the artisan had achieved. A leopard, rampant, so—" Knees bent, Twain leaned forward with his hands together at eye level.

Maintaining the posture for a moment, he ceremoniously removed a key from his pocket. Flourishing it over the box, he said, "How the artisan achieved his masterpiece remains a mystery to this day. There is not a trace of a seam to show how he did it."

"M'Lords, m'Ladies, ladies and gentlemen," he said dramatically, opening the box to reveal its contents. "Behold, the Phantom Leopard."

In spite of herself, Abigail gasped. Blazing as though it would set the room afire, the Punjat's Ruby was clutched in the jadeite leopard's paws.

Candlestick in hand, her hair in a single braid over her shoulder, the marchioness appeared like a diminutive ghost at the marquess's bedside. She touched his shoulder gently.

Instantly alert, he raised himself on his elbow, "Is this a social call?" he asked coquettishly.

"No, my Poopsie Woopsie," she replied huskily. "Not entirely."

He swung wide the covers and slid from the huge bed to help her out of her dressing gown. Kissing the nape of her neck, his voice lost its tremor. "It has been a long time."

When they were snuggled together underneath the covers, she purred, "The Punjat's Ruby is a splendid gift for the Prince."

"Do you think he will like it?"

"I am certain of it. Did you put it in the safe?"

"Of course. And the key to the box is around my neck."

"I am so pleased for Frederick," she said, fingering the golden chain at his throat. "He seems so happy at last."

"Yes," he said, his hand wandering underneath her gown. "Miss Danforth is a lovely girl."

"And she seems obedient."

"Are you obedient, my kitten?"

"Oh, my, me, my," she moaned. "Oh, yes, yes, yes."

The Nawab Ahanti Khabir Abdulsamad began to sweat. Shoving the eiderdown comforter aside, he shifted his position yet again, yanking at his nightshirt. Loath to forgo the fortune to be realized by reselling the Punjat's Ruby when he reached New York, he did not suffer these sudden changes in plans easily. Muttering curses, he listened to Aref's contented snores.

Fergus and Max conferred in Max's rooms about methods to use to finish off Miss Arrington, should she regain consciousness. A quarrel then ensued, which lasted most of the night, when they differed violently about how much of a threat Abigail had become, and what to do about her should she not relinquish her suspicions.

J.C. and Maurice slept.

Stork lay on his cot, staring at the ceiling, dreading the new day.

Rodney groaned. The bed lurched. Closing his eyes to halt the room transferred the whirling to his stomach and skull, stirring the red behind his eyeballs. If only he could grasp that red ruby and, kneeling before his father, present it to him. Thus did his impossible dream of pleasing his father seize him once more and lure him to sleep.

Having left word to be called if Miss Arrington awakened during the night, Abigail was asleep before her head touched the pillow.

Frederick punched his satin-cased pillow again, pulled another from the other side of the bed, and hugged both. Sleep would not come. Miss Danforth's warm brown eyes smiled at him and her sweet mouth, her lovely voice, her slim and graceful figure, her fresh-smelling hair swirled in his brain, conspiring to create a not unpleasant torment.

Miss Arrington's condition remained unchanged.

Chapter Four

Given a line and a point, one and only one line can be drawn through the point so that both lines are parallel.

Euclid

Except when the given line and point are drawn on hyperbolic or elliptic surfaces.

Author

Awake since first light, Abigail lay abed and whimpered.

The under housemaid had been in to black the grate and start the fire. Well-trained and discreet, she had paid no heed to the moans issuing from the canopied bed.

With an energetic rustle of petticoat, Jacqueline entered bearing a tea tray.

"Is that you, Jacqueline?" Abigail sounded as if she were trying to stifle tears.

"Mon Dieu, Mlle.!" Silver clattered against silver as Jacqueline dropped the tray on the nightstand. "What is the matter, Miss?" She stood on tiptoe to reach Abigail's forehead with her cool hand. "Are you ill?"

"I don't know," Abigail moaned. "Fetch the marchioness." Tears threatened again. "Tell her to summon the doctor."

"Oui!" Jacqueline ran to the door. Returning to Abigail's

bedside, she said, "I send for the marchioness. I do not know the way."

"What am I to do?" Abigail bit her lower lip. Tears spilled down her cheeks. "I do not want to die in England."

"There, there, *Mlle.* I cannot feel the fever. Maybe it is not so bad as you think."

The door swung wide. Jacqueline sprang away from Abigail's side, curtsied, and hurried to stand respectfully at the foot of the bed.

The speed with which the marchioness crossed the room breathed life into the brilliantly threaded peacock that adorned the back of her kimono.

Pink tongue hanging out, Oliver was tucked under her right arm, having the time of his life.

"Oh, my, me, my, Miss Danforth," the marchioness's voice was sympathetic. "Are you ill? Is it something you ate?"

"No, m'Lady." Abigail sniffed, her voice faint. "I am paralyzed."

"What exactly do you mean, child?" Some of the sympathy drained from her voice. "Can you literally not move or are you merely sore?"

"I don't know," Abigail shrank from the marchioness's piercing gaze.

"Ridiculous!" The marchioness yanked the covers off, dumping the puppy at Abigail's feet. Tail wagging, Oliver attacked her exposed toes. Abigail jerked her feet into her gown, crying out in pain.

"Don't be such a sissy!" the marchioness barked. "Get out of that bed at once!"

To Jacqueline's amazement, Abigail stood. She winced and groaned and was obviously in great pain, but she stood.

"Stop your gawking," The marchioness pointed at Jacqueline. "Fetch Miss Danforth's robe and order her bath."

"But what is *wrong* with me?" Abigail asked as Jacqueline assisted her with her dressing gown.

"As I said yesterday, nothing that a sit in a hot tub and a short ride won't cure."

"On horseback?" Abigail collapsed against the bed, caressing Oliver's ears. "Ohhh, your Ladyship, I couldn't possibly!"

"I told you that you might be a trifle uncomfortable today."

"But I have ridden all my life."

"Astride?"

"But, m'Lady, please," Abigail held the pug close, her eyes wide, "I am not ruined?"

"Your soreness is nothing, I assure you." The marchioness reached for Oliver. "Wait till you whelp. Then you'll know what pain is." She tucked the squirming dog under her arm. "I'll order Crosspatches. You need ride him for only a few minutes. Stay in the paddock." The magnificent peacock shimmered as she called over her shoulder. "And for Jove's sake, don't fall off like that stupid girl who can't even sit a *bicycle!*"

"Did Miss Arrington awaken?" Abigail called after her, chagrined that all her thoughts had been focused selfishly on her own condition.

"Not yet." The marchioness was gone.

Trying not to wince or moan now that she knew the cause of her pain was not serious, Abigail hobbled toward the fireplace. The tweenie had produced the tub and was standing by in case she could help Jacqueline further. Gingerly easing into the hot water, Abigail chided herself for allowing her imagination to run riot.

Kinkade had not slept well. Dank and sour accommodations, considerably beneath his usual lot, had offended him. A fastidious man, he'd arisen even earlier than usual and had made the most careful toilet he could under the circumstances.

To the snoring of Lord Pepper's valet, he quietly unpacked Rodney's coffee kit and mounted the narrow stairs to the kitchen. Amazed to find no one about, he had selected a pan from a hanging rack, filled it with water, and placed it on the back burner of the well-lit stove. Checking his watch, he estimated how long he had for a stroll before the water's boil.

He selected a cloak from one of the pegs by the servants' entrance. It was much too short, but warm enough. The freshness of the air restored him like a tonic. Hoarfrost had whitewashed everything it touched, and the crunch of his shoes on gravel echoed in the morning stillness. He absently stroked the lump on his nose and the thoughts that had been nattering at him all night came into focus.

Clearly Jacqueline was undesirable. She could not be faulted on her job; Miss Abigail was turned out flawlessly. But she was man-crazy. Worse still, men liked her. Far from having been put off by his warning of her preference for the master of the house, J.C. had seemed to be all the more intrigued by her. And then the brazen thing just sat there and ate! That particular memory made his gorge rise again, and he looked up to check how far away from the house he'd gotten. He did not turn back, but slowed his steps. The solution was obvious.

He must encourage J.C. Whichever way the affair progressed, he'd be rid of her before Mr. Danforth discovered that Miss Abigail had made such a dreadful mistake in judgment. Innocent girl, how could she know? If J.C. could seduce Jacqueline, and Kinkade did not doubt for an instant that he, or any man, could, especially with the many opportunities that were sure to be provided on the forthcoming voyage, then she'd be dismissed automatically. Should J.C. go so far as to make an honest woman of her, she'd leave to marry him. Certainly Master Rodney wouldn't miss her. When Rodney had been in his inebriated, talkative state last night, he'd done some careful prying. Brushing his hands together as though dusting her away, he smiled a rare smile and turned back toward the house.

As he lengthened his stride, he shook his head impatiently to try and turn off his mind. Time enough on board ship to worry about Master Rodney's behavior while in London, and how much of it to reveal to Mr. Danforth. Nor did he want to be the one to tell him about Miss Abigail's outlandish visit with Dr. Conan Doyle. There again, if he did not, and someone else did, Mr. Danforth would, and right-fully so, question his competence as a protector of his children. Closing the door, he hung the cloak on its peg and sighed heavily. At least all the reports on Lord Hunterswell were favorable. Now, if that romance would only develop fast enough, there might be no need to tell him at all.

His reverie was interrupted by a female shriek. A crash of metal on wood was followed by wailing that sounded like a dog had been kicked. He dashed up the stairs, two at a time, grabbing the kitchen door frame to stop his headlong flight.

On the other side of the room, two kitchen maids cowered by the huge oblong table that split the kitchen in half. The enormous cook was bent double, snatching at whatever was underneath a corner table where the wailing was coming from.

" 'Twarn't no ghost who put that pot of water on my stove!'' The cook yelled as loudly as her awkward position would permit.

"But 'twarn't meeeee!'' the terrified voice whined from under the table.

"What's the fuss?'' Kinkade called across the room.

Cook righted herself. She peered toward him shortsight-edly, her face red with exertion and outrage, ''Somebody's put a pot of water on my stove!''

"I did,'' Kinkade confessed.

"Who are you?'' she bellowed, taking a step toward him.

"Mr. Danforth's valet. We had tea yesterday. Don't you remember?''

Brandishing a cast iron skillet, she stalked toward him, "How dare you put a pot on my morning stove?'' she bellowed as she bore down on him. ''I'll have your head!''

It was not until he had actually been forced to duck to keep from getting hit by the heavy black missile she wielded, and had felt the breeze that bespoke of just how close he'd come to leaving his brains on the floor of this alien kitchen, that it occurred to Kinkade that she was serious and meant to do him bodily harm. He ran.

The kitchen maids clutched one another, screaming, while

the wailing from under the table sounded like the kicked dog was dying.

Once alert to his danger, Kinkade outdistanced her easily and reached the far end of the table near the weeping kitchen maids before Cook could reach halfway. He called over his shoulder as calmly as the situation permitted, "But Mr. Danforth likes coffee in the morning as his wake-me-up, and I thought—"

"You thought wrong!" She had clasped her skirts in one hand to chase after him, holding the skillet overhead in the other, "Nobody but myself touches my morning stove! Nobody but me and the scully as cleans it!"

Kinkade stopped at the corner of the table to watch her progress, "But all I did was—"

"All you did was *use my stove!*" She stopped to emphasize the horror of his crime. "Without my permission!"

Kinkade held out his hands in an exaggerated supplication, "May I *please* use your stove?"

"No!" She smacked the table with the skillet. The maids screeched when it struck. "Not without you ask Mrs. Budge proper!" She left her weapon where it had landed to prop both hands on her ample hips. "Then she'll ask me polite-like, and then I'll get my scully to do it."

"But why do I have to ask Mrs. Budge when it's your stove? Why can't I just ask you?"

"Because she keeps strangers like you outa my kitchen!" As she reached for the skillet again, she glanced toward the doorway. "Ah, there you are!" she cried.

Kinkade looked beyond her great hulk to see the stern Mrs. Budge returning his stare. The butler stood behind her.

"What is going on in here!" Mrs. Budge demanded, marching into the room.

Pointing to Kinkade as if he were a loathsome bug crawling on her fresh-made pie, the cook accused Mrs. Budge, "What is this furriner doin' in my kitchen?"

Mrs. Budge addressed Kinkade, "What are you doing in the kitchen, Mr. Kinkade?" From her tone of voice, she could have been asking him why he was walking on the ceiling.

"No one was here to tell me nay," he explained, looking from one to the other. "So I thought I'd brew Mr. Danforth's—"

"Don't you believe a word of it!" the cook exploded. "I've been here since cock's crow. My scully was here before me, lightin' the stove." She turned to shout toward the corner table, "Come outta there!" As the girl crawled from underneath the table, rubbing her nose on her apron, cook glared balefully at Kinkade. "He's just trying to say we wasn't on duty to cause trouble!"

Mrs. Budge asked Kinkade in disbelief, "Didn't Timothy show you the stillroom?"

Before Kinkade could answer, the butler shouted indignantly, "Now you hold on a minute, Mrs. Budge! I'll be the one to inquire after Timothy, if you please."

With an impatient gesture toward the stillroom, Mrs. Budge whirled to face the butler, "Will you please tell me why Mr. Kinkade can't brew his coffee in the stillroom same as anyone else? Does he need special morning privileges, too?"

The cook strode toward them, punctuating her speech with her hands, "First I gotta share my stove with his high and mightiness, the French Chef, who thinks he's ooo la la, and now my morning's not got a minute's peace with furriners barging in like they own my stove, too!"

While the cook was approaching, delivering her tirade, the butler drew himself up to his considerable height and talked down to Mrs. Budge, "Are you trying to tell me I don't know how to train my footmen?"

The kitchen maids and scullery girl wailed an accompaniment to the bickering of their superiors.

"You can't tell me I didn't warn you there'd be trouble," Mrs. Budge snapped at the butler. "I told you, commoners don't know how to behave in a grand house!"

The cook complained more loudly so that she'd be heard over the butler's retort. No one noticed Kinkade as he tiptoed to the stove. Using his handkerchief as a potholder, he removed the pan of boiling water, collected his coffee pot, and slipped off in the direction of the stillroom.

Maurice eased himself out of the backstairs into the servants' yard of the south courtyard. Truth be told, pretending to be Fergus's valet wasn't so bad. It sure beat hauling rich peoples' luggage about in fancy hotels. The work was easy, once he'd got the hang of ironing, especially in a big house like this, crawling with servants. Naturally Fergus squirted his own toothpaste, dressed himself, and things like that. He had drawn the line at being a valet in the privacy of Fergus's rooms, unless Lord Hunterswell was present, which was seldom. He was strictly for show. And after he'd pressed the man's clothes and shined his boots, there wasn't much to do. J.C. passed his spare time chasing skirts.

Maurice would have never admitted it, even to J.C., but he wasn't sure he could have played Max's or Fergus's part, keeping up with the gentry's conversations without slipping, or yawning. His manners were too rough to fool anybody for long. But watching Fergus and Max ride every day, while he was confined to the house, was another matter. Short straw or no, a man had limits. Well-placed bribery had gained him access to the stables and these early morning rides had proved all the more pleasurable for being secret from his cohorts. And it gave him time to think.

Things had changed. In the beginning, the four of them had spent a lot of time together, talking and planning. Almost like friends. But ever since they'd set up Stork in Rangoon, he only saw Fergus when he brought him his clothes. Plotting to steal the Punjat's Ruby had begun as a lark, a game almost. Never once was killing anybody so much as mentioned. And now Fergus had jumped clear past the talking stage and tried it. No question, the man had changed. Maybe it was the taste of the high life? Maurice scratched his head, recalling the expression that had crossed Fergus's face when he'd told him that he wanted out when he'd delivered his dinner clothes the night before. Never before had he seen that look, and it was gone so fast, he'd doubted he'd seen it. He had allowed himself to be persuaded to stick it out until they got to America. Fergus was right. Why give up his share after he'd worked so hard? Nobody was getting paid until they were onboard the ship, and J.C. handed over the ruby to the Nawab. Besides, free passage to America didn't grow on trees.

Familiar with the inside of the stable, Maurice entered the darkness without slowing his step. Too late, he heard a grunt of effort and a whir in the air. He was dead before his crushed skull hit the ground.

Abigail had subdued the pain in her limbs by the time she finished her ride in the paddock and returned to the south courtyard. Puzzled that no stable boy rushed forward to help her dismount, she nudged Crosspatches into a walk around to the servants' side.

Crowded together in the stable doorway, none of the stable hands noticed her. Curious, she rode closer.

"No, Miss!" one of the men shouted as he looked up. "Don't come near." Starting toward her, he continued, "There's been a fearful accident."

Ignoring his protest, Abigail dismounted and, handing him the reins, strode to the doorway.

"What happened?" she demanded.

"A pulley hook, Miss." Accustomed to obeying the marchioness, a stable boy responded to Abigail's imperious manner. "Musta come loose and fell square on his head."

"Stand aside!" Abigail commanded.

Muttering among themselves, the stable hands made room for Abigail.

Ignoring the ache in her limbs, she stooped for a better view. The side of the man's head was an unnatural shape, caved in instead of rounded. Not much blood at all. Therefore, she was unprepared for the ringing in her ears and the blackness that threatened to envelop her. Wondering how she had managed to remain so composed with Miss Arrington, she forced the threatened fainting spell to recede by asking, "Who is he?" Shaking her head, she dismissed her queasiness. "He's not in livery. I do not recognize him as a guest."

Knowing that heads would roll if the horsemaster caught them letting a servant ride the marquess's horses, even those grooms who knew the secret refused to answer.

"Poor bloke," one of them said. "Rotten luck to pass by when he did." He crossed himself. "Lord have mercy, it coulda been me."

She shuddered as she rose and looked up to see the marquess, trailing groomsmen and footmen, striding toward the stables. Max and Lord Hunterswell followed not far behind. "Thank heaven you're here, your Lordship," she said as he drew near.

Summoned in haste, the marquess had not taken the time to don a cap and the early morning sun glinted on his silver hair. "What are you doing here, Miss Danforth?" his expression was stern. Without waiting for her response, he bent over the body.

Max and Frederick ran the last few yards to join them. Frederick rushed to Abigail's side while Max stooped next to the marquess who was examining the dead man.

"Who is this?" The marquess demanded.

"Oh, my god!" Max exclaimed. "It's Maurice!"

"Who is that?" The marquess asked.

"Mr. Buchanan's valet."

"What is a house servant doing in my stables?"

Wide-eyed, none of the stablehands spoke.

"Perhaps he came looking for Fergus?" Brushing the knees of his trousers, Max stood. "And I suppose you're going to accuse Fergus of murder, Miss Danforth?"

"Murder a servant! Whatever for?" Frederick looked at Abigail in bewilderment. "Just sack the man."

Flummoxed by Max's pronouncement, the marquess stood also, a look of distaste on his face. "Why would anyone want to kill a servant?"

Max looked down at the body. "One can plainly see that it was an unfortunate accident."

"Oh, I pray you, sir—" Abigail exclaimed.

"Escort Miss Danforth to the house at once, son." The

marquess commanded. "I must find out who let this person in here."

Frederick's grip on Abigail's elbow was firm. "Now, now, Miss Danforth," he turned her toward the south entrance. "I insist we go in to breakfast. You are not to tire your pretty little head worrying about a servant. Poor Fergus will have to make do with sharing Max's valet."

"But, your Lordship—"

"If the man were titled," Frederick overrode her protestations as he walked her toward the house, "it might be amusing to allow you to indulge your overactive imagination. But under the circumstances, it is quite out of the question for you to pursue the matter. Furthermore," he stopped to look her square in the eye, "I must insist that you tell no one of your morbid suspicions. I'll not have a scandal associated with this house over a valet that one of my friends picked up in Rangoon."

Abigail was so angry that she dared not speak. Max had cleverly cast her as a busybodying fool, accusing Fergus of murder again, when she had spoken not a single word. And although she could not help but admire the manliness of Frederick's demeanor as he escorted her to the house, she was furious that he had not noticed how she'd been outmaneuvered. Why had Max done it? That Maurice might have been murdered hadn't entered her mind. Until now.

In Max's bedchamber, after an interminable day wherein Max and Fergus had occupied themselves with hunting, cycling, eating, and games with the other guests, J.C. jabbed at the dying embers in the grate with the poker. "Just a servant!" he exclaimed. "We couldn't even make sure he had a decent burial."

Fergus had settled his lanky frame on the settee near the fire. "He had no business being at the stables," he said calmly. "No real servant would have dared. If he'd been caught, there would have been questions. He could have nixed it for all of us."

"But carted off to London like so much baggage?" J.C. smacked the coals, sending sparks onto the hearth.

Max slammed his hairbrush on the mirrored dresser after passing it through his blond curls. "Stop poking at that bloody fire, will you?"

"I'm gonna miss Maurice!" J.C. said, shaking the poker at Max as he crossed the room toward Fergus. "With him for company, I could remind myself I'm not really just a valet."

Max sat beside Fergus. "Think of it this way," he said, stroking his beard thoughtfully. "We can split his share."

"Did you kill him?" J.C. glared at Fergus.

Fergus tensed. "Are you accusing me?"

"Well, there's Miss Arrington at death's door," J.C. said. "And we all know *that* was no accident."

"May I remind you that she's not dead," Fergus said with a sardonic smile.

"Not yet, she ain't, but she will be soon, if you have your way."

Fergus shrugged. "But why should I kill Maurice?" He gestured lazily toward Max. "It could just as easily have been Max. Just because he looks so innocent, with his cupid's hair and smile, doesn't mean he isn't capable of murder. After all, he is the mastermind for this whole scam."

"Hey!" Max exclaimed. He held up his hands to stop the quarrel before it heated up. "Nobody killed Maurice. He was just in the wrong place at the wrong time."

J.C. was about to voice his disbelief when he suddenly realized that if Fergus did indeed kill Maurice, he'd best not let on he believed it, lest his own head be the next one smashed. "Well, now that that's settled," he said heartily, replacing the poker and firescreen, "want to hear a real corker?" Hands behind his back, warming his back at what little heat remained, he faced them. "Kinkade—that's Mr. Danforth's man—put a curious proposition to me today."

"Oh, really?" Fergus yawned.

"He wants I should seduce Jacqueline—Miss Danforth's maid."

"And you said no, of course," Max said.

108

"I did no such thing."

Max leaned forward. "I forbid it!"

"You *what?*" J.C. laughed.

"What do you want to get mixed up with a girl for?" Fergus asked. "It could complicate things."

"It would give me something to do on the voyage," J.C. smiled. "A reward for all the waiting."

"You'll have enough to do attending the two of us," Fergus said.

"Up yours, Fergus, if you think I'm polishing your boots!"

"Steady, boys!" Max stood, stretched, and scratched his beard. "Let's not spoil everything at the last minute. All we need do is wait for our plan to unfold. You had best be gone to the servants' quarters, J.C., so you'll be ready when Stork has done the deed. Fergus, you get some sleep. It cannot be much longer now."

"You better be right," Fergus rose to leave.

Max accompanied them to the door. "It's not doing us any good to get overwrought over Maurice's bad luck."

Closing the door behind them, Max returned to the fire. He stared deep into the small remaining glow and anxiously bit his fingernails.

The marchioness's flickering candle lit a path through the vast expanse of darkness that separated the door of her bedchamber from her husband's.

As her light drew near his bedside, he asked somewhat dubiously, "What can I do for my Dearie tonight?" Slipping out of bed, he put on his robe.

"I know I am being a foolish old woman," she said, lighting his candle on the nightstand with hers. "But I would like one more itsy bitsy peek at that gorgeous ruby before you give it to the Prince."

"Of course, Dearie." Opening the safe, he placed the box on the nightstand. "I wanted to see it again myself," he said, removing the golden chain holding the key from around his neck.

When the lid parted, he snatched the box from the table to peer into it more closely and gasped, "It's not in there!"

"What did you say?" Her voice rose dangerously.

"It's gone!" he cried, holding out the empty box for her to see. "The Punjat's Ruby has been stolen!"

She blinked once at the empty box and swooned.

For one nonplussed moment, the marquess looked at the empty case in his hands, then at his unconscious wife at his feet. He dropped the case, nearly striking her on the head, and ran to the door to summon help.

Stork drew his right foot up and rubbed his stiff ankle against his left calf. Glancing at Frederick, he longed to tell his master what J.C. was forcing him to do, but dared not. As certain as death, he would be dismissed should Frederick discover what J.C. knew. There was nothing he could do about it, but go through with his part of the bargain. Would this long day never end? He sighed.

"You've been mooning about all day." Frederick said, without looking at him. "You're not coming down with something are you?"

"Why, no, m'Lord," Stork replied, trying not to let the guilt show in his voice.

"Good! Must make a ripping impression on Miss Danforth's father. Can't have you laid up."

"Yes, m'Lord." Stork buried his melancholy underneath his professional manner. "I've packed the crested chocolates in your valise that will stay in your cabin, sir, should you wish to give some away while on board ship. The cases of Chateau d'Yquem '58 and Chateau Lafite Rothschild '74 will go in the hold for gifts in New York, as you say you are willing to try the wines on board the *St. Louis.*"

"That is at least the third time you have told me that useless information," Frederick said impatiently. "You may go. Nothing more for you to fidget with here. We have an early rise on the morrow."

Placing his hand on the doorknob, Stork turned toward

Frederick. "Sir?" he said, thinking he might risk a confession after all.

Busy plumping his pillows, Frederick did not hear him. Stork cleared his throat to speak again when he heard a commotion in the hall.

Opening the door, he watched the uncommon sight of the marquess carrying his own candle as he and the marchioness rushed past him. Closing the door, he sped down the corridor as fast as his limp would allow. Apparently, the plan was working.

"What is the matter?" Alarmed by his parents' obvious distress, Frederick drew on his robe.

"I don't know how to tell you, after all you've been through to get it for me," the marquess said.

"Tell me what, sir?" Frederick said with as much impatience as he dared.

The marquess squared his shoulders. "The Punjat's Ruby has been stolen!"

"No!" Frederick looked at each in turn.

They silently assured him that the dreadful news was true.

"But how could anyone take it from your safe?"

"The case was not gone," the marquess answered.

"But when your father opened it, the box was empty!"

"The ruby must have been taken before we put it away for safekeeping." The marquess patted his wife's shoulder.

"May I please see the case, sir?"

"I left it in my chambers."

"Unguarded?"

"There is nothing to steal!"

"I would like to see for myself, sir," Frederick started for the door. "With your permission."

"Wait! I'll go," the marquess called after him. "You take care of your mother, I cannot bear it when women faint."

Stork dared not use his candle in the night black corridors. He knew the way well enough and darkness was his ally, but it slowed him terribly. When he finally reached the marquess's bedchamber, he was relieved to discover that the door had been left partially closed. A faint glow confirmed his dread of the light from a burning candle left on the nightstand, but the door would shield him from observation from the hallway.

Desperate to retrieve the box before the marquess, or worse, Lord Hunterswell, came for it, he sidled into the room. Staying in the shadows, he crept to the foot of the bed. Without entering the circle of candlelight, he squinted. Imagining he heard footsteps, he had almost despaired of spotting the case and was about to bolt. As he turned his head, a glint of gold caught his eye. It was buried in the shadow cast by the nightstand. He could not reach it without stepping into the light. Holding his breath, he fell to his knees and stretched full length. He could barely touch the box without exposure to the light. As his fingers gained purchase, the footsteps that he had heard in his imagination became a reality.

He snatched the box. Scrambling into the blackness, he clutched it to his chest, his heart pounding so hard he was sure it could be overheard from his shelter behind a chair.

The door swung wide. Unaccustomed to any burden, the marquess's hand was remarkably steady as it held the candlestick. Humming and muttering, he sounded as though he might actually be enjoying himself.

Stork crouched until the marquess reached the nightstand. The light from his candle projected wildly gyrating figures on the ceiling as he searched for the box. Unable to hear beyond the thumping in his ears, Stork prayed that he made no noise as he scurried toward the exit.

"Who's there!" the marquess demanded, whirling to face the door. The menacing shadows made him suddenly realize that he was alone and helpless, and the trembling in his hands returned.

But Stork was gone. With the case hidden under his jacket, he raced to the servants' quarters.

J.C. joined him at their prearranged meeting place.

"Aw, Stork," J.C. said, holding out his hand for the box with a sardonic smile. "Don't take it so hard."

"This discharges my debt to you forever." Stork handed the case over. "Don't you ever come to me again for anything, or I'll—I'll kill you! So help me on my mother's grave."

Had he dared, the footman would have complained. Once put to bed, guests should stay put, not call for candles and an escort. And this one had the sauce to demand that he hurry. Didn't she know the flames would gutter and go out if he went any faster?

Following behind the slow, muttering footman, Abigail fumed at herself for not having insisted upon visiting Miss Arrington during the day. But whenever she'd asked about the girl's condition, she'd always been told that visitors would not be welcome. She would be deterred no longer. At dawn on the morrow, they'd all depart for Southampton and, even if Miss Arrington were unconscious, she wished to bid the unfortunate girl farewell. If she should awaken and speak, so much the better.

Abigail heard the door close in the shadows before she saw Fergus, candlestick in hand, emerge from Miss Arrington's room.

"How is she?" She asked as she drew near.

The footman stepped back and held his candelabra high to light the scene. "What are you doing here?" Fergus asked, his face tense.

His menacing tone sent shivers down Abigail's spine. She decided to answer his question rather than challenge his right to know. "I came to wish Miss Arrington well, and to tell her good-bye."

"It is really best that you do not disturb her. I just finished reading her to sleep." Fergus's voice was all unctuous civility.

Abigail placed her hand on the doorknob. "I would like to see her," she insisted.

Fergus's hand closed over hers. "There is nothing you can do." He squeezed her hand tight enough to hurt.

Wincing, Abigail pulled her hand away. She did not believe Fergus, but realized that he would not hesitate to harm her if she insisted upon opening the door. Without further ado, she signaled to the footman and repaired to her own quarters, her thoughts in turmoil. Was Miss Arrington sleeping as Fergus claimed? Or had Fergus killed her. But why? Was he that jealous? If so, it would seem that love was as dangerous as becoming an old-maid detective.

The intermittent drizzle did nothing to dampen the chaos at quayside. Dripping snarls of black umbrellas compounded the general uproar that accompanied any transatlantic vessel's imminent sailing. Amid the squalling din, the ubiquitous horse-pulled carts, drays, wagons, and carriages, stopping wherever their drivers happened to rein them in. Scores of passengers and their well-wishers were discharged from the vehicles. Endless piles of baggage appeared, disappeared, and reappeared.

The chaos and noise were even greater on board the double-masted *St. Louis*. Even though she was five hundred feet long, her twin funnels were considered disproportionately tall, therefore she was not ranked with the great beauties among ocean liners. But the power of her twin screws promised a crossing of less than a week.

Turning sideways, Jacqueline squeezed past two young ladies standing in the doorway to Abigail's deluxe suite. Excusing herself in French, she dashed off to her second-class cabin to see if one of Abigail's pieces of luggage had been sent there by mistake.

Someone had brought Abigail a potted tulip and its red blossoms dominated the rest of the gifts on the small round table next to the settee.

In the middle of the room, surrounded by Abigail's chattering friends and acquaintances, Lady Pepper dabbed at her moist eyes with a handkerchief. It had been only moments before departing Hunterswell House that she had learned of Miss Arrington's demise, when her husband had insisted that she attend Abigail while he stayed behind to begin making arrangements with Miss Arrington's family.

The shocking news and Abigail's departure had upset her composure as she pulled Abigail aside to pour out some last-minute advice. "Under no circumstances are you to enter the dining room without your brother to escort you." Blowing her nose, she nodded toward Rodney. "I am certain that Lord Hunterswell is much too much a gentleman to compromise you by trying to see you alone." She unfurled her fan so that it concealed their conversation. "He is in love with you, you know. Perhaps you will be back with us soon, hmmmmm?"

Abigail wanted to scream. Of course she would never consider going to the dining room alone. Didn't the addle-headed old partridge credit her with *any* sense? Did everyone think her daft, just because she wanted to be a detective? And why was it that everyone took it for granted that Lord Hunterswell's feelings for her were the only ones that mattered. Weren't her feelings for him important, too? She didn't even know what her feelings were! And how could they all take Miss Arrington's death so calmly? No one had so much as mentioned her name. Smiling, she maneuvered Lady Pepper toward some friends without permitting the soreness in her limbs to show.

Abigail's plain heavy wool sailing costume contrasted with the elaborate morning dresses of the two friends who had replaced Lady Pepper for a farewell hug. Releasing her from their delicate embrace, they agreed that she was the luckiest of women to have the most eligible bachelor in London, as well as his attractive companions, pursuing her to America.

"Except for having that ogre of a marchioness for a mother-in-law!" the one nearest the door said, her face suddenly scarlet. "Oh, please, floor, swallow me!" She frantically fanned herself.

"It is a deck, you goose!" the other replied. Following her companion's stare, she unfurled her fan to hide her embarrassment.

Swathed in pearls, the marchioness glared in their direction.

"Oh, dear, we really must go, Miss Danforth." Grabbing each other by the hand, they fled.

After greeting the marchioness, the few remaining young people bade their farewells as quickly as etiquette could be served. When the marquess invited Lady Pepper and Rodney for a last-minute promenade, Abigail's heart sank, realizing she'd be alone with the marchioness.

Watching fondly as Abigail kissed Lady Pepper a tearful good-bye, the marquess closed the door behind them.

The marchioness used her parasol to sweep a place clear on the settee. "Come sit near me, child," she patted the spot beside her. When Abigail managed to seat herself next to her without wincing, the marchioness whispered, "A serious matter is at hand."

"Yes, ma'am." Certain that she was about to be questioned again about Lord Frederick, Abigail tried to think of something noncommittal to say.

"I fear I do not know what to do." The marchioness sighed. "We shall be ruined if the Prince of Wales finds out." She paused for such a length of time that Abigail finally realized that she was supposed to say something.

Relieved that her feelings were not the topic, she asked, "Is it about Miss Arrington?"

"More serious than that." The marchioness's voice was full of scorn. "If the stupid girl couldn't sit a bicycle, she shouldn't have been riding."

"Has something happened to the Punjat's Ruby?" Forgetting how painful it was to do so, Abigail stood.

"My, my, me my." The marchioness was impressed. "What a clever girl you are."

"Has it been stolen?" Abigail could scarcely contain her excitement.

"Purloined!" The marchioness fanned herself violently.

Ignoring her protesting muscles, Abigail sat next to the marchioness again. Her eyes alight with curiosity, she said, "Tell me the particulars."

Outside, the rain had stopped. Flattered by the marquess's attention, Rodney was pleased to be seen by the other passengers in the company of the titled Englishman.

116

The promenade deck was jammed with people saying their farewells. So polished were the marquess's manners, that Rodney did not realize that he and Lady Pepper had been left talking with some friends of Abigail.

With that distracted look in his eye that brooked no interference, the marquess rushed back to Abigail's cabin and knocked on the door.

Abigail hurried to let him in.

"Has my wife told you?" he asked, placing his top hat and cane next to the tulips.

"Yes, m'Lord," Abigail replied, returning to sit by the marchioness. "I was about to tell her Ladyship that I think you were victims of the magic box trick."

"The what?" the marquess exclaimed.

"I suspect that the box containing the ruby was a double," Abigail explained. "Such a case can be opened two ways, to reveal either the ruby or an empty chamber." She looked at the marquess sympathetically. "Depending upon which of two keys is used, it would appear as though the ruby had vanished when indeed it would be reposing in the base."

"Are you trying to tell us that the Phantom Leopard was still in the case when I left it in my chambers?"

"It is possible, your Lordship," Abigail replied. "That the entire case was missing upon your return indicates that the thief was watching your movements closely."

The marchioness collapsed in a faint. The marquess started for the electric bell to summon a steward. Producing a vial of smelling salts from her reticule, Abigail reassured him that further help was unnecessary.

Just as the marchioness was reviving, a loud blast from the ship's horn announced the first all-ashore call.

"Then it is settled," the marquess said when he could be heard.

"Beg pardon, m'Lord, but what is settled?" Abigail asked, returning the vial to her reticule.

"Didn't my wife tell you? We want you to recover the ruby for us."

"*Me?*" Abigail slowly sank onto the settee beside the marchioness. Her dream had come true. Too late. "Recover the ruby?"

"You are the only one who can help us," the marquess said earnestly. "Surely you have learned some methods of detection."

"I will soon be in New York, under my father's protection—and direct supervision." Abigail's disappointment brought tears to her eyes as she continued, "I will not be able to do anything without his permission."

"Even though we must ask that you keep your search a secret, you should be able to find it quite easily during the crossing," the marquess assured her.

"Yes," the marchioness interrupted, fingering her pearls. "We know who has it."

"The Nawab Abdulsamad?" Abigail asked.

"Clever girl!" The marquess exclaimed. "How did you guess?"

"I never guess." Abigail said as huffily as she dared. "Had you not wished to see the ruby again, m'Lady, you would not have known it was gone until the Nawab was safely in America." Her smile was ironic as she stood and took the few steps to the table. "And now I know the real reason for the Nawab's journey. To sell it again." She frowned. "But then, why do you need me? Why don't you just have him arrested?"

"He would not be foolish enough to bring it on board on his person," the marquess said.

"The Nawab must have an accomplice," the marchioness interrupted, again. "We cannot stop the ship from sailing. We have no proof."

Abigail was about to accept when another all-ashore gong made speech impossible. Waiting the few moments for the noise to abate gave her time to reflect and, when she could speak, she responded with unfeigned regret. "I know my father would not approve of my accepting the task you propose. Had we remained in England, it would have been a different matter, but now—?"

"See?" the marchioness whispered at the marquess from behind her fan. "Didn't I tell you she was obedient?"

"But my dear Miss Danforth," the marquess responded smoothly. "When you already know who has the ruby, wouldn't it be a simple matter to find it in his cabin before you reach New York?"

"Your father need never know!" the marchioness winked at her.

Placing his hat on his head and retrieving his cane, the marquess held his arm for his wife. "She's right, you know, Miss Danforth." The marchioness joined him. They looked at her expectantly.

Abigail hesitated, frowning down at the tulips.

"Well, Miss Danforth," the marquess's voice was gentle. "Will you help us?"

With a decisive nod, she responded, "I will do what I can." The realization that she had accepted her first case washed over her, making her quite giddy.

"Good!" the marchioness said. "We will reward you handsomely."

"But the moment we dock, I must abandon the search, even if I fail."

Stepping over the threshold, the marchioness turned to Abigail. "Do be careful, my child," she said solemnly.

"Yes, m'Lady," Abigail replied sincerely. "I will."

"Be careful of what, m'Lady?" Rodney came forward to take his sister's arm.

Desperately wishing she had asked Rodney's question, Abigail smiled as she took Rodney's arm to escort them to the gangplank. If the marchioness believed Miss Arrington's death had been an accident, why the warning? Where did the danger lie? Could her death be connected with the missing idol? Could the valet's?

"I was wishing your sister a safe voyage," the marchioness said with a questioning glance at her husband.

Their consternation amused Rodney. Noticing the marquess's absence, he had returned to Abigail's cabin and stationed himself at her draped, but open, porthole. He had overheard everything.

* * *

With a nonchalance he was far from feeling, Max glanced at Frederick again, then risked exchanging a glance with Fergus. Their errand belowdecks had taken longer than anticipated, and the first all-ashore whistle had sounded. Both Max and Fergus had expected Frederick to be in a rush to rejoin the Danforths, but he appeared to be enjoying their leisurely promenade and in no hurry to reach Miss Danforth's cabin. Could this be a game to make them worry? Could his Lordship be testing them somehow? Had Stork talked? But Stork did not know about their involvement. Only J.C. knew the connection, and he wouldn't tell. Or would he? Max was bursting, yet he dared not ask any questions. They were supposed to be the best of friends. No secrets. So why hadn't Frederick mentioned that the ruby had been stolen?

Except for his visored cap, J.C. looked fashionable enough to be a gentleman as he let himself out of the Nawab's cabin. Patting the bulging pocket of his greatcoat, he celebrated with a few minutes' leisure at the railing, watching the receding shoreline. Then he set off to find the second-class saloon.

Inside the Nawab's deluxe quarters, Aref spread a spotless linen cloth and lit a ceremonial candle beside the box. The fragrance of burning incense permeated the cabin as the Nawab sat at the table and muttered their prayers. Aref stood beside him, his eyes closed. Completing the ritual, the Nawab took a key from his vest pocket and, with a quick glance at Aref, opened the box.

"What's this?" the Nawab gasped, when the box fell open to reveal an empty chamber. "Have I used the wrong key? Aref! Fetch me the other key!"

Aref was burrowing in their luggage before the Nawab had finished issuing the command.

"Hurry!"

Aref placed a tiny sack in his master's outstretched, trembling palm.

The Nawab closed the case and locked it with the first key. Breathing deeply to control his mounting panic, the tremor in his hands increased, and he had difficulty inserting the second key. He stopped breathing entirely and squinted his eyes shut when he turned it. The box lay open for some moments before he dared to look. His face sagged. "It is gone." He shivered. "The *pujari* will kill me."

In desperation, the Nawab hefted the case, feeling its weight. "Fetch me a pick, Aref!" he cried.

Soon there was black velvet and bits of gold and teak spread all over the linen.

As a secret member of the *pujari* sect sent to guard the ruby. Aref's beautiful face was ice.

"If I do not possess it," the Nawab's voice was thin with terror. "Where can it be?"

Chapter Five

Given any point as a center, and any radius, a circle
can be drawn.

Euclid

Abigail felt like a sneak thief. The instant she had bid the marchioness farewell, she had begun planning this moment with much delight. And everything had gone according to plan. The men were enjoying their after-dinner brandy and cigars in the smoking room, and she need not fear interruption. Yet when the door clicked behind her, and the Nawab's cabin was revealed in the light from the candle she held high, her enthusiasm vanished into the shadows. Even the victory of managing to be alone did not ease this unforeseen distaste for invading another's privacy. Her zeal was also hampered by her newfound opinion that her search might be in vain.

She had watched the Nawab carefully at dinner. He had seemed distracted and, for the first time since she had met him, he had little to say. It seemed to her that a man who had executed such a coup would have cause to preen himself like a peacock, and a man of the Nawab's disposition would have acted thus.

Determined not to fail so simple a task as finding a distinctive box in such small quarters, she dismissed her squeamishness as female weakness, and took special care to be thorough. The bureau and nightstand drawers revealed nothing except a stunning array of jewels for a man. Near the bottom of the half-empty trunk, she could scarcely believe her luck when she discovered a leather case much like the one that held the ruby. To her dismay it rattled when she shook it, but she opened it anyway, just to be sure. It contained rubber items, one much like a cock's comb, which puzzled her, and she resolved to ask Frederick their purpose as she carefully restored the box to its original position. Wincing with pain, she knelt and was lifting the coverlet to look under the bed when a glint of gold caught her eye. When she managed to grasp the tiny object with her gloved fingertips and hold it closer to the candlelight, it proved to be a golden screw. She recognized the intricate design on its head as coming from the case that had held the ruby. Concentrating intently upon the tiny object, she was startled by male voices outside the cabin. They had stopped at the door. Her heart thumped wildly. She blew out the candle and slipped the screw into her reticule. To her vast relief, after a few moments wherein a wager seemed to be struck, the voices continued down the corridor.

With the screw as evidence, she was all but certain the case had been destroyed. The idol could be hidden in almost anything, anywhere. She needed another plan and, unwilling to risk another such fright while making one, she opened the door a crack. The corridor being clear, she returned to her suite to further ponder the implications of her tiny burden.

Conveying the permanence of his banker's office, the mahogany-panelled smoking room comfortably insulated the male voyager from any hint of his inherent vulnerability while on board so puny an object as a ship on sail across the North Atlantic. Further comfort was no doubt to be found in the sameness of the black and white of dinner dress by all who inhabited it.

As Aref lit his after-dinner cigar, the Nawab scrutinized his companions who were seated comfortably in their leather chairs. After several indifferent courses, the turkey in oyster sauce had begun to assuage his terror. He knew himself to be a voluptuary and, as an aphrodisiac, he had often listened to the shrieking of a man tortured beyond endurance. He preferred live sounds piped into his bedchamber. On site, it was apt to get smelly. Professional torturers subscribed to the theory that the stench of a victim's own irredeemably burnt flesh added mental anguish to physical torment, and thus a subtle, ineffable hopelessness to his cries.

The Nawab also knew himself to be a coward. For the crime of losing the Punjat's Ruby, punishment was certain. Prolonged agony at the hands of a specialist. Perhaps a team, which might even include a consultant in the use of the newfangled electricity. He knew he would succumb as surely as had the priest he'd broken to gain possession of the ruby. Dreading his loss of dignity and that excruciating descent into mewling infancy, he had extracted Aref's promise to dispatch him hastily with a stiletto should they prove unable to reclaim it.

Immediately upon recovering from the shock of its disappearance, his first thought had been that the marquess had—through Stork's defection—intercepted it, and that the idol reposed in London. His subsequent discreet effort to disembark had failed.

Frederick disturbed his reverie by toasting the Queen, which the Nawab acknowledged with his tea while the others hoisted glasses of brandy. Placing his teacup on the small table they shared in the middle of their circle of chairs, the Nawab cast a vicious glance at Fergus. "You look a bit peckish, if I may say, Mr. Buchanan. Are you grieving over the demise of the lovely Miss Arrington, or the loss of the services of your valet?"

Still unaware that the Nawab did not have the ruby, Fergus wondered vaguely why he'd brought up such delicate questions in so cutting a tone. But, truth be told, at that moment he cared for nothing except that he be allowed to escape the subtle, yet incessant, motion of the ship. He was growing queasier by the minute.

"I say!" Thinking his friend's silence meant that he was

searching for a suitably devastating response to the Nawab's insensitive questions, Frederick interrupted before Fergus could begin an unpleasant quarrel. Having no desire to recall the scene of the clumsy Miss Arrington's accident that such a quarrel would induce, he switched the subject as best he could. "I feel an awful duffer," he frowned.

"What makes you say that, my boy." With little choice but to respond to Frederick, the Nawab was all unctuous sympathy.

Examining the tip of his cigar, Frederick replied, "I sat directly across from Miss Danforth all during dinner and could not think of one single remark to amuse her."

Fergus groaned and sank deeper in his chair, relieved at having their attention thus withdrawn from him.

Max smiled nervously and smoothed his beard.

"I am surprised to hear that, Lord Hunterswell," the Nawab said. "I have never considered you a man at a loss for words, or courage for that matter. Why I'll not soon forget that night in the bush when—"

"Oh, but your Highness," Frederick glanced at Max and Fergus. "If Miss Danforth were a leopard, I would know what to do. It is because she is a woman that I am tongue-tied."

"Ahhhh!" Rodney could restrain himself no longer. "She is only a girl!"

"Allow me to remind you, Mr. Danforth," Frederick replied stiffly, his dislike of Abigail's brother deepening. "Our beloved Queen was merely eighteen when she ascended the throne."

Max's voice was soothing as he smiled at Rodney. "Her brother is no doubt remembering Miss Danforth as the pesky little sister who left home—as brothers will."

"Yes," Fergus roused himself enough to add. "Perhaps to Master Danforth, she will never quite grow up."

"How astute!" Rodney's smile pulled down the corner of his mouth. "why don't you play a game with her, your Lordship?"

"A game?" Frederick wondered if his companions had been discussing his predicament behind his back.

The Nawab puffed on his cigar and watched.

"You know of my sister's morbid interest in the art of detection?"

Frederick nodded grimly, resolving to strike Rodney on the chin forthwith if he mocked her again.

Rodney glanced at the Nawab. "You could volunteer to be her Dr. Watson, your Lordship. Then there would occur the necessity of consulting with her often. A mystery to solve would automatically supply you with a subject to discuss."

Frederick's smile transformed his craggy features.

Rodney continued, "May I suggest a case for you to solve?" Pretending not to notice that he had everyone's eager attention, he prolonged his sense of power by relighting his cigar. After a long pause wherein he exhaled quite a lot of smoke, he said, "You could pretend that the ruby had been stolen."

The superb ventilating system swiftly removed the smokey haze that Rodney had intended for refuge and his cigar had grown too hot to further draw upon. Hooking it in his index finger, he reached for his brandy and, rolling the glass in both hands in front of his face, he watched the men over its rim, delighted with the effect he had created.

In his effort to observe both Frederick and Abdulsamad simultaneously, Max might have been at a tennis match.

Fergus groaned and closed his eyes.

The Nawab stared at Frederick, stunned.

Frederick was first to recover his aplomb, "By jingo! You are clever, Mr. Danforth!" he exclaimed, returning the Nawab's stare, puzzled by the fellow's inability to conceal his guilt. "I shall approach her after breakfast tomorrow."

Aghast that the Nawab was showing any feelings whatever, Max's laugh was overhearty as he stood, glass extended toward Rodney, "I say, capital idea, old boy. You deserve a toast!"

"Hear! Hear!" Frederick sipped his brandy while the Nawab indicated that his teacup was empty.

Although Rodney shrank deeper into his chair, his voice was firm when he spoke. "But I am not finished, gentlemen. Wouldn't it add to the fun if his Lordship told my sister that he already had a suspect? A red herring I believe it is called.'' He lowered his glass so that the Nawab could see that he was smiling, ''Would you like to volunteer, your Highness?''

''What?'' The opal in the Nawab's turban flashed as he straightened in his chair and turned toward Rodney.

''Volunteer to be the suspect.'' With his hand holding the cigar and wineglass, Rodney casually gestured toward Lord Frederick, ''Allow his Lordship to pretend that he suspects you of stealing the ruby.''

Max was forced to sit abruptly as the Nawab stood, consuming all the space at the small table. ''I am not amused, gentlemen.'' He stared coldly at Frederick, ''I cannot stop you, your Lordship, if you wish to pursue such foolishness, but in the interest of a pleasant voyage, I am going to pretend that this conversation never took place. Now if you gentlemen will excuse me, I shall have a little wash before the recital.''

Abandoning his cigar and brandy, Rodney leapt to his feet. Apologizing profusely, he escorted the Nawab to the door.

''What was that all about?'' Max asked anxiously, watching their retreating figures.

Frederick looked directly at Max, then Fergus. ''I haven't the faintest idea,'' he lied.

As Frederick opened the door to his cabin, his jaw dropped. With boxes still strewn about and the bed looking more slept-in than turned-down, his quarters were definitely not shipshape. Pleased with himself for remembering its location, he jabbed at the steward's call button. ''What's this!'' The exclamation escaped his lips, and he stooped to retrieve what appeared to be a lady's handkerchief as a steward knocked and called softly, ''You rang, m'Lord?''

Telling the voice to summon his valet, Frederick recognized the delicate initials woven into the sheer linen as Miss Danforth's. Pressing it to his lips, he wondered whether he should chide her for her carelessness or keep the gossamer fabric as a talisman. Grumbling at his lack of privacy, he swiftly glanced about the room for a hiding place. He was patting the pillow and congratulating himself on having found the perfect spot, when Stork knocked softly and entered. Frederick started guiltily. Quickly stepping away from the bed, he snapped. "Where have you been!"

Stunned by the disarray, Stork mumbled. "I don't know, m'Lord."

"What rot!" Frederick snapped. "Don't *know?* You were there!"

Stork consulted his watch. "Over an hour ago a steward told me I was invited to inspect the bootblacking facilities. I followed his directions to below decks, but there was no such place. A regular rabbit warren down there, if I may say so, m'Lord."

"Seems you might have been called away on purpose," Frederick smiled, filled with admiration at how skillfully Miss Danforth had lured him out of the way, although he could but wonder why she would look for the ruby in *his* quarters.

"On purpose, your Lordship?" Stork's face lost what little color it possessed.

"It is my guess that my accommodations have been searched." Occupied with washing his face, Frederick failed to notice Stork's near collapse.

Accompanying himself with an off-color rendition of "The Blue Bells of Scotland," Max danced a jig near the railing to stamp some warmth into his thinly shod feet. Involved with his efforts to keep from freezing, he felt a smart rap on his shoulder. He wheeled around, but the moonlight was too dim to see by. Alarmed, he whispered hoarsely, "Who is it?"

"It is I, Ahanti Abdulsamad," a voice said from the shadows provided by a staircase. "Stop that stupid hopping about. Can't you ever be serious?"

"Where are you?" Max peered into the darkness.

"Turn around and look at the ocean!"

With a weary sigh, Max complied. "Why did you want to see me?"

"Where is the Punjat's Ruby?"

"Is this a joke?"

"I assure you that I am not trying to be funny, Mr. Driscoll. I am so serious, that you might say I am deadly serious."

The menace in the Nawab's voice made Max's skin crawl. "But J.C. gave you the ruby when we sailed."

"J.C. handed me an empty box, Mr. Driscoll."

"What?"

"I repeat, where is the Punjat's Ruby?"

Max whirled to face the voice. "I don't know!"

"Turn around!" the Nawab snapped. When Max had resumed his stance at the railing, he continued, "It is as well that troublemaker Maurice is dead, or I would suspect him. Now I hold you personally responsible for its disappearance."

"But I—"

"Make no mistake, Mr. Driscoll. I do not want my money returned. I want that idol! J.C. will begin by questioning Stork. Aref will help."

Max shuddered, but not from the cold.

"And furthermore," the Nawab's voice seemed to come from a greater distance. "Keep that silly girl away from me."

"Miss Danforth?"

"Who else could I mean?" he snarled. "If you do not, I shall have Aref see to her as well."

A dashing figure in his checked Norfolk jacket, breeches, and six-button gaiters, Frederick cleared his throat and spoke in a paternal way designed to palliate the effect of an intrusion. "May I join you, Miss Danforth?" Flustered by her closeness, he was certain everyone in the Grand Saloon was staring at his awkwardness.

Seated behind her mistress, Jacqueline smiled to herself and concentrated upon her mending.

As Abigail nodded her assent, she wished he were more observant; he might then play the role of her Dr. Watson. "Is the sea air agreeing with you, Lord Hunterswell?" She already had made many deductions from her discovery in the Nawab's suite that needed recording. That is, if she could persuade him to assume such a task.

"Oh, yes, quite!" Frederick sat on the edge of the chair, not daring to be so bold as to draw it close. "Bracing and all that. And you, Miss Danforth?"

With a graceful flutter of her fan, Abigail concealed her impatience at being interrupted at a fascinating passage in *Pudd'nhead Wilson* only to exchange banalities. Casting about for a topic of conversation—without mentioning the missing ruby until he broached the subject—she asked, "Do you find your aunt difficult?"

"Aunt? What aunt? I have no aunts."

"The marchioness referred several times to her sister. It was her sister's riding costume I was wearing when we met in Tapestry Hall. Your mother's sister would be your aunt, would she not?"

He eased back into his chair, "But I assure you, Miss Danforth, my mother has no sister, nor does my father." He spread his empty hands. "Ergo, no aunts."

"Why would the marchioness be so—ah—creative, do you suppose?"

"Oh, mother has her own whys and wherefores for doing things," he laughed. "She finds it boring to be direct, especially if another tack will provide her with an excuse to spend more money."

"At the risk of contradicting you, m'Lord, I found her to be quite direct. But, of course, you know her more intimately than I."

"Perhaps she wanted to see if you would be brave enough to ride astride and did not want you to plead the lack of a riding habit as a reason not to. It is quite like mother to invent a sister it belonged to."

"How did she know my size?"

"I might have told her."

"How observant you are," Abigail blushed. Although

delighted by this evidence of his powers of observation, she was embarrassed by the implied intimacy of his, so thoroughly scanning her figure that he could gauge her size.

Frederick leaned forward, "Observant enough to act as your Dr. Watson, while you attempt to recover the Punjat's Ruby?"

Astonished, Abigail fluttered her fan coquettishly. She was trying to think of a graceful quote that would include a subtle reference to destiny, when it occurred to her that his mother might have ordered him to volunteer. "Is this the marchioness's idea?" she asked, dreading the answer.

Unwilling to credit her brother with the idea, he replied, somewhat huffily. "Of course not! It was mine. And I must say," he continued quickly, "I am impressed with how swiftly you set about your assignment."

Abigail stilled her fan. "Whatever can you mean, sir?"

"I have proof," he chided her, tenderly drawing the handkerchief from his jacket pocket. "I found this in my suite."

"Oh, Miss Danforth!" Jacqueline exclaimed. "I think I forget how to count."

If Jacqueline's chair had spoken, Frederick's expression would not have been more amazed.

Abashed by his stare, Jacqueline whispered to Abigail, "I packaged eight handkerchief cases for the voyage, but only seven come out of the box."

"Dr. Conan Doyle was right." Abigail wondered once again if Frederick would prove sufficiently astute to play Watson. She smiled, "There is nothing so deceptive as an obvious fact."

"I beg your pardon?" Frederick frowned.

"Did you not wonder why I would select your most unlikely suite to search?" Her fan fluttered dangerously. "Oh, no. Just because the handkerchief is obviously mine, you assumed that I dropped it."

"And did you not?" His tone was indignant.

"Your obvious fact deceived you, your Lordship. Furthermore," she concealed her ire with the fan, "if you think

131

me clever enough to recover the Punjat's Ruby, how could you believe I would be so careless?''

"Pray forgive me, Miss Danforth." Frederick stood. For one awful moment Abigail thought he might fling himself at her feet. "I confess I did not see the contradiction." He paused, "But if not you, who then?"

"When Rodney called for me for dinner last night, he had to wait in the sitting room while we finished my toilette . . ." Frowning, she did not conclude the thought out loud.

Frederick clenched his fists and forced himself to sit.

"I'm not sure I agree with your parents that the Nawab purloined the ruby," Abigail continued, paying no attention to his grim-faced silence. "At dinner last night, he seemed deflated rather than puffed out with accomplishment."

"I fear you are blessed with an overabundance of women's intuition, Miss Danforth."

"He did not appear for breakfast," she protested.

"He is no doubt seasick, as is Mr. Buchanan."

"A discreet inquiry has negated that possibility." With an air of triumph, she held out the tiny screw.

"What's this?" Frederick squinted as he reached for it.

"I'm convinced it is a screw from the case that held the Punjat's Ruby."

"Where did you find it?"

"In the Nawab's suite."

"See!" Frederick exclaimed. "Mother was right!"

"Not so!" Her eyes were alight with excitement. "The case must be in pieces, if this indeed is one of the screws that held it together. That must mean that the Nawab took it apart." She paused for emphasis. "Looking for the idol!"

"But then who has it?"

Looking over her shoulders to make sure no one, except Jacqueline, was nearby, she asked, "How long have you known your travelling companions, m'Lord?"

"Max and Fergie?" He placed the screw in her outstretched, gloved palm and continued emphatically, "You may under no circumstances suspect them, Miss Danforth." He sat back in his chair. "They don't even know the ruby is missing."

"You still suspect no foul play in the death of Miss Arrington or Mr. Buchanan's valet?"

"Certainly not!" Frederick's mouth was a firm line of righteous indignation.

Abigail glared at him, her dark eyes ablaze with anger, " 'Tis a pity, but perhaps you shall not do as Dr. Watson, after all, your Lordship!" She fanned herself vigorously. "Far from being constrained by him, Mr. Holmes is unbound by ordinary conventions, and certainly has never been forbidden to conduct an investigation by his chronicler. Nor shall I be!"

Abigail's anger quite unsettled Frederick's objections. Realizing he'd nearly spoiled his opportunity to be with her, he apologized profusely.

Thus immersed, they did not notice the Nawab's entrance into the Grand Saloon. A striking figure in Western garb and bejeweled turban, he spotted the two huddled figures in earnest discourse and hurried on before they might look up and see him.

On the third day out the weather turned foul. J.C. told himself that he was queasy only because of the ship's roll, as he tiptoed behind Aref toward Stork's cabin. Praying that Stork would confess before Aref hurt him, he knocked softly on the door.

"What do you want?" Stork peered at them through the crack in the door.

"I'm here to apologize, old man," J.C. swallowed hard and made himself smile.

Stork did not slam the door shut, nor did he open it in welcome. His shirtsleeves were rolled past his elbows and an apron protected his clothes. As they entered and J.C. closed the door, he moved warily to the washstand and deposited Frederick's shoe on the rim.

A white blur streaked through the air. Landing on the tall man's back, Aref wrapped his legs around Stork's waist and pressed a chloroform-soaked rag to his nostrils. Flailing his arms, Stork tried to dislodge him, but the drug took effect immediately. Aref nimbly jumped to the floor and caught him under the arms, grunting to J.C. to lift him by the legs.

They bound him, spread-eagle, on the bottom bunk. Stuffing his mouth with a piece of cloth, Aref squatted at his midsection and withdrew a razor-sharp stiletto.

J.C. began to sweat. Glancing at Aref's leering face, he nearly fainted. Obscene noises issued from a gaping red cavity where his tongue should have been. The stiletto flashed in the glare of the electric bulb as Stork groaned and opened his eyes.

Aref severed Stork's apron strings as if opening a gift. The heavy green fabric parted as he lightly ran the knife down past Stork's crotch.

Realizing that he was unarmed and unable to control Aref, J.C. pleaded with Stork, "Don't scream. Please, don't scream. I'll take the gag out so you can answer some questions, but promise not to scream."

Frantically nodding his head, Stork kept his eye on the knife.

Using the tip of the blade, Aref removed the gag and held it aloft.

Raising himself up on his knees so that his face was near Stork's, J.C. whispered, "Where is it?"

Moving his tongue around to lubricate his mouth, Stork croaked, "Wha? Wha? What?" His voice was dry and hoarse, "Where is what?" Wrenching his head from side to side, he tried to avoid the gag.

Aref waited until Stork opened his mouth to scream and, striking like a cobra, silenced him with the cloth.

Stork's face turned crimson as he gnawed on the gag to keep it from choking him. Eyes wide, he twisted his head trying to watch the progress of the knife and look at J.C. at the same time.

Aref flicked the buttons from Stork's vest with the stiletto, while J.C. whispered in Stork's ear. "The Punjat's Ruby wasn't in the box, old pal," J.C. said as, with the point of the knife, Aref shoved back Stork's vest so that it lay on the torn apron. "You had an opportunity to nick it. Where is it?" Aref lovingly cut the waistband of Stork's trousers. J.C. continued in a rush, "What did you do with it?"

Slitting Stork's shirt and undershirt, Aref left his collar and tie intact. Mouth agape, he dandled the knife over Stork's face, as if to pluck out an eye. Stork squeezed his eyes shut, while J.C. cringed at the sound of Aref's laughter.

His stomach as roiled as the sea, J.C.'s voice was gruff as he pleaded with Stork, "Don't scream. Please, please don't scream. Just tell us where the ruby is."

When he felt his mouth free, Stork squinted his eyes to look at J.C. "No, no, no, no, no," he gulped. "I didn't, not me. I swear it, not me, not me, I swear it. I didn't. Not me."

J.C. was frantic, "Please tell us, Stork old pal!"

Shaking his head violently, Stork cried, "I don't know, I don't know, I don't know—"

Poking the cloth into Stork's mouth in midsentence, Aref's expression was strangely at peace. He bounded to the floor and—before J.C. knew what was happening—slashed Stork's trousers and undersuit, exposing his manhood. The reek of urine filled the cabin.

All color drained from Stork's face as he moaned and fainted.

"Stop!" J.C. surprised himself by grabbing Aref's wrist. Returning the boy's crazed stare with one of his own, he said, "Stork doesn't have it! He would have confessed by now. If you cut him, his Highness will be dragged into it!"

Aref's small-boned arm was much stronger than J.C. had anticipated. He sighed with relief as Aref pulled away and reluctantly cut the ropes.

Staring hungrily at Stork's nakedness, Aref sheathed the knife, bowed, and left.

The door shut behind Aref and J.C.'s stomach revolted in earnest. He staggered toward the washstand, but the trajectory of his vomit missed the washbowl, filling Frederick's shoe.

* * *

Awake in the semidarkness, Ahanti Abdulsamad heard Aref creep into the suite and lock the door. Sensing Aref's excitement, he moaned and held out his arms. Aref slipped out of his clothes and raced to the double bed.

"Do not be gentle tonight, my boy," the Nawab groaned. "Do not be gentle. Ahhhhhhhhh."

When Abigail entered Fergus's cabin the next afternoon, she nearly swooned from the smell. The incessant motion of the ship had done its work. Lying on his sweat-soaked bunk, Fergus longed for death to intervene. Every muscle on his lanky frame ached from its involuntary participation with retching. Ceaseless nausea kept his raw and empty stomach in flames. A shot of morphia the day before had induced such terrifying nightmares that he had hysterically refused another.

Dressed for tea, Abigail hoped the odor would not so permeate her costume that it would necessitate yet another change. She cautiously approached his side. "Mr. Buchanan?" She drew upon her hours of training to produce a passable smile. Determined not to be put off by the sympathy she was feeling for his plight, she sat in the straight-backed chair next to his bunk bed. "I thought I might help pass the time by reading to you." She held out a copy of Tennyson's poems.

"Wha—?" Fergus peered up at her. The violence of his illness had broken the blood vessels across his forehead and under his eyes. "Miss Danforth?"

"Yes," Abigail forced another smile, larger this time. "I also wished to express my condolences to you for Miss Arringtons's demise. It must have come as a terrible shock." Her tone was ironic. "In fact, I was not a little surprised that you would continue such a journey as this, upon suffering so great a loss."

Fergus groaned and feebly held out his hands, "Oh, Miss Danforth," he said, his voice hoarse. "Help me."

"Help you, Mr. Buchanan?" Repulsed, Abigail pulled back.

"Yes, oh, God, yes," he sobbed. "I want to die."

"Mr. Buchanan!" Abigail was shocked. Had he really cared so much for her? Had it really been an accident?

Trying to sit up on one elbow, but too weak to do so, he cried, "Help me get up." He held out his hand toward her. "Help me get up and walk to the railing. Please! I want to jump."

"Now, now, Mr. Buchanan." Although Abigail's heart went out to him, she stayed well out of his reach. "You will get over your loss in time. Soon you will be in America—"

"No, no, you stupid girl." Fergus collapsed back onto his pillows. Tears streamed down his face. "Get this hell-hole of a ship to stop moving. Or toss me overboard. I can't stand it any longer."

After a long moment wherein she realized that he probably thought himself at death's door, Abigail stood and looked down at the moaning figure of misery. "Did you kill her?" she asked, hoping against hope for a deathbed confession.

"What does it matter?" he sobbed. "Nothing matters but that I die soon." The spasms began again.

Realizing that she'd get nothing further from him, Abigail turned to go. As she crossed the small room, he heaved. And heaved.

Closing the door, she turned to join Jacqueline who'd been waiting just outside.

"How is he, Miss?" Jacqueline asked.

"Not well," Abigail smiled. This time it was genuine.

That night, dinner was followed by dancing, and Abigail had decided that, like her sick call to Fergus, she would use the excuse of dancing with Max to question him, without Frederick's being the wiser. Unless, of course Max revealed something of sufficient significance to record.

Much to her surprise, she found him to be a clumsy dancer for one who ordinarily moved so smoothly. He had protested his awkwardness in advance, but all gentlemen

137

did so out of a proper modesty. Max had meant it. She was forced to concentrate so hard upon following him, even on so simple a rhythm as the waltz, that she had difficulty speaking. Finally, when she felt she could trust where his feet would next fall, and thus keep hers out of the way, she opened their discourse by remarking upon Fergus's condition.

Max mumbled an unintelligible response, apparently utterly involved in guiding her around the crowded floor without bumping into others. Unbeknownst to Abigail, of course, ballroom dancing had not been included in Max's upbringing. He'd not dared decline to write his name on her card, and thus risk exposing his ignorance. Many gentlemen were inept dancers after years of lessons and practice, and he hoped to get away with being numbered among them.

"I wonder if you'd mind telling me, Mr. Driscoll," Abigail said, somewhat breathless from the exertion. The waltz was about to end, and she did not want what was proving to be an unpleasant experience to have been in vain. "Just exactly what were the circumstances of your meeting Lord Hunterswell?"

Abigail never was sure whether Max's foot ground down upon her toes deliberately, or if he had indeed lost his balance and so misstepped. However it happened, she was led limping from the dance floor, the answer to her question forever lost in Max's profuse apologies.

The next morning the sky was blue to the horizon. Bundled in her second-best furs, gloved hands in a matching muff, Abigail relished her stroll alone on the promenade deck, with Jacqueline a few paces behind. The simple matter of finding the Punjat's Ruby in the Nawab's suite had become quite complicated, and with many activities to attend to, privacy to think was at a premium.

She'd been able to get no real information from Fergus, and Max had been so steadfast in keeping his distance, she suspected that Frederick had warned him away. And that left J.C. and Aref. But how could she manage to question a manservant not in her own household. Or a mute?

Startled by the unctuous voice speaking her name in her ear, she whirled to search for Jacqueline, only to see her several yards away in a charade with Aref.

To an onlooker, with his cane swinging jauntily, the Nawab's hand upon Abigail's elbow would have seemed a gentlemanly gesture, however, his grip had caught the nerve and was exceedingly painful. With a smile for all to see, his thin voice was sharp with malice. "You know that I find you a pretty and charming girl, Miss Danforth?"

"Your Highness?" Abigail's feet scarcely touched the deck as he steered her, helplessly, toward the railing.

Reaching the rail, he released her elbow, yanked a handkerchief from his pocket, and waved it at her. "Emblazoned as it is with your initials, I am correct in assuming this is yours, is it not?"

Shocked, she could but stare at it as she withdrew a hand from her muff and rubbed her tender elbow.

"I need not tell you that I found it in my suite!" With great drama, he held the handkerchief over the railing and released it. Pointedly watching the wind dash it into the ocean, he scowled. "Should I have reason to suspect that you are spying upon me any further, I shall have to take steps to stop you."

"But, your Highness—"

"Unpleasant steps. I hope I make myself clear, Miss Danforth. It would be a singular pity to mar your physical beauty to put a curb upon your morbidly curious nature." Turning his back on her in a most ungentlemanly fashion, swinging his cane, he stalked away.

Cheeks aflame, Abigail watched his retreating figure and recalled her quarrel with Rodney. He had been loudly indignant in his denial of so much as touching her handkerchief cases. Toying with the golden screw in her muff, she longed for his skill at dissembling and vowed to have it out with him again.

Staring at the ocean, she shook her head dejectedly. The art of detection was proving to be more difficult to master than Dr. Conan Doyle made it appear in his stories. Even the purpose of the contents of the leather case among the Nawab's things was still a mystery. A red-faced and speechless Frederick had not even allowed her to complete a description. From his reaction, she had deduced that it must have had something to do with the impenetrable mystery of the marriage bed. Which made it all the more mysterious, since the Nawab was not married.

As Jacqueline rushed toward her, she turned away and proceeded with her walk in that aloof manner which no servant would dare interrupt.

Kinkade was in exceptionally high spirits. On this, the fourth evening of the crossing, he knew J.C. to be in Jacqueline's company in the second-class saloon and their romance seemed to be progressing apace. Hurrying along the alleyway, he kept his voice low as he sang, "Fe, fi, fo, fum, I smell the blood of an Englishman." He thought himself droll to be chanting that particular ditty while on his way to visit an Englishman's man.

Kinkade relished these missions on behalf of the senior Mr. Danforth, a man he admired extravagantly. Valeting Master Rodney was rendered tolerable by knowing that his father relied on him to protect his son as well as report on his behavior. The responsibility of subtly quizzing Stork to determine Lord Hunterswell's more intimate qualifications as suitor for Miss Abigail made him feel important. While resolved to be thorough, he also anticipated a bit of relaxation with a fellow professional.

Immediately upon hearing the approaching voice in the hall, Stork had taken two quick steps to the doorway. Gripping a belaying pin like a cricket bat, he stood poised to smite anyone who entered his cabin.

Kinkade rattled the doorknob as he intoned, "Be he alive or be he dead—" To his surprise, the door was unlocked, and he shoved it open while forcing his voice to sing as deep as it would go, "I'll grind his bones to make my bread—"

Stork recognized him in mid-swing. In his effort to miss Kinkade, his weak ankle gave, and he stumbled forward, crashing his hip into the small table.

"What the devil!" Kinkade exclaimed, as he jumped back into the open doorway.

Stork slumped into a chair at the table. The belaying pin clanked as it struck the metal deck, which was covered by a thin rug. "I am so sorry." Unable to look Kinkade in the face, Stork waved him inside as he added, "Do come in."

Closing the door, Kinkade pulled a flask from an inside pocket. "You look like a man who could use a drink." Unscrewing the top, he took a deep, appreciative sniff. "Have a dram of this." The kindness in his eyes softened his pugnacious features and bespoke his concern. "None of this ship's swill, mind you, but from Mr. Danforth's private stock."

"Then it deserves a proper glass." Stork bestirred himself to rummage in his travel locker and produced two brandy snifters.

Both men took a moment to admire the color and fragrance of the fine brandy before they hoisted their glasses. "To the Queen," they chorused.

Kinkade blinked as Stork tossed his drink down in one gulp. As they sat at the table, Kinkade poured him another and watched Stork as he muttered to himself and studied the glass before draining it.

Again Kinkade poured and Stork drank.

Watching the man stare at still another brandy, Kinkade asked softly, "Want to tell me about it, old boy?"

Stork cradled his chin in his hands. Tilting his head, he looked directly at Kinkade, "Know when you're in service, how nobody sees you as a human being?"

Kinkade pursed his lips and nodded ruefully. He knew only too well what Stork meant.

"You're not supposed to have any feelings," Stork sighed heavily, sat back, and stared into the brandy. "I'm not a man what has a heavy burden of passion. But I am a human, by Jove." With another sigh, he drained the glass, and stared into its emptiness so long that Kinkade thought he'd passed out with his eyes open. At last he spoke, "J.C. caught me in an indiscretion. In Rangoon. He threatened to tell Lord Hunterswell. If his Lordship found out, he'd sack me."

"Not after all the years you've been with them!"

"Especially after so many years! Some things just ain't done." He held out the glass for a refill. Kinkade obliged. Stork's voice was firm, "I won't tell you what the indiscretion was." He snorted, "Don't want another blackmailer bleedin' me."

"Blackmail!" Kinkade was horrified.

Tears welled in Stork's eyes, "He made me betray the family!" He gulped the brandy and shuddered. "I'll never forgive myself." He choked back a sob.

"Aw, come on, old boy. Nothing's that bad."

After a long pause peering at Kinkade as though assessing his trustworthiness, Stork continued, "You know that li'l chap, Aref? Him so pretty an' all?"

Kinkade nodded.

Stork shuddered. "Him and J.C. come bustin' in here, chloroformed me, an' tied me to that bunk." With his eyes shut tight, he pointed toward the double berth. Hugging himself, he opened his eyes and stared into space. "When I come to, Aref was squatting over me with a chiv, sharp like a razor it was. He threatened to—" Stork shuddered again. "He cut my apron, shirt, an' pants, so I had to make a bundle an' throw 'em overboard so no one would see an' wonder what happened." Stork's voice grew faint. "His Lordship's slipper still ain't dry."

Kinkade reached out to touch Stork's shoulder. "Did they hurt you?"

Shrugging Kinkade's arm off, Stork whispered, "They was gonna unman me."

Kinkade gasped. Mouth agape, he sat back. What had he done? While Jacqueline might have deserved dismissal, her crimes did not warrant being thrown into the arms of a violent blackmailer.

"I don't know what to do, Mr. Kinkade," Stork sobbed. "I don't know what to do." Burying his face in his hands, he cried, "I'm so scared. I can't sleep. That knife goin' for my parts will haunt me 'till I die." He raised his head to look Kinkade in the eye. "Don't tell a soul! Swear it!"

One hand on his heart, the other pointed heavenward, Kinkade stood over him. "I swear it, Stork old boy. What do you want me to do?"

Stork hiccoughed a great gasping sigh and whispered, "Help me," and passed out.

Vigorously applying two brushes to subdue his blond curls, Max grimaced at his reflection in the washstand mirror. Miss Danforth's efforts to pry into his past had been so transparent that it had been an easy matter to keep her at arm's length. He had tried to reassure Fergus, but the poor bastard had been too sick to care. And thank God for that; no need to alarm Frederick by having Fergus threaten her.

He slid the silver-backed brushes into the fitted straps of their leather travelling case—a gift from the marchioness—and extracted a silver-trimmed, tortoiseshell comb to groom his dark beard. If only Fergus had not gotten himself involved with Miss Arrington, she would not have gotten in the way. Why couldn't Fergus, and J.C. for that matter, leave the troublesome creatures alone? Or at least wait until after Miss Danforth's debut and they had dumped Frederick.

Donning a heavy satin dressing gown with a quilted collar—a gift from the marquess—he had just turned off the bright electric bulbs and lit the softer oil lamp when J.C. knocked on the door and entered without waiting for a response. Instantly on guard, Max gestured casually toward the decanter of port. "Want a drink?"

J.C. declined with a shake of his head.

"It's late," Max said impatiently when J.C. remained silent. "What's on your mind?"

J.C. ran a finger down a perfectly trimmed sideburn. "I can't take anymore of this." He cleared his throat. "I didn't mind some Robin Hood flimflam, but when things get physical? Hell, I puked all over that poor bastard's washstand, and it was him who was tied." He shook his head. "That Aref is loony."

"But don't you see?" Max lounged on the settee. "The Punjat's Ruby really is missing. Puts a whole new light on everything."

"Not for me, Max." J.C. sat on the edge of the bed and leaned forward. "When we set up this scam in Rangoon, I was different. Down on my luck and hungry. Now I've had a few squares, you know?" He hesitated, "And don't think I ain't grateful." Again, he shook his head. "But it ain't been the same without Maurice."

Max did not speak. Sneering, he raked J.C. with a contemptuous glance.

"I, too, am different now," J.C. protested.

"Oh, come on," Max said scornfully. "You had a bully time putting the pinch on Stork."

"But to almost cut his pecker off? With him awake and watching? Max, I tell you that Aref had a hard-on when he was waving that toadstabber around!"

"Yeah, sure," Max stood. "I'll bet you've changed." He poured himself a glass of port. Taking a sip, he said, "You've got the ruby stashed somewhere."

J.C. threw back his head and laughed heartily.

"Why else would you be talking such tomfoolery?"

"For all I know, you and Fergus have it."

Max just glared at him.

"Listen, Max." J.C. sobered. "I'm still young," he said earnestly. "I've chased a lot of skirts in my time, but now I'm getting to know the refining sweetness of true womanhood as exemplified by Miss Bordeaux—"

"I don't believe a word I'm hearing," Max interrupted. "Of all the sentimental claptrap. Women are empty-headed, expensive creatures that only gentlemen of leisure can afford to keep."

"Not the likes of Miss Bordeaux." J.C. sat tall. "I ain't

fit to kiss the hem of her skirt. But I could be. And when you and Fergus move on, I'll be wanting to stay in New York. My share from the caper with the Nawab is near enough to start a business. And if it ain't, queer thing is, much as I hated drawing that short straw, I've got a profession now. I could go into service with a rich family, get my rake-offs, and in a year, be in a position to marry her. Start a family of my own.'' He grasped his crotch. ''While I still can.''

''Well, well, well.'' Max stood and stretched. ''So you've found your own true love,'' he said as he forced himself to smile. ''Congratulations!''

''You're sure you don't mind?'' Relieved, J.C. stood and walked toward the door.

''I only ask that you take Jacqueline out of the Danforths' household.'' Max joined him at the door.

''No wife of mine will work!'' J.C. said, holding out his hand to seal the bargain. ''I'll promise you that.''

Max sighed as he leaned against the door after closing it behind J.C. The man was a fool and then some. Like Maurice. How could J.C. possibly think that they would risk leaving him behind to spill his guts. Pity Fergus was so sick, they'd have to wait until New York for an opportunity to stage another accident.

Free for the rest of the evening, Kinkade was hurrying past Miss Danforth's door when he heard a feminine voice call his name and turned to see Jacqueline beckoning to him. Intrigued, he followed her below deck. They reached the second-class saloon only to discover that a boisterous rendition of ''Sally in Our Alley'' was in progress, making conversation impossible. Kinkade was for joining in the fun, but Jacqueline made him understand that she would fetch her coat and bonnet and meet him outside at the railing.

Awaiting Jacqueline's arrival, Kinkade gazed at the stars. Assuming she'd asked for this interview to plead her case, he decided to forgive her if she would promise to leave Master Rodney alone in the future, and steer the conversation so that he could somehow warn her against J.C., without betraying Stork's confidence. As Jacqueline drew near, with a perky bonnet replacing her servant's cap, he was astonished to realize just how pretty she was. Feeling expansive, he reached out his hand to pat her shoulder. "I can understand why Master Rodney was attracted to you."

She backed away from his touch. "He tells you that?"

Clasping his hands behind his back, Kinkade resumed a more formal manner, "Not exactly, but—"

Her gaze was fierce as she looked up at him. "He forces me to say Miss Danforth's secret to him! Then he makes me promise not to tell her. When I promise I won't tell is when he grabs me and kisses me!" She screwed up her face in disgust. "Ugh!"

His mouth ajar, Kinkade stared at her, speechless.

"Hah!" she exclaimed. "You say you understand!" She stamped her foot. "But no, you do not. It is not my beauty. Master Rodney is happy he upsmarted me!"

"I see—" To his vast embarrassment, Kinkade blushed. She peered at him.

"No," he was quick to insist. "I do understand. Really, I do."

Mollified, she glanced at her muff, then turned to gaze at the star-lit ocean and sigh, "Ah, Miss Danforth. She is perfection, no?" Tilting her head slightly, she looked up at him from underneath her dark fluttering lashes.

"She is?" Accustomed to being in control, especially with the female servants, Kinkade was uncomfortable at having been caught off guard so completely. Hearing the question in his voice, Jacqueline glanced at him sharply and he swiftly corrected himself, "I mean, yes, she is, but why—"

"She did not give me a sack after all," Jacqueline said with pride, gazing at the ocean again.

"You told Miss Abigail what you'd done?" Kinkade was flabbergasted.

"*Oui.* I have no brains for the secret. Better Miss Danforth know it about me now. And you, too, *Monsieur.*"

"Does Master Rodney know?"

"Not yet. That is why I tell you. When he finds out, he will have anger at me and will want to give me the boot."

Sympathy for her plight was clear in his expression, and when he patted her muffed hands resting on the railing, she did not recoil. "The stars are beautiful," he said softly.

"Oui, Monsieur," she replied without looking at him. "But now I must go—"

"No, stay, please," he implored. "Just for a moment. There is something I would ask you."

"Monsieur?"

Dropping his pretense at nonchalance, Kinkade huddled close to her so that he could not be overheard. "What would you say, if I told you that I had a conversation with someone who described a situation similar to yours? But this person truly believes he cannot tell his master. Perhaps it would have to do with the missing ruby."

"Could this person be the Stork?" she whispered.

Startled, Kinkade stepped back. "How did you know?"

"Miss Danforth notices how liverish he looks. She was going to ask Lord Hunterswell to give him a physic."

"I hope she did not call his Lordship's attention to Stork's condition."

She laughed, "No matter." In a surprisingly rich voice for one so tiny she sang, *"L'amour, l'amour fait tourner le monde."*

Absolutely enchanted by her lovely voice, Kinkade asked, "What do the words mean?"

"It's love, it's love that makes the world go round," she sang in English, then laughed merrily. "Lord Hunterswell is so in love, he goes in circles and sees only the face of Miss Danforth at the center to his universe. Stork could confess to the murder and his Lordship would not see."

"Murder!"

"Non, non, non, I mean—"

"Ah," he laughed. "You exaggerate."

"Oui," she laughed in turn. *"Merci beaucoup* for understanding, *Monsieur* Kinkade. Now I must go. It is late."

"Please do not tell Miss Abigail about Stork. I promised him—"

147

"Hmpff!" The twinkle in her eyes told him she was teasing as she shook her finger at him. "Fine keeper of the secret you are!"

"Ah, but no, Miss Bordeaux," he said with a gallant bow. "If you recall, I did not have to tell. You were too clever for me."

"*Touché, Monsieur.*" After a brief hesitation she continued, "What can it matter? No need to tell Miss Danforth what she already knows. No?"

To his amazement, Kinkade heard himself asking politely, "May I escort you to your cabin, Miss Bordeaux?"

Her refusal was so graceful that he did not feel rejected until she had disappeared. Cursing his missed opportunity to warn her about J.C., he struck the railing. Did she care for the scoundrel?

The petals had begun to wilt on the potted tulips in Abigail's suite. She felt as forlorn as they looked. Dressed for disembarking in a squirrel-trimmed coat with shoulder cape, she had escaped the hubbub on deck for a few moments of solitude. Failure was a distasteful experience. Yet it must be faced. The *St. Louis* would be docking within the hour, and she had no real knowledge of the whereabouts of the ruby. Worse, she suspected everyone, including her brother, though she could scarcely credit him with the required cleverness.

Reposing on the settee, she closed her eyes and, removing her gloves, lightly stroked her grandmother muff of squirrel. Instead of sleeping the night before, she had read Frederick's manuscript of his version of her investigation. His handwriting was brisk, with little embellishment, and easy to read. Unfortunately, his writing style held none of the terse excitement of Dr. Conan Doyle's prose. Detailing every gown and hat she'd worn on the voyage and extolling the beauty of her feminine nature, his report was more suitable to a lover than a chronicler of a detective's adventures. If she had succeeded and there had been a reason to publish, the manuscript would have been unacceptable.

148

Parting her lashes slightly, she absently blew on the muff, watching the random tracks her breath made in the soft fur. His narrative had not included one word of her misgivings about Max and Fergus. Or J.C. Nor had he mentioned Miss Arrington's death, even as an accident. Or the death of the valet Maurice. Her fingers traced the patterns her breath made in the fur. Had she not expressed her suspicions strongly enough?

And then she remembered dancing with Frederick. Unlike Max, he was a superb dancer, and although he'd held her correctly, his eyes had searched her face, and mouth, hungrily. Her cheeks grew warm with the memory, and those odd feelings she'd felt stirred again. Was this what love felt like? She shivered to dispel the feelings, suddenly relieved that she need not reveal to him that his writing was unsuitable.

Erasing the furrows on the muff with her fingertips, she took a deep breath and forced herself to end her brooding over the dismal fashion in which her first case was ending. Ever since she had left New York, a homesick young girl, she had been anticipating her homecoming as a grown woman. Yet today she had not been particularly thrilled at her first sighting of the Statue of Liberty. Nor had the spires of Trinity Church soaring into the New York skyline along with the Produce Exchange Building inspired her. She was allowing disappointment in herself and Frederick's performance as a journalist to spoil her return.

Drawing on her gloves, she realized anew that Rodney was certain to tell their father of her meeting with Dr. Conan Doyle, and the fiasco of her search for the ruby. She despaired of finding a way to diffuse his anger. Although he had never treated her with the scorn he seemed to reserve for Rodney, she had no wish to provoke him; especially now that she was to be so utterly dependent upon him. Now that her dream was over.

Resolutely straightening herself, she dispelled a threatened recurrence of melancholy and checked in the mirror to see if her hat had remained at its most becoming angle during her reverie. Perhaps her father would be at the pier and, perhaps, if she looked her very best, he'd break his cool reserve and clasp her in his arms in welcome.

Heralding their impending arrival, the first of several ear-shattering blasts from the ship's whistle startled her. As she turned to retrieve her muff, the cabin door opened. Expecting Jacqueline, she was startled anew when the Nawab sidled in and locked the door. With gloved fingertips to his lips, he signaled that they might as well remain silent until the racket abated.

Knowing that the noise would render useless any attempt to scream for help, she calmed herself to better face the danger. As she casually positioned herself to put the table between them, the flower pot in easy reach to hurl at him if necessary, she really looked at him.

From the fire opal centered on his white turban, to the highly polished points of his small, modish shoes, his grooming was impeccable. Yet his Western suit seemed loose, as though he'd suffered a weight loss too precipitate to summon his tailor. When she dared look at his eyes, she cautioned herself to remain on guard as her sympathy went out to him. Forsaking her desire to escape, she relaxed to listen to what he had to say.

The final echoes of the ship's horn had not yet finished reverberating as he spoke. Despite his haggard appearance, his voice retained its surprising lightness, "I have come to most humbly apologize to you, Miss Danforth, and to ask your forgiveness. I know now that you did not search my cabin."

Guilt-stricken, but unable to tell him the truth, she unfurled her fan and concealed her blushing cheeks. She curtsied slightly and murmured, "Your Highness."

"I now know that your handkerchief was deliberately left in my quarters to embarrass you. I would not blame you overmuch, if you could not see your way clear to forgive my horribly suspicious mind, but I implore you to hear me out." Approaching her, he indicated with his cane that she sit on the settee.

"Your Highness, the warning whistle," she protested, but his expression was so grave that she sat.

150

"I have been given to understand that you accepted an assignment from the marquess and marchioness to recover the Punjat's Ruby, which was stolen from them. This is true?"

No longer seeing a need to maintain the secret, Abigail nodded her assent.

"Well?" In spite of his effort at control, the Nawab's tone grew impatient. "Have you found it?"

"No, your Highness. I have been unable to locate it. But why should its disappearance concern you?"

"I hasten to explain." With one hand, he turned a chair to face her and sat on its edge. His words tumbled forth, "Just as Mr. Twain said, the idol has been an object of worship since its creation. It was I who cast the deciding vote in favor of bartering it. On one condition. It was to be given to a great queen or king who, in gratitude, would come to our defense should the need arise. That is its real price, Miss Danforth. I will be held responsible for its return to its rightful new owners, so that the unspoken debt can be collected. Or it is I who will be suspected of its theft by my own people." He thumped his cane on the deck for emphasis, "So you can see, its disappearance is as embarrassing to me as your purloined handkerchiefs were to you. Though the consequences will be infinitely more severe in my case."

Certain that he was trying to bamboozle her by the rapidity of his outpouring, she waited for him to reach his point.

Standing, he nonchalantly used his cane to maneuver the chair back to its spot at the table. "I had intended to begin my travels in your wonderful country almost at once, Miss Danforth. However, I would like to change my plans and remain in New York indefinitely."

Abigail stood and gathered her muff and parasol. "In that case, I shall see that you receive an invitation to my debut."

"I would be honored. But my dear Miss Danforth, I need your help."

She turned to face him. "You do?" Her surprise was genuine.

"I have just explained. My life is in danger."

"I do not understand, your Highness. How can I help you?"

"Please, Miss Danforth, find the Punjat's Ruby. For me!"

"You flatter me, sir." Abigail shook her head. "The time has come for me to set aside my dream of becoming a detective. Soon, I will be under my father's direction protection." Even as she spoke, she wondered if she might be hiding behind the necessity of obeying her father. Having been unable to find the idol on board so small a ship, how could she hope to recover it in the huge city of New York? "I know without asking that he would not grant his permission."

"Miss Danforth, I beg you," the Nawab moved to stop her. "Name your price."

"Forgive me, your Highness," she said, brushing past him. "My father has been most generous to me." Reaching the door, she turned to face him with a wry smile. "I will not further risk his displeasure by disobeying him while living under his roof." It was with no small amount of pleasure that she discovered herself to be truly saddened to be thus coerced into refusing him.

Chapter Six

Things equal to the same thing are equal to each other.
                                                    Euclid

The customs shed in Hoboken was wildly disorganized.
The long-coated, helmeted inspectors seemed to relish their
moment of power, holding people hostage who had riches
and leisure enough to circle the globe, while they pawed
through the most intimate depths of their trunks, searching
for undeclared trinkets.

With only Rodney's two trunks and his own meager luggage to watch after, with a gentlemanly fingertip to cap in
salute to the diminutive Jacqueline—who was looking especially pretty in a perky bonnet that complemented her
modest cloak—Kinkade had taken charge of the stevedores
carrying Abigail's trunks to quayside. All too willing to take
advantage of a few moments to be alone with the pretty
maid, he had also volunteered to help her search the heaps
of luggage on the dock that had been off-loaded from the
ship's hold, for the rest of Abigail's belongings.

To keep up appearances, J.C. was busy with managing
both Max's and Fergus's luggage, and thus helpless to assist
Jacqueline. He grumbled to himself as he watched the way
she flirted with Kinkade as they searched for Abigail's luggage. Preoccupied with keeping them in sight while wres-
tling with unaccustomed feelings of jealousy, he quite forgot
about the missing ruby.

Stork kept a wary eye out for Aref, who managed astonishingly well to make his wants known to the stevedores without speaking a word. He also kept J.C. in sight, at one point following J.C.'s fixed gaze to the byplay with Jacqueline and Kinkade. Although it was with great delight that he noted J.C.'s distress, he knew that he'd not have a moment's true peace until the ruby was found. Being thus distracted, his experience in disembarking did him in good stead. A generous tip in the hold had placed his Lordship's luggage miraculously close to the customs shed.

Frederick and Max had been last seen standing at the ship's railing, and were nowhere to be found when it was time to disembark, so it was Rodney, hat askew, all the while admonishing Abigail not to walk too fast, who followed her down the gangplank, as he supported an exhausted, stumbling Fergus. None too gently depositing the man on a crate, brandishing his cane, he raced off after Abigail, who had vanished into the shed.

Inside, bedlam reigned. Dogs barked, children wailed, people shouted, and quarrels were plentiful. Although she could have waited outside in the relative calm while the servants took care of the baggage, Abigail could not resist pacing along the column of inspectors on the slender chance that an extraordinarily lucky one would discover the ruby. She was not surprised to find the Nawab similarly occupied. Then Rodney caught up to her.

"You stupid silly girl!" he shouted. "I told you not to leave my sight." Grabbing her elbow he turned her around. "I've got you this close to home, and I'll not lose you before we get there!" Releasing her elbow, he proffered his arm for her to take. "Come with me this instant!"

With a significant glance at the Nawab to convey her hapless situation, Abigail shrugged. "Yes, Rodney," she said, suddenly docile. With a great sigh, she gave up her last faint hope of finding the ruby as she took Rodney's arm and allowed him to lead her outside to join Fergus.

Still seated on the crate, Fergus was regaining his strength with each breath he drew, now that the earth was stationary. Just as Rodney and Abigail reached him, Frederick and Max broke through the crowd, leading Crosspatches.

Letting go of Rodney's arm, all decorum forgotten, Abigail ran to meet them. Patting Crosspatches's nose, her smile was one of pure delight as she glanced up at Frederick. "What a lovely surprise!"

Frederick's blush of pleasure was so deep, it showed beneath his tan as he tipped his hat. "A gift from my mother, Miss Danforth."

"For me?" Thrilled beyond measure, Abigail gasped. "But I cannot—"

"It is but a small token of her appreciation for your efforts," he interrupted with a wink to indicate their secret pact.

"But I failed—"

Again he interrupted. "My dear Miss Danforth," he said, with a smile of his own so large that it transformed his craggy features. "In my opinion there is no possible way that you can fail at anything you do."

"Your Lordship." Abigail blushed furiously, her heart suddenly warmed by the heat of his glance. It was not the gift of Crosspatches that so bedazzled her, it was his tacit approval of her riding astride that the gift implied that suddenly made her wonder if she could not indeed love this man. She was about to blow him a flirtatious kiss, when Fergus let out a howl of pure anguish.

Max had just broken the news to him that they must board the Christopher Street Ferry to reach the city. Still seated, holding on to his cane as though it could root him to the ground, Fergus vowed earnestly that he'd rather die in Hoboken than board yet another ship, no matter it was a stable, slow-moving ferry.

No sooner had Fergus quieted his moaning than a hullabaloo and ruckus, louder than any others before, issued from the shed, with the Nawab's voice loudly raised above them all. Abigail rushed to the doorway in time to see the Nawab nose to nose in disagreement with an inspector. The Nawab raised his cane to strike the man, and the situation threatened to deteriorate when, before their hot words could culminate in fisticuffs, Kinkade intervened, and by turns charmed, cajoled, and intimidated the customs officers. Abigail suspected that he also crossed a palm or two with silver.

Howsoever he accomplished it, he soon had everyone, their innumerable possessions, and the horse, aboard the Christopher Street Ferry. As they embarked upon their short journey across the Hudson River, their ferry was but one vessel among the innumerable barges, tugboats, packets, and side-wheel steamers that plied their way in one of the busiest ports in the world.

After a smooth docking, as Abigail emerged from the ferry's terminal on the New York side, she looked back in awe. The rigging from clippers, sloops, and frigates moored at the pier seemed to enmesh the very heavens.

Piled high with vast stacks of cargo of every imaginable kind, the docks were aswarm with stevedores, teamsters, porters, sailors, and roustabouts, as well as passengers, all of whom had to shout to be heard over a fearsome din of iron-clad wheels and horses' hooves on cobblestones.

Even more oppressive than the noise was the reek of overheated horseflesh mingling with ancient and new droppings. Combined with the stench of ripe fish, the horrendous odors overwhelmed senses relaxed by a week's fresh air at sea.

Handkerchief to her nostrils, Abigail trailed a step behind her brother, searching the crowd, in vain, for her father. Rodney drew up short. Abigail nearly bumped into him.

"You stay here, Abigail," he ordered, pointing his walking stick at the ground as though pinning her to the spot. "There is something I must ask his Highness before he disappears to the Plaza Hotel." Hurrying back to the terminal toward a large carriage which Kinkade had hailed for the Nawab, Aref, and their baggage, Rodney shouted at her over his shoulder, "Don't move!"

Sweltering in December's unseasonable sixty-degree heat, she looked for Jacqueline near the household dray, which seemed to have arrived before their own carriage. Wishing to give Jacqueline the cape portion of her cloak and muff, but unable to attract her attention, she made her way over the rubble toward the dray. Pausing to see if she could discover what had so engaged her maid, she observed Jacqueline's open admiration of Kinkade's skill in ordering the porters about, and its salubrious effect upon him. She took a moment to go behind the dray, where Crosspatches was hitched, to pat his nose, and also noticed that while the still liverish Stork seemed content to have Kinkade in command, J.C. comported himself much like a jealous lover. Admonishing herself for her vivid imagination, she gave Jacqueline her unwanted garments and returned to the spot that Rodney had demanded she stand.

Having momentarily lost sight of her again as he was returning from his errand with the Nawab, Rodney frowned, but withheld comment as he grabbed her firmly by the elbow.

Exhausted and enormously grateful to be on firm ground again, Fergus allowed Frederick and Max to support him as they followed Rodney and Abigail, who were threading their way through the crowd toward a strange machine that might have been a carriage except that it had no horses mounted in front.

"How jolly!" Abigail exclaimed, not allowing her disappointment at not being met by her father to show. "Father has sent Oscar for us in a motor car! I did not know he owned one." Withdrawing her arm from Rodney's grip, she extended her hand to the chauffeur.

"Good to have you home, Miss Danforth." Cap under his arm, his eyes misty, Oscar saluted when she released his hand.

"It's a Woods Electric Station Wagon," Rodney proclaimed loudly, his good humor restored at the impression the expensive vehicle was making on the nobleman and his friends. "It can go twelve miles an hour!"

A liveried footman settled Abigail and Rodney in the back seat with Frederick, Max, and Fergus facing them. Closing the doors, he joined Oscar up front in the driver's seat. While Abigail admired the fresh roses in their bud vases, Rodney showed off the car's coat rail, mirror box, card case, hat brush, watch, and bragged about its seventeen coats of body paint.

Ignoring the derisive shouts of "Get a horse!", Oscar did not wait for the luggage dray and servants as he maneuvered the car through the curious onlookers, past row upon row of solid brick and stone commercial buildings. As the motor labored up the incline of Christopher Street, urchins, their rags flapping, ran beside them. Before Abigail could ask Rodney for an American coin to toss to an exceptionally pretty, red-haired match girl, they had reached the top of the hill. Traffic speeded up, enabling them to follow in the wake of a coach-and-four, and the child could no longer keep pace.

Grateful that street noise made conversation impossible, Abigail gazed out of the window, exhilarated by the vitality of a city that had grown and changed much more than she since their separation.

But the thrill of the ride changed to dread when they turned off Park Avenue into Gramercy Park and she saw the heavy layers of straw scattered in front of her house. Ben's condition must still be grave to warrant such silencing of horse and buggy.

Although appearances were important to him, Andrew Benjamin Danforth had disdained building what he considered a pretentious mausoleum on Millionaire's Row along Fifth Avenue. With a cellar unmatched in the city (which contained, among other rarities, cases of vintage pre-phylloxera clarets) his modest nine-bedroom mansion was grand enough to entertain a future marquess and his entourage as house guests without apology. Fully electrified, it had every convenience including the telephone, and was most remarkable for its modern facilities for servants. He provided well for them, not out of kindness, but in the expectation of loyalty and graft-free, thus relatively cheap, service in return.

Finally giving up all pretense of reading the New York *Herald,* Andrew Danforth folded the paper neatly, made room for it sideways on the cluttered table, and compared his pocket watch with the clock on the mantelpiece, again. Standing, he strolled from the tufted-satin, fringed sofa to a matching blue Turkish seater and straightened it a fraction to more exactly face its mate. His tailor had no flaw to conceal in his tall, well-muscled physique, and his posture was so stiffly correct that when he turned his head, his broad shoulders turned also. Years of manicures and creams had erased all trace of physical work in the mines from his strong, square hands. Their only adornment was a signet ring wrought in heavy gold worn on his right ring finger. It had been a wedding gift from his beloved, late wife.

Still a vigorous russet color, his unparted hair waved back from his forehead. Its youthful abundance pleased him. While he would have vehemently denied this vanity, he always placed his hat precisely within the trough of a wave so that when he tipped it to salute a lady, his hair remained undisturbed.

Because of his tonsorial skill, Kinkade had nearly been denied his voyage to London, until Samuel, a second footman in the household, was discovered to have uncommon talent with scissors. It had been in the privacy of his dressing room where Samuel had persuaded him to grow his moustache. The same russet shade as his hair, it was now full and curved upwards at the corners of his mouth, which lightened his expression. His eyes were the deep brown of burnt sienna and seemed to harbor a perpetual sadness. His occasional smile was apt to be more danger signal than sign of friendliness.

From his vantage point near the fireplace he proudly surveyed his drawing room, from the elaborate frieze which surrounded the ornate ceiling, to the Polar bear skin, its fangs agleam, on the Bokhara carpet. An insatiable collector, he considered himself, and was sought out by others, as a connoisseur. Countless objets d'art vied with short-leaf palmettos in grotesquely shaped china pots and ruffle-shaded lamps for space on the numerous, scarf-covered tables.

Looking at his pretty things gave him much pleasure, and he anticipated Abigail's return more than he cared to admit, so that she could wear her mother's jewels. He had removed the sapphires and some of the lesser pearls from the bank vault. The blue gems had been his engagement gift to his wife. Time enough to fetch the others after the New Year.

Although momentarily expecting the announcement that the voyagers had arrived, he had yet to come to a decision about Samuel's permanently replacing Kinkade. Seldom at a loss, the unresolved question had him somewhat disturbed. He was relieved that his daughter was returning to him full grown. Soon after her debut on New Year's, she would take over the responsibility for the smooth running of the household. If, by then, he did decide to retain Samuel, the onerous task of telling Kinkade would rightfully be hers.

Impatient for Abigail's arrival, he was about to break his vow and make a sentimental fool of himself by going outside to wait for her, when he heard the faint sounds of the butler Gregory welcoming people in the foyer. Starting forward eagerly, he stopped himself in the middle of the room. He had waited so long, another minute wouldn't matter.

Even though Abigail was followed by others who vied for his attention, the moment she entered the room he was stricken with an unmanly giddiness at the uncanny resemblance she bore her mother. Dizziness enveloped him to the threshold of collapse. Stiffening his spine to overcome it, he was barely able to say, "Abigail, you are home."

Seeing only his withdrawal, and surmising that she had somehow displeased him, Abigail swiftly smothered her smile and mirrored his aloofness. Impeccable manners masked her pain at the chill of his greeting as she stopped short to turn and formally present Lord Hunterswell, Mr. Driscoll, and Mr. Buchanan.

In his struggle to gain control, Andrew Danforth refrained from looking at Abigail and, turning his gracious attention to his male guests, he spared a kind word of welcome for Rodney.

Longing to ask her father if the straw-laden street meant that Benjamin's condition had worsened, Abigail unfurled her fan and bided her time for that inevitable pause to occur in their gentlemanly discourse. Not wishing to ask a direct question that could be rebuffed, yet in hopes of some explanation, she addressed her father's back when the opening in their conversation finally appeared, "Sir, if I may be excused, please. I would like to see Benjamin."

The timbre of her voice was so like her mother's that Andrew Danforth could not risk looking at her. His yes sounded stern even to his own ears.

Hurt and bewildered by his curt dismissal, her back was as rigid as his as she walked to the door.

When, by the rustle of her skirts, he'd judged her to be near the door, Andrew Danforth glanced her way, but could not summon the strength to call out for her to return.

Basking in his father's unusual friendliness, Rodney was oblivious to the situation. Only Frederick noticed Andrew Danforth's fleeting expression of inconsolable grief as the door closed behind his daughter. He worried anew at his chances of winning Abigail's hand.

Breathless after dashing up two flights of stairs, Abigail paused in front of Benjamin's door to still the questions surrounding her father's greeting. Why had he been so aloof? Had he somehow found out her secret dream? But how? And if this was his manner with her without knowing, how was he going to react when Rodney finally told him?

Composing herself, concerned that she might be disturbing Benjamin, she knocked gently while holding her ear to the door for his response. Certain that she heard his voice, she entered.

Expecting the worst, she was delighted to find him sitting up on a chaise lounge near a brisk fire, reading. Although the room was warm, he wore a woolen dressing gown and had a comforter about his knees. He resembled a melted-down version of their father, except that his vivid hair seemed out of place on a person so shrunken. Seeing who it was, he laid the book on his lap and held out his arms.

Rushing to sit on the edge of the chaise, Abigail felt like she was embracing a skeleton.

His voice was husky with emotion as he whispered in her ear, "Forgive me for not standing, my sweet Abby."

She found it difficult to keep the tears of joy at bay as she pulled away to look at him. "Dearest Ben, it's so good to see you." Her smile was tremulous, relieved that someone was, at last, glad to see her. "Typhoid fever!" She exclaimed. "It could have killed you."

"I'm fine. I'm fine." He patted her hand and sighed. "Father must have had a nasty shock when he saw you."

She stood abruptly. The pain from their father's aloofness returned, and she worried anew about what she'd done to incur it. "What do you mean?"

"You look exactly like mother."

"I do?" Genuinely surprised and pleased by the compliment, she relaxed somewhat.

"Didn't Rodney say anything?" Ben looked at her, puzzled. "Don't you remember her portrait? You must have passed it on the staircase."

She shook her head. "I'm afraid I rushed by it without looking. I remember it as so beautiful. You mean that I—"

"Such becoming modesty." Smiling, he made a circling motion with his fingers. "Turn around, Miss Gabby Abby, and let me see your pretty frock. Show me what they taught you—a broad?" he chuckled.

"Oh, it's erect posture and a regal sweep you want?" She winked at him and ran to the fireplace. Grabbing the hearth brush, she swept an imaginary path in front of her as she returned to the chaise.

Helpless with merriment, Ben hugged his sides. Catching his breath, he said, "So that's what Father paid a fortune for!"

"You should have seen the regal manner in which I swept from the drawing room just now," she said over her shoulder as she returned the brush. She paused with her back toward him. "Oh, Ben," she said, suddenly near tears. "Father was so cold." She turned to face him, trying to smile. "And that moustache!"

"Don't be too hard on him, Sis." Ben beckoned for her

162

to come closer to the chaise, draw up the wicker chair, and sit beside him. He gazed at her quietly while she removed her hat and placed it on the foot of the chaise. Finally, he said, "I don't know about Father. He comes in here several times a day. Probably more often than I realize, because I spend much of my time sleeping."

Suddenly concerned that she'd overstayed, she reached for her hat. "I should go, Ben. I don't want to—"

"No, stay." Ben held out his hand to stop her. "He always looks at me like he's on the verge of confiding something, but he never does."

"No doubt he's been worried about you."

"I know that to be true. But one thing I do not understand is his liking for that Pecksniffian creep, Samuel."

"Oh?"

"Samuel is responsible for the moustache."

"Aha. Well, sir. I have the most delightful new lady's maid. She's French, quite tireless, and talented."

"I know. You wrote. But you didn't say, is she pretty?"

"Yes." In a mock severe tone, she continued, "Now promise you won't give her difficulties."

"I?" Ben was all innocence.

"Rodney behaved a perfect scoundrel."

"That's my twin for you." Ben shook his head sadly. "By the by, was Miss Cunningham in the drawing room?"

"Miss Cunningham? Why no. Who is she?"

"You mean you honestly don't know? Rodney didn't tell you?"

"Don't you do that to me, Ben!" She threatened to pounce on him. "Tell me!"

"She is to be your chaperon."

Abigail groaned and slumped back in her chair.

"She is some kind of distant cousin of mother's," Ben explained. "When she came for a visit, I think father tried to finagle her into running the household for him. She wouldn't, though she would nurse me whenever the real nurse didn't show. She's sort of stayed on."

"Penniless I suppose?"

"I don't think so, but I don't know. I was too sick when

she arrived, and it didn't seem worth the candle to find out since.''

"Do you think father might be . . . '' she paused. "How can I express it delicately?'' Her smile was impish, "Ah, dallying, with her?''

"Abigail! What a divinely devious mind you have! Next you'll be subscribing to *The Police Gazette* and causing father apoplexy.'' He smiled. "No. There's no dalliance there. Quite the contrary. She could be the reason father's so nettlesome these days. She has to be one of the most dour women I have ever met. Keeps to her rooms with the vapors.''

"How dreary for you. And me.'' Abigail sighed disgustedly. "I had thought that Jacqueline could be all the chaperon I'd require.''

"Now, now, Abby,'' he tried to soothe her. "For all her dreariness, Miss Cunningham has made you the most fantastic schedule of luncheons, morning calls, dinners, and balls. I shall never see you.''

With an annoyed swirl of petticoats, she stood. "Now that's precisely what I told Dr. Conan Doyle would happen!'' she exclaimed.

"What's that you say?'' Benjamin sat forward. "You actually met Dr. Conan Doyle? You didn't write about that!''

"It was but a short while before we sailed,'' she said, looking at him solemnly. "If I tell you something, will you promise me not to tell father?''

Without speaking, Ben crossed his heart.

Making herself comfortable in the wicker chair, Abigail began with Conan Doyle's rejection, and swiftly recounted her suspicions regarding Miss Arrington's accident, her attempts to find the missing ruby, and ended her story with the Nawab's request.

"Wow! The Punjat's Ruby!'' Ben exclaimed when she was through. "If father had known there'd been a chance to see it—never mind meet Wales—he would have gone for you himself.'' He stifled a yawn. "I can't wait to meet Crosspatches. And, of course, his Lordship.''

Interrupted by a knock at the door, he called out, "Come in."

Liveried in the Danforths' dark blue with red piping, the servant came forward, "Miss Danforth's presence is requested at tea in the solarium at 4:00."

Abigail dismissed him with a curt nod and, as soon as the door closed behind him, reached for Ben's hand, "I hate to leave. There is more to tell."

"Not now. You must go and change. I am weary and father is still testy when it comes to being punctual. Come and see me again before dinner."

"Won't you dine with us?"

"I still take meals in the solitude and comfort of my rooms."

Retrieving her hat from the foot of the chaise, she looked down at him thoughtfully. "Do you have any idea why father has not remarried?"

"No, my dear. Furthermore, I've never had nerve enough to ask. Now scat!" He fanned his book at her.

She stopped at the door to blow him an extravagant farewell kiss.

His voice was husky as he called after her, "It's wonderful having you home, Abby!"

Stork was impressed. He considered himself a well-traveled man, but he'd never seen accommodations such as these. A water closet for the servants. A bathing room, complete with shower stall. With hot and cold running water! One belowstairs in the menservant's quarters and, presumably, one upstairs for the females. Furthermore, he had his very own room to himself. It made no matter that it was scarcely large enough for a cot and wardrobe, it had a door and provided that rarest commodity of all for a servant—privacy.

The kitchen was a wonderland of the latest inventions, but most wondrous of all, it was ruled by a cheerful cook, who did not begrudge an unscheduled snack and had insisted that they sit in the comfortable servants' parlor for a bite before resuming their duties. The fragrance of her spicy apple pie was too seductive to resist. Although he'd have preferred tea, he did not risk spoiling her good nature by refusing her cocoa and was glad. With a gob of marshmallow on top, it was rich and delicious.

Smiling to himself, he sat a little taller as he became aware of the smothered giggles as the maids took a peek into the room. It reminded him of his youth, when he'd stared in awe at His Royal Majesty's valet, when Albert had visited the marquess. Proud of his rank, his tangled nerves began to unwind, and even his lame foot began to thaw in the warmth.

Kinkade had been acting the perfect host. His pugilist's face wreathed in smiles, he had joshed with everyone while making introductions. Only a critical eye would have noticed that his expansiveness had diminished when Jacqueline had departed for the upper regions of the house wherein lay her new lodgings.

However, his sociability had ceased entirely when he had discovered that Samuel had moved into his bedsitter the day he'd left and had no intention of moving out. Dropping his host's role, his expression fierce, he had excused himself to find Gregory to brace him for an explanation.

J.C. had the fidgets, Stork was pleased to observe. The cad had actually tried to draw him aside on the ferry and apologize, but Stork would have none of it. Instead, he'd threatened to tell his Lordship the truth, and J.C. had slunk off. Of course, he never would commit such a rash act, but J.C. couldn't call that for certain. He wished he had the nerve to kill the man and be done with it. Stage an accident like that poor Miss Arrington had. Never before had he wanted to do another man harm.

Stork had no way of knowing that J.C.'s distress was due to Jacqueline's and Kinkade's absence—together. Unable to stand the suspense another minute, J.C. excused himself from the table, leaving his pie half-eaten. He had no idea where to start looking for Jacqueline, so he stood at the bottom of the backstairs where she'd vanished and, as she'd been invited for pie also, prayed that she'd reappear before he'd be called for duty. He did not have long to wait.

J.C.'s expression was so bleak that when Jacqueline saw him, she sent her escort ahead so that she could stop and speak to him alone. *"Monsieur* J.C.?" She frowned with concern. "Are you all right?"

Without preamble, J.C.'s jealous heart burst. "You think that Mr. Kinkade is so swell, do you? Well, let me tell you about him!" he said in a rush, keeping his voice low so he wouldn't be overheard. "Kinkade is the one who dragooned me into calling on you. He said you was a tart. Only went for the master. But you might provide some fun on the voyage, he said. There's a copper in it for you, if you get her in the family way, he said."

The instant the words were out of his mouth, he realized his mistake. Anger at Kinkade's betrayal had blinded him to the effect his revelations might have upon her.

Jacqueline had turned to stone.

Desperately, he swiftly explained how he'd immediately known her for a virtuous woman. That she was, in fact, the girl of his dreams. He loved her.

Without a word or gesture to indicate whether she'd heard him, Jacqueline turned on her heel, lifted her skirts just high enough to clear the tread, and dashed up the stairs.

Gregory was nowhere to be found and, suspecting he'd just had the runaround from some of his supposed pals in the household, Kinkade raced down the backstairs, heading toward the servants' parlor and his long-awaited pie. To his delight, he saw Jacqueline mounting the stairs toward him.

Smiling, he opened his mouth to speak, but before he could utter a word, she burst into a barrage of French, jabbing the air with her expressive hands. Although he could not understand one word, he did comprehend that she was angry. That his ancestry was in question. That she was very angry, indeed. With him.

Then he heard J.C.'s name mentioned accompanied by

a kissing-her-fingertips gesture of total disgust, and it dawned on him what must have happened.

Kinkade's heart filled with remorse at the pain he had caused her. His arms ached to hold her and soothe her savaged feelings, but he felt helpless in the face of her rage. He was near tears as, speechless, he watched her storm past him and continue up the stairs. He was also quite ready to kill J.C.

Concerned that she'd be late for tea, Abigail sped down the corridor leading to her rooms. As she turned the corner, the door next to hers opened and a woman stepped out.

"Why, hello. You must be Miss Danforth," the woman said with a nod. "I am Maude Cunningham."

Abigail nodded in response.

"How astonishing," Maude said. "You look exactly like the portrait of my cousin."

"Thank you," Abigail said as she examined this new person in her life. No expression had escaped Maude's gray eyes, nor had she smiled in greeting. Pulled back so severely that it straightened the natural wave, her honey-streaked hair was unfashionably wound into a thick coil pinned to the back of her head. Gowned in her invariable black, her ample waist defied fashion as well. As she refused the service of a lady's maid, no one could guess her unthinkable secret of not wearing a corset. Her shapely wrists and hands were bare.

"I'd like to consult with you at your earliest convenience, Miss Danforth." Maude's voice was as expressionless as her eyes. "I have an extensive agenda planned. I also would like to show you the calling cards I've ordered, subject to your approval."

"I've brought calling cards from London," Abigail said in a haughty tone, her heart sinking as the itinerary she had so dreaded seemed about to close in upon her. "You may come with me while I change."

"I think not," Maude said, once again her voice was flat,

168

without expression. "I'd prefer to wait until I have your full attention."

"After tea, then?"

"Good enough." Without further ado, she departed.

Opening the door to her rooms, Abigail wondered what Miss Cunningham's underslips were made of that they allowed her to steal away so quietly. She also wondered if the old spinster always got the last word.

Rodney approached his father's study cautiously and knocked on the door. Although the remainder of their brief visit in the drawing room had been felicitous, his father has ignored him once Frederick had mentioned his gift of the cases of Chateau D'Yquem '58 and Chateau Lafite Rothschild '74, and had concentrated his immense charm upon Frederick, Fergus, and Max.

During one of the later, innumerable rehearsals for this dreaded meeting, Rodney had decided to save Abigail's foibles for a later interview wherein he could be more certain of not being blamed for allowing her to get thus involved. Drawing a final, deep breath, he knocked on the door. Opening it, he was so immersed in his thoughts that he did not notice no voice had invited him to enter.

Regal as any king, Andrew Danforth sat behind his desk, which was as much sculpture as furniture with its kneeling Atlas supports. To Rodney's chagrin, Kinkade was sitting opposite, a glass of sherry in hand.

"Don't you know the purpose of knocking on doors?" his father growled. "It is to gain permission to enter. Even a servant knows better. Leave at once. I'll summon you when I am ready."

Mortified, Rodney fled.

Embarrassed for Rodney, Kinkade finished his sherry and cleared his throat, "As I was saying, sir," he continued, "when I get my Kodak back from Rochester, I'll have some dandy pictures to show you."

"Good job, Kinkade," Andrew Danforth said and, by shifting his position in his chair, placing his empty glass on the desk decisively, and repeating, "Good job," he indicated that the interview was over.

On his feet at once, his manner tentative, Kinkade cleared his throat. "It will be a pleasure to be valeting you once more, sir," he said. "Not that I didn't enjoy my little jaunt—"

"Didn't Gregory speak to you?"

"Beg pardon, sir, but I haven't been able to find Gregory."

"Well then." Andrew Danforth stood, a definite sign of dismissal that one ignored at his peril. "You do that, Kinkade. He'll instruct you."

Even though he knew he was on dangerous ground, Kinkade pressed. "Then am I to continue to valet Master Rodney, sir? And, if so, what about Master Benjamin?"

"Ben still needs a nurse, not a valet!" Andrew Danforth waved him away impatiently. "I must talk to Rodney now."

"Very good, sir." Kinkade bowed slightly. "I'll be getting along then, sir." With Jacqueline's anger echoing in his brain and his status in the household suddenly in question, Kinkade came perilously close to slamming the door on his way out. Only the knowledge that such a display of temper would cost him his job deterred him. Too distraught to notice Rodney, he hurried off to try and locate Gregory.

Unnerved by his father's temper, Rodney stood rooted by the hall table. Watching Kinkade disappear down the corridor, he hesitated, not knowing if he should go right in. But his father's words had been that he'd summon him, so, satisfied that he was following instructions, he carefully poised himself near the door to listen. When he finally heard it, his name sounded like an angry curse.

As he opened the door, his father bellowed, "Why do you make me shout for you? Didn't you see Kinkade leave!"

Discombobulated, yet eager to prove that he was not just a bungler, Rodney approached his father's desk to take the chair that Kinkade had vacated.

"No, don't sit." Removing his watch from his vest pocket, Andrew Danforth looked at it and not his son.

"Haven't time," his voice was brusque. "Must dress for tea."

Insulted beyond endurance by having to wait while his father drank sherry with a servant before seeing him, and by his allowing that servant to sit in his presence while he was made to stand before him like a schoolboy, Rodney's gorge rose. He could scarcely stammer, "Well, there's not too much to report, sir." His voice was uncertain. "We had a smooth crossing except for—"

Snapping his watch shut, Andrew Danforth looked at him with a smile. "If you insist on giving me a description of every ocean's wave in detail, Rodney, I'm afraid you'll have to wait until after dinner."

"But, sir—"

"Right now I only have time for a concise summary. I care not whether the crossing was smooth or the roughest since the flood!" He thundered. "You are excused!"

His heart racing and his face inflamed, Rodney strode from the room, and closed the door softly.

Aref moved with a languorous grace. He had no need to hurry. A substantial potion of laudanum ensured the Nawab's slumber until dinner.

Using the Plaza Hotel's stationery, he practiced writing his faultless English so that he would appear proficient in the transatlantic cable office downstairs. When he was content that his message would be clear to the receiver yet unintelligible to the uninitiated, he gathered the used pieces of paper, tossed them into the fire, watched them burn, then scattered the ashes with a poker.

Pinning the Nawab's diamond-encircled opal in the center of his turban and loading his slender fingers with precious rings, he slipped out of their suite and rang for the elevator.

Bent over his desk, the clerk in the cable office did not look up when Aref entered. The balding top of his head was scattered with sparse long hairs combed from a deep part, while bushy mutton chops proved that he could grow hair.

When at last he did deign to glance at Aref, his imperious manner melted in the glow of so many precious gems on such an exotic personage.

By use of notes, which he retrieved once the clerk had read them, Aref sent his cable. When his transaction was complete, he held out a final note with the question, "How much?"

"We'll just charge this to your room, sir," the clerk said obsequiously.

"No!" Aref scrawled across the paper. Disdainfully tossing a heavy gold piece onto the clerk's desk. He wrote swiftly, "For your silence!"

Noting that the coin represented more than a month's wages, the clerk said, "I quite understand, sir." He nodded emphatically as he picked it up. "Yes, of course. Not a word."

Aref had no doubt that the man would prattle to his family and cohorts. That was no matter. But it was essential that Ahanti Abdulsamad not discover his communication.

Andrew Danforth had consigned Fergus to bed rest with trays in his room, so he had not appeared at tea. Poor fellow had protested not a whit, but the house was becoming more like a hospital than a home, Andrew Danforth muttered on his way to Ben's rooms. He had found Max personable enough. Certainly the tale of the panther's being shot in the nick of time had been invigorating. He'd have fetched Abigail himself for the chance to see Punjat's Ruby. But he was most pleased with himself in having foiled Frederick's attempts to seek a private interview to plead his obvious intentions to ask for Abigail's hand. And what was Frederick's mother up to, giving his daughter an expensive piece of horseflesh? Didn't she trust her son to do his own courting?

Slipping into Benjamin's darkened rooms, Andrew Danforth tiptoed toward the canopied bed. As he drew near, Ben stirred.

"Shhhhhh, my son," he whispered. "Don't disturb yourself. I wanted to see if you'd finished your tea."

"Now, father, you know I'm trying to eat," Ben responded as crankily as he dared at the all too familiar nagging. Plumping his pillow to prop himself up, his voice was groggy as he continued, "It's wonderful to have Abby home again, isn't it?"

On his way to the window, Andrew Danforth said casually, "She was in here quite a long time today, wasn't she?"

Ben shrugged.

Opening the drapes as he spoke, Andrew Danforth asked, "What did she have to say about Lord Hunterswell?"

Unable to speak of Frederick's failure as chronicler of Abigail's forbidden adventure, Ben said, "Actually very little. She promised to tell me more before dinner tonight. We had so many other things to discuss," he finished lamely.

"Really?" He sat on the foot of Ben's bed, facing him, "What things?"

Desperate for a topic that would not compromise his sister, Ben coughed into his hand and said, "We were wondering why you never married again."

His father winced, then rose and slowly retraced his steps to the window. He stared out of it for such a long time without speaking, that Ben was certain that his question had been unforgivably personal.

Still staring out of the window, his voice was extraordinarily tender when he finally spoke. "I worshipped your mother. She was so gay and full of life." He looked at Ben. "I am cursed with a lusty nature, son."

Flabbergasted by such an intimate remark, Ben swallowed hard, and nodded manfully.

Turning his gaze toward the window again, his father continued. "While she wished to please me in all things, your mother did not really care for the conjugal bed. I tried all I knew, but I could never change her. She loved me, though, and never denied me." He sighed. "I think it was her Puritan upbringing and that she was such a lady." He rubbed his eye with a knuckle, and took a deep breath. "But then you and Rodney were born." He sighed heavily.

"After seventy-two hours of labor, you were born at one twenty-five in the morning. Rodney finally came at six. Imagine if you will," his voice cracked, "she tried not to scream in order not to upset me."

Never having seen his father so overwrought, Ben dared not move.

Swiftly pulling out a handkerchief from his pants' pocket, Andrew Danforth blew his nose, "She denied me her bed after that." He replaced the handkerchief. "And rightly so." Staring straight ahead, his voice was more composed. "Gave me my freedom, as long as I was discreet."

Ben watched in silence as his father returned to sit at the foot of his bed.

"Four years later, we'd been at a party together. We did everything together except—that. She'd had a little wine and I was—persuasive." His smile was bitter. "It was torment to be with her all the time and not be able to bed her." Andrew Danforth glanced at his son as if seeking his understanding. "I could bear it no longer."

Standing, he paced to the window and, once again, his silence was so lengthy that Ben almost interrupted. At long last he spoke, his voice so subdued that Ben had to lean forward to hear him. "Nine months later, your mother died giving birth to Abigail."

Too moved to speak, Ben crawled out of bed and, in his nightshirt, stumbled over to the window. Gingerly placing his arm around his father's shoulders, he finally found words, "But it wasn't your fault, sir."

Overcome with anguish, Andrew Danforth's voice was even more faint as he said, "I could never live like that again with a woman I loved."

"But father," Ben said reasonably, "not all women are that delicate."

"I could never take the chance. To love like that again, and then kill her? No." He shook his head vehemently. "I've managed to control my base nature." He moved away from Ben's arm. "It has cost me a price I will not speak of." He shook himself as though coming out of a dream. "Here, here!" he exclaimed, turning on Ben. "What are

174

you doing out of bed without your dressing gown? You'll catch your death." Shooing his son back to bed, he said, "And whatever in blue blazes got us started on this morbid subject?"

Sliding under the covers, warmed by his father's confiding in him, Ben smiled. "We were talking about the possibility of your remarrying."

"Out of the question. I'll not marry. Nor will I allow Abigail to marry."

"What?" Ben's smile froze.

"Don't you understand?" Andrew Danforth looked down upon Ben as though he'd suddenly turned daft. "She has probably inherited her mother's frailty."

"Then why did you allow Lord Hunterswell to come all the way from London to court her?"

"Makes good reading in the society columns, son." Andrew Danforth frowned, his aloof manner upon him as though he'd never spoken of his pain. "Besides, Abigail is much too young to marry yet, and that's final." He turned to go. "Furthermore, I need her with me for now, as my hostess." Nearing the door he stopped and turned to face the bed. "Swear you'll not tell her why. I'll not have her worry unnecessarily."

Ben promised.

"Now get some sleep."

Ben closed his eyes obediently, but he lay awake long after his father's departure.

"Oh, Abigail, you take my breath away!" Benjamin exclaimed when Abigail appeared at his bedside, dressed for dinner in rose-colored silk.

"I've brought your dinner," she said, helping him on with his robe. He scuffed on his slippers and, placing her hand on the crook of his arm, she unfurled her fan and flirted with him as they strolled to the table set by his sitting room fire, just as if they were entering an elegant dining room.

When, after serving Ben, the footman stationed himself

by the buffet as though he meant to stay, Abigail instructed him to wait in the hall until she rang. While Ben ate with a heartier appetite than he'd had since his illness began, Abigail confessed to bewilderment when it came to her feelings for Frederick. Their father's skill in putting him off at tea had not been lost on her.

The footman had returned, cleared the table, and departed for Ben's ice cream when she said, "By the by, you were right about Miss Cunningham."

"So you've met her," he grinned.

She grimaced. "A regular prune."

"Father came to see me after tea today." Ben sat back, folding and unfolding the huge linen napkin in his lap. "You realize, of course, any plans you may have for your life will depend entirely upon father's wishes."

Abigail grew still. "I know."

"He'd certainly not listen to the idea of your becoming a sleuth."

"I know."

She sounded so dejected that Ben hated himself for being blunt. He had agonized over what he could ethically reveal, while keeping their father's confidence, and had finally decided that she deserved a warning before she truly fell in love. "It is as well your feelings for Lord Hunterswell are unsettled," he said as he continued to stare at the napkin in his lap. "Father will forbid you to marry him."

"Oh?" Surprised, Abigail frowned. "But why?" She was genuinely puzzled. Having thought all along that a titled marriage was what he'd wanted for her, she wondered if her bringing Lord Hunterswell home had been the source of his aloofness toward her.

Ben looked at her beseechingly, silently shaking his head. "I am not at liberty to say."

"But why did father give his permission for him to visit, if his mind was already made up?"

"Not everyone in New York can have a future marquess as houseguest, dear sister." Ben shrugged. "His Lordship's every move, and consequently father's, are being detailed in all the society columns."

176

"But I think, now that they've met, that father likes his Lordship. They seemed old friends at tea."

"Liking the chap has nothing to do with it. Father wants you to be his hostess."

The first notes of the great brass dinner gong sounded. Slowly, she stood to go.

Standing also, Ben kissed her lightly on her cheek, he said, "Please try to understand. Father does love you. It's for your own good."

"I know," she replied, sighing as though shouldering a huge burden. "I know."

A splendid figure in his evening clothes, Andrew Danforth was annoyed with himself as he strode down the corridor toward the drawing room. Having seen Abigail at tea, and just now at dinner, where she seemed able to hold her own as an amusing dinner partner, he thought he should be inured to her resemblance to her mother, but he was unaccountably nervous at the necessity of speaking with her alone. Pausing a moment to collect himself, he entered the drawing room without knocking.

Abigail stood near a table on the far side of the room, looking through a stereopticon.

Gowned in her usual high-necked black, Maude relaxed on one of the Turkish seaters, listlessly thumbing through a copy of *Harper's*.

Asking Maude briskly if she could find an errand elsewhere for a few minutes, he watched her wraithlike exit impatiently. "Can't stand that woman!" he exclaimed as soon as the door closed behind her. "Not natural for a lady not to make noise when she walks."

Replacing the stereopticon, Abigail remained by the table. "Then why, pray, do you not ask her to leave for good?" she asked.

"Can't," he snapped. "Obliged."

Not wishing to risk his ire by questioning him further, Abigail made no further comment.

"Besides, she'll be an excellent chaperon for you." He

guffawed gleefully. "None but the most serious beaux will be willing to brook that sour puss of hers."

Abigail kept her amusement at his cruel, and accurate, assessment to herself.

"Well, no time to pursue that topic." He beckoned for Abigail to join him on the sofa. "Only a few minutes to talk to you before the gentlemen rejoin us." Waiting until she was seated before seating himself beside her, he said, "I want you to know where I stand before you get too attached to this earl you dragged home."

"Yes, father." Gazing at her hands folded in her lap, Abigail sat ramrod straight.

"It will do you no good to protest." Disarmed by her quiet composure, his manner softened. "You can keep the horse. That was a gift from his mother." He stood and, hands behind his back, faced her, but his gaze was toward the fire. "I forbid you to marry. You are too young. Perhaps in a few years." Looking directly at her, he said, "In the meantime, you'll act as my hostess. After your debut, of course."

Abigail's eyes were warm as she returned his gaze. "Thank you, father," she said demurely.

"What's that you say?"

Blessing Ben for the warning, she rose and, with a smile, went to him. "Thank you so much, Father. I shall try to be worthy of your generosity."

"You mean you don't mind?"

"You are my father. You know what is best for me. I would be rushing the decision of a lifetime to marry now. I am grateful for your protection."

Having assumed that a lover does not pursue a lady across an ocean without encouragement, he had expected some objection from Abigail, and was dumbfounded by her gracious acquiescence—nay—her appreciation of his wisdom.

Kissing him on the cheek, Abigail asked for permission to retire, pleading weariness and the requisite early rise in the morn.

He could but grant her leave. When she'd closed the door behind her, he turned to the fire and, pulling the screen

178

aside, grabbed the heavy brass poker and vigorously thrashed and shifted the flaming logs. Sparks flew as feelings he'd thought long since dead overwhelmed him.

"Another hundred strokes, if you please, Jacqueline." Ready for bed in a frilly, beribboned nightgown and matching peignoir, Abigail was seated at her dressing table. "There was much grit on the street today." The melancholy that had stricken her on the ship had returned in full force. While it was marvelous to see Ben so near recovery, her conversations with him had only served to highlight the hopelessness of her position. Her father had made it all too clear that she'd be a prisoner in his house until he decided that she could marry. The empty social life that was to be her lot, and that she so dreaded, would begin in earnest on the morrow.

"Yes, Miss," Jacqueline said automatically. Of all the chores she performed for her mistress, this was her favorite, but her thoughts this night were elsewhere.

Because her maid's face was always a study in concentration while brushing her hair, Abigail seldom interrupted her during the operation. She assumed, and rightly, that Jacqueline practiced counting the brushstrokes to herself in English. Abigail knew when she had reached fifty, because Jacqueline would invariably pause to check the bristles of the brush. She would carefully remove the hairs and tuck them into a hole in the silver rim of a squat, crystal jar. At week's end, the jar's contents would be transferred to a larger container. Some lady's maids sold their mistress's hair to a wigmaker, but Jacqueline was planning to accumulate Abigail's until she had enough to make a sentimental pillow.

"Double braids tonight, if you please," Abigail ordered before Jacqueline could ask.

"Yes, Miss." Trading the brush for a comb, Jacqueline parted Abigail's waist-length hair down the middle and began plaiting it loosely. "I have done it again, Miss Danforth," she sighed heavily.

"Done what, Jacqueline?"

"I do not like the tattle tittle, Miss, but I heard about the Stork something maybe you should know. From the ship."

"What is it, Jacqueline? Pray, do not maunder so! Tell me the particulars."

When Jacqueline had finished telling her Kinkade's story about Stork, Abigail gazed into the mirror as if fascinated watching Jacqueline's task. Dozens of questions vied for her attention, including several regarding Jacqueline's motives in speaking so candidly. She sighed heavily. If only she could consult with Dr. Conan Doyle. If only there were someone in New York she could talk to.

"Miss?" Exhausted by her long day, Abigail ready to retire with the second braid complete, Jacqueline stood waiting to be dismissed.

Suddenly inspired, Abigail shook herself from her reverie and looked at Jacqueline in the mirror as she asked, "Are you in love with Kinkade?"

"Mon Dieu, Mademoiselle!" Horrified, Jacqueline clapped both hands to her mouth the moment the vulgarism had escaped.

"In that case, fetch him for me." Suspecting that Jacqueline might be protesting a mite too strongly, Abigail nonetheless decided to act upon her inspiration.

Although she'd been instructed in its use belowstairs, Jacqueline approached the newfangled intercom with trepidation.

"And quickly!" Abigail added, as she hurried to the writing desk in her sitting room to pen a note. She was sealing the envelope with wax when Jacqueline let Kinkade in.

He gazed at Jacqueline beseechingly, but she ignored him as he approached Abigail at her desk.

"I need someone I can trust, Kinkade," Abigail said, as he stood before her without a hint that he felt anything amiss at being summoned at this late hour by the young mistress of the house. "I have a letter I want you, personally, to deliver for me tonight. Before I tell you who it is for, you must make me a promise."

"Yes, Miss." A smile softened his expression, realizing

that Jacqueline was also interested in his response. "Of course, Miss."

"You must swear to me that you'll not breathe a word of this to my father." Her dark eyes were solemn, her expression grim. Before he could respond, she thrust a gold piece into his hand.

Curiosity at what could be worth such a sum along with a burning desire to please Jacqueline overcame his loyalty. "You have my promise, Miss Danforth," he said, hand to his heart. "Not a word."

"You must deliver this to Mr. William Gillette at the Plaza Hotel."

Kinkade departed, only to stand in the corridor and debate long and hard with his conscience. Writing to an actor? To what purpose? Mr. Danforth would have a conniption. If he found out. But Jacqueline had clearly wanted him to obey. At long last he decided to deliver Abigail's missive without telling her father.

As the door closed behind him, Abigail climbed into bed. "The first thing I want you to do tomorrow is to refurbish my gentleman's costume, Jacqueline."

"Yes, Miss."

"Have Kinkade order Crosspatches saddled by two o'clock in the afternoon. I did not want to overtax his loyalty too much by asking him myself tonight." Abigail's smile was wicked. "Then you must station yourself in here, so that I do not have to summon you. Is that clear?"

"Yes, Miss Danforth."

"Good." Abigail yawned mightily and smacked the pillow. She smiled as she rested her head in the hollow she had created. "When it is time for Miss Cunningham and me to leave for morning calls, I am going to be stricken with a most dreadful headache."

Chapter Seven

All right angles are equal to each other.
                                    Euclid

While the rich had blamed the sluggishness of their Season's commencement upon the uncommon mildness of the weather, those whose lot it was to endure poverty were grateful for its continuing yet one more day.

Since her two younger sisters had been carried off by the cholera, Molly O'Brien had somewhat more to eat, but she sorely missed their body heat at night, and December's warmth had been a real boon. She hated the cold more than the hunger that was occasionally her lot since her father had been shanghaied. Her mother brought home piecework from the factory where she labored twelve hours a day, but no matter how long or hard she worked, her wages barely paid the exorbitant rent for the single room in their West Side tenement. The pittance that the twelve-year-old Molly earned selling matches often made the difference between a cold potato for supper or nothing at all.

Frazzled by the effort required to feed and clothe her brood of four surviving children, Mrs. O'Brien had no time to spare for the reading lessons her husband had begun before he'd disappeared. With him had vanished all hope of Molly's acquiring an education, however scanty.

But he had not taken Molly's dreams. With an imagination as vivid as her red hair, Molly firmly believed in leprechauns, and that she'd see one some day, if she looked hard enough. She believed just as strongly that her father would reappear, if only she looked hard enough for him at the docks. Sure and this was a world full of miracles and queer sights. Just yesterday hadn't she seen a lady as pretty as any princess climb into a magic coach that carried her away, with nary a horse in sight?

Her mother had called her daft and full of her father's blarney. She'd had to embellish her story to place the incident elsewhere so she'd not catch another beating for loitering around the riverfront again.

Molly knew she was luckier than most. She had a mother and a home and, most of the time, a good meal at the end of her dawn-to-dusk trek about the city. There were thousands of waifs younger than she roaming in packs, eking out an existence, who ate what they could scavenge and slept where they fell. Molly had joined one such gang, at first for protection, and now by dint of her intelligence had become its leader.

The tickle of a louse in her armpit woke her at last. Scratching at the mite, she yawned and stretched. She'd have to take extra care cleaning herself today. Her route included the Plaza Hotel, and the rich wouldn't come near if they saw you scratching, and suspected you had lice.

As Abigail hurried down the main staircase, the brass gong assembling the Danforth household for breakfast reverberated throughout the house. Kinkade's mission had been a success. Humming to herself with delight, Abigail anticipated an interesting day. Just as she reached the main landing, she heard someone call her name from above and turned to see Rodney close behind.

"Last one down is a rotten egg," he teased as he had when they were children.

"Oh, Rodney, it's you," she said, smiling. Keeping her voice down, she continued. "I had wanted to thank you for not telling father about—" she looked over the banister, and even though she could see no one, she kept her remarks cryptic, "well, about, you know."

He did not speak as he descended the stairs, and his smile was sour. As he drew close, he slowly withdrew a handkerchief from his wristcuff. With a malicious giggle, he wafted it under her nose.

"So it was you!" she exclaimed, recognizing it as her own. Furious, she grabbed for it.

He whisked it away and dangled it above her head.

"But why?" she cried, abandoning the attempt to wrest it from him.

"I wanted to find the ruby myself," he said coolly. "What better stalking horse than dropping your hankies behind me after I did some searching of my own?" Seeing that she'd not grab for it again, he stuffed her handkerchief into the pocket of his trousers. "Furthermore, I know who has it!"

She gasped. All but certain he was merely taunting her, Abigail dared not risk contradicting him on the chance that he had indeed somehow found out who had it. After all, he had been fraternizing with Frederick's friends much more freely than she'd been able to, and perhaps had learned something. "Oh, Rodney," she exclaimed as though genuinely impressed. "How terribly clever of you. Do tell."

"You don't imagine that I'd help you, do you?"

"But why not, Rodney?"

"Don't you know?"

"Oh, Rodney, stop it. No, I do not know."

"Can't you even guess?"

"Please, Rodney, I pray you. No, I cannot. You are my brother. I love you."

"Oh, no, you don't," he said petulantly. "You love Benjamin. You wished he would have fetched you, not me."

Blushing furiously because Rodney's words were true, she said, "Of course, I love Ben, too—"

"Oh, shut up, Abigail!" he shouted, pointing dramatically over her shoulder. "Just look behind you!"

Abigail whirled around and gasped. Focusing on the full-length oil painting for the first time since she'd arrived home, she saw her own features, slightly matured, gazing back at her. Stunned by the resemblance, she faced Rodney. "Mother?"

"Of course, Mother!" he snarled, his eyes full of hate. "If it hadn't been for you, she'd still be alive! I took one look at you in London and knew you'd come back and try to take her place. Well, you can't! Not with me!"

Shocked, Abigail could but stare at him. She had been told that her mother had died from childbed fever, a quite common, although tragic, occurrence. She had never before blamed herself. The very thought was too painful to bear, and she refused it utterly. "It was not my fault!" she cried.

"I'll never forgive you." His voice was venomous. "Furthermore, you need never fear. I intend to tell father about your escapade." He paused ominously. "But in my own time." Wheeling around, he raced down the stairs.

Abigail stared after him.

Neither of them had noticed Max who had stayed out of sight, but not out of earshot, at the top of the stairs.

Later that afternoon, slim and dapper, a bewhiskered Abigail, impeccably dressed—complete with top hat, riding gloves, and cane—in a gentleman's costume, paused by a poinsettia-laden table in the lobby of the Plaza Hotel. She smiled as she recalled the horrified tailor's expression whence she'd had the outfit made on Saville Row. Even though she'd claimed a costume ball as reason for dressing as a man, he'd scarcely been able to conceal his disapproval beneath his professional demeanor during the several fittings. She thought he'd be pleased with the results, since no one so much as glanced at her awry as she made her way across the magnificent lobby—which was in partial disarray as the finishing touches were being completed on the lavish Christmas decorations—to announce her arrival to Mr. Gillette.

When Gillette himself swung the door wide to his suite, they both stepped back in surprise.

The actor had been expecting a demure young lady with chaperon in tow.

With his clear-cut, hawklike features and piercing eyes, Abigail felt she was meeting the estimable detective himself.

As they settled comfortably in his sitting room, while the waiter served tea, in a wondrous voice that set Abigail atingle, the actor conceded the necessity of her incognito, which gave her the freedom to visit him without others in the household the wiser. Abigail needed little encouragement to pour out all that had happened since her interview with Conan Doyle.

"I am surprised that Conan Doyle took that attitude with you, Miss Danforth," Gillette said, as he placed his empty teacup on the table when she had finished. "His mother is quite strong-willed, and his sisters have careers of their own."

Concerned that it might have loosened during her lengthy discourse, Abigail gave a delicate pat to her moustache. "Perhaps it was his intense dislike of his fictional character?" she ventured, reaching for her teacup.

"No matter," Gillette leaned back in his chair. Gazing into the distance, elbows on the arms of the chair, he touched his fingertips together, forming a tent. "Without question, the Punjat's Ruby is prize enough for the most horrific skullduggery," he said thoughtfully, tapping his fingers together. "Which would not preclude staging an accident for the unfortunate Miss Arrington. Or the valet, for that matter."

"I quite agree," Abigail said, her dark eyes sad. "But with each passing day, I feel my fate closing in. I shall be able to plead the vapors only so often to escape those boring calls." She sighed heavily as she replaced her cup and saucer on the table.

Gillette nodded sympathetically. "I know a great deal about having a burning desire to do some particular thing with your life, only to be met with opposition at every turn," he said. "I shall always be grateful to Mr. Clemens for getting me my first acting job, when my family threatened to disown me."

"But what am I to do?"

"I say." He leaned forward. "It's not much, but it may

186

help. Why don't I hold a reception for you and your guests? I'll see that you get choice tickets to the play. That way your father can see for himself what an actual consulting detective does. Afterwards, I shall do all I can to impress him with the efficacy of the profession. At the very least we may be able to take some sting out of your brother Rodney's treachery."

"Oh, Mr. Gillette!" she exclaimed. Clapping her hands together with delight, she stood. "Would you?"

Standing, he tried to penetrate her disguise with his piercing gaze. "I must meet you again, Miss Danforth," he said, his voice husky. "If nothing else, I must learn what you truly look like without all the whiskers."

Blushing furiously underneath her disguise from the heat of his gaze, Abigail agreed upon the day after Christmas for the reception, and bid him a hurried good-bye.

Crossing the festive lobby, adjusting her top hat, delighted with the outcome of her interview, Abigail spotted Max and Fergus in a heated discussion with the Nawab Abdulsamad next to a potted palm. Amazed to see Fergus in public since he'd claimed to be too weak to come down for breakfast, she had rushed into the revolving doors and was out on the busy street before realizing that it was unlikely that they'd recognize her.

Walking slowly toward Crosspatches at the hitching post, she longed to remain incognito and follow them. She was about to mount when a redheaded girl approached her.

"Wanna buy a match, Mister?" the child asked.

Abigail recognized the ragged, but clean, urchin as the one who had run after her from the wharf the day before. Impressed by the territory she had traversed, Abigail had a sudden inspiration. Still holding the reins, she bent down to the girl's level. "How would you like to earn some money, lass?"

"Sure, Mister!" Molly replied. "And what is it you'll be wanting me to do?"

"I want you to follow someone. Have you any friends who could help?"

"It's friends I have, sir." Molly stuck out her chest. "I lead me own gang, I do."

"Excellent!" Rehitching Crosspatches, Abigail hurriedly paid the child a small advance, negotiated financial arrangements and a trysting place. Business complete, Molly ran off to round up her gang members.

Crosspatches grew restive. Abigail began to worry that the urchin had run off with her money. Soon, the men would leave the hotel and scatter. She was about to mount up and begone when Molly materialized out of the crowd.

"I've got me spotters placed, sir," Molly said. "All what's needed is for you to be showing me who it is you're wanting trailed."

"You're back just in time." Abigail pointed her crop toward the canopied steps of the hotel. "There they come now." The Nawab, followed by Aref, descended the stairs well ahead of Max and Fergus, as though they were strangers to one another.

"I'll take the fat one meself," Molly said, vanishing into the congested street.

Immensely pleased with her day's accomplishment, Abigail maneuvered Crosspatches through the horrendous traffic, thoroughly enjoying her ride home from the vantage point of a man on horseback.

Still dressed for a night on the town, Rodney strolled toward the backstairs hoping to catch Jacqueline on her way up. She'd been sly, that one, avoiding him, but he hadn't forgotten. After waiting awhile, he assumed that she'd already retired, but decided against mounting the stairs. More than one underhouse parlormaid had succumbed to his importuning, too terrified to cry out and be blamed for enticing him to her quarters. Caught in the family way, one of them had been dismissed without references. He'd been rather sorry about that as she'd been willing enough after the first time, and quite pretty. While Rodney wanted to get Jacqueline fired, seducing her as a means to that end seemed too risky.

He was about to turn away and summon Kinkade to ready him for bed when he thought he heard a furtive step approach. Hiding in the shadows, he watched as J.C. stealthily climbed the forbidden stairs that could lead to a manservant's immediate dismissal were he part of his father's household. Max and Fergus would probably consider J.C.'s escapade a lark, but discovering the man in Jacqueline's chamber would seal her doom.

Allowing his imagination to slowly disrobe Jacqueline, Rodney tiptoed after him. He waited at the top of the stairs until J.C. would have had ample time to tumble her into bed. Excited by the prospect of what he would see, he tiptoed to her door and, without knocking, threw it open.

The room was empty. The gloom from a light down the hall shone on a white square of paper on the floor. Swiftly picking it up, he turned on the light and read the contents. Suddenly conscious of doors gently closing and of the position he would be in were he caught, he threw J.C.'s note on the floor, and fled.

Christmas Eve morning found Jacqueline hiding behind the man-sized palm in the corridor across from Frederick's rooms. She had taken the precaution of loading her arms with one of Abigail's gowns so that, if seen, she could pretend to have gotten lost, which occasionally still happened in the huge house. Consumed with curiosity, she could scarcely contain her excitement. Quite aside from the thrill of acting the spy, she had just overheard Stork assuring Kinkade that, this being Christmas Eve, he was finally on his way to Lord Hunterswell's chambers to confess and throw himself on his Lordship's mercy. Feeling responsible for, and worried about, the outcome, she wanted to hear Lord Hunterswell's reactions for herself.

She liked Stork. Although they had never had a true conversation, he was devoted to his master. A quality she much admired. Besides, he had much better manners than those two scoundrels, Kinkade and J.C., put together. She was still angry with herself for having relaxed her guard enough to enjoy J.C.'s companionship on board ship, and had not bothered to have his note translated.

Hearing someone approach, she parted the palm leaves, nearly dropping Abigail's gown in fright as she spotted Samuel. The only good thing about that oily one was that he had unseated the villainous Kinkade, or so the vine of grapes said. She sighed with relief as, whistling a Christmas carol to himself, he turned the corner toward Mr. Danforth's rooms.

The dress grew heavy, and she was about to give up her vigil when she heard Stork's distinctive footsteps. Her heart went out to him. Looking much like a man approaching the guillotine, he hesitated before his master's door, straightening imaginary flaws in his perfect attire before knocking.

The instant the door closed behind him, Jacqueline started across the hall. She no sooner had reached the middle of the corridor when she heard Samuel's cheery whistle. Reversing herself, she made it back behind the tree before Samuel turned the corner. As soon as he was out of sight again, she scooted across the hall to press her ear against the panel. Frustrated by hearing only the drone of voices and not the words, she eased open the door a crack. Her heart was thumping so loudly that she doubted her own ears when she heard Lord Hunterswell's hearty laughter. But when his merriment ceased, she heard quite clearly that he wished to leave his rooms at once. Thrilled by the happy ending, she closed the door swiftly and raced toward the backstairs, much relieved that his Lordship had taken Stork's confession with such apparent good humor. All of which set her to wondering. If the spirit of Christmas was thus respected by her betters, perhaps she should relent and have J.C.'s note translated.

Abigail grumbled to herself as she trailed Maude toward the side porch entrance. The days and nights since she'd been home had proved as tedious as she had predicted. Every conversation seemed to pertain to some facet of her appearance; either how lovely she looked at any given moment, or how beautiful she would be if she were to buy that frock or add that feather. The most daring topic, which consumed hours of conversation among the young ladies she'd met, was just how much ankle of boot to show accidentally, how to accomplish showing it without seeming to notice it was on view, or to notice the gentlemen noticing. What with preparations for the holidays, her debut, and certainly while doing some last-minute shopping, she had despaired of hearing from the match girl, consequently she was not listening for the bird call, which was their signal for a rendezvous.

The resourceful Molly threw a handful of pebbles, which scattered on the steps just behind Maude, and ran to the back of the house to their trysting place.

Maude was for chasing the urchin, but Abigail persuaded her to go on inside with the packages while she returned to the carriage house for her suddenly missed reticule.

Excitement, and the effort of running, had put color in Abigail's cheeks by the time she reached Molly. "Well?" she asked breathlessly.

"I put One-eyed Jack to followin' the skinny one."

"Mr. Buchanan?"

Nodding, Molly spoke rapidly. "He went to Grand Central yesterday and was buying himself tickets for Chicago."

"Oh, I knew that." Disappointed, Abigail turned to go. "They're leaving after my debut."

"And is your debut being on the day after Christmas?" Molly called after her.

"I thought I had told you." Impatient, Abigail faced the child. "My debut is on New Year's Day."

"Well, for sure Mr. Buchanan ain't gonna be there." Hands on her hips, Molly held her chin high. "He got two tickets for the twenty-seventh."

"Just two tickets?" Abigail frowned. "Are you sure?"

"It's Jack's eye what's bad, Miss, not his ears."

Promising Molly a bonus, Abigail hurried back toward the house, her thoughts in turmoil. Gentlemen did not run their own errands. If Mr. Buchanan had not wanted to alert the household to his early departure by asking one of the

Danforth's servants to purchase the tickets, why hadn't he sent J.C.? Had he, or Mr. Driscoll, already informed her father about their early departure and she hadn't been told? As she nodded her greeting to Gregory when he let her into the house, she wondered with a sense of foreboding, why only two tickets? Who was going to stay behind?

The day proved to be a long one for Molly, and as she wearily mounted the five flights to her home, it was far from over. She hoped that her brothers would still be out. The surprise she carried was too grand to be giving to her mother with them being rowdy and jumping all over.

"And where is it you've been, me girl?" her mother asked without looking up from her sewing when Molly let herself into the apartment.

"Merry Christmas, Ma." Molly stooped to kiss her mother on the cheek, happy to note that her noisy brothers were not home.

"What's this?" Mrs. O'Brien rested her sewing in her lap and eyed her daughter suspiciously. Displays of affection were rare since the disappearance of Mr. O'Brien.

"You're closing your eyes for me, Ma." When her mother continued to stare at her, Molly clasped her hands under her chin and begged, "Please, Ma."

With a weary sigh, Mrs. O'Brien complied.

"Now hold out your hand." Molly giggled. When her mother stuck out her hand, she carefully placed a gold coin onto her palm. "Open your eyes!" Molly danced around the room.

After staring, dumbfounded, at the twenty-dollar gold piece in her hand, and then at her daughter as she happily skipped about the room, dodging the piecework, Mrs. O'Brien suddenly stood. Waiting until Molly was in arm's reach, she swung with all her might, striking the child full force on the face. "Whore!" she spat.

Molly spun and skidded across the floor, landing in a heap near a bed. Too stunned to cry out, she pressed her hand to her flaming cheek and cowered on the floor as her mother bore down on her.

"Now you'll not be lying to me, me girl," her mother thrust the coin at her. "Where did you get this?"

Molly started to get up. "I worked for it, I did." She stuck out her jaw defiantly.

Before Molly could regain her feet, her mother hit her on the mouth, yelling, "Liar!" She struck her again, with the back of her hand. The blow landed on Molly's ear, setting it to ringing. "Thief!" she cried as she struck again. "Slut!"

"I'm not lying to ye!" Molly sobbed, hurt more by the insults than by the physical blows. "I'm not! I'm not!" Molly scrambled to her feet.

"Then you must've stole it!" her mother yelled, her arm raised to strike again. "Me only girl left, a common thief?"

"No!" Molly ducked and ran to the other side of the table. "No, no, no!" she cried.

Her mother started after her, but too tired to give chase around the table, she slumped into the chair, sobbing.

When her mother had calmed down somewhat, still keeping her distance, Molly called to her. "It's all right, Ma," she said. "I have a job."

"It's a job you call it!" her mother wailed. "And you're supposed to be me good girl." Her mother's anguish was almost more than Molly could bear. "Don't I take you to Mass every Sunday? I bring you up right to be pure for some nice Catholic boy to marry, and *this* is how you repay me?"

"But, mama, I earned it," Molly cried. "I worked for it!"

"And it's *how* you earned it." Burying her face in her arms on the table, she sobbed, "It's my heart you're breaking."

Rubbing her throbbing cheek, Molly watched her mother as she wept. When her sobs began to subside, she knelt at her side. "Mama?" she called to her softly.

Without responding, Mrs. O'Brien wiped her face on her apron.

"It's all right, Ma." Molly continued soothingly, "I have

a job of real work. You'll be thinking me full of Papa's blarney, when you hear what it is.''

Her mother looked down on Molly, her face as stern as her voice, "The whole world knows that whorin' or thievin's the only ways a girl can come by as much money as you've brought home.''

Red hair agleam in the light from the single candle on the table, Molly slid into the chair opposite her mother, "I'm being an Irregular, Ma,'' she said.

"Go on, lass,'' her mother said disparagingly. "There's no such thing.''

"Oh, yes, ma'am, there is,'' Molly said. "In London. A detective bloke what lives on Baker Street has 'em.''

"Has what?''

"That's what I'm trying to tell you. They're called Baker Street Irregulars. They do errands and spying and such for him.''

"Spying!''

"I don't do nothing wrong, Ma!'' Molly insisted. "I just follow a fat man what wears a towel wrapped around his head with a jewel beaming big as a lantern stuck in the middle.''

"Aw, go on,'' her mother replied in disbelief.

"Then I report to me boss where he's been.''

"And who might that be?''

"You'll be remembering I told you about a beautiful princess what drove off in the horseless carriage?''

In spite of herself, Molly's mother was intrigued.

"Well, she's the one! Only she was playing the gentleman when she hired me at the Plaza Hotel.''

"Go on with your blarney, Miss Molly.'' Mrs. O'Brien half-raised her hand as if to strike her daughter again. "I'll tan ye, but fair!''

"No, Ma. 'Tis sooth,'' Molly said, hand on her heart. "Bewhiskered like you'd dare not pull 'em off, they were that real. And she rode a horse astride like a man!''

"No!'' Mrs. O'Brien recoiled in horror.

"I swear it.'' One hand to her heart, Molly's other hand pointed to heaven. "She lives in a house, grand as any

194

castle, on Gramercy Park. And we are called the Gramercy Park Irregulars.''

"You're puttin me on, child. Are you trying to tell me that there's more than one of you what got paid a twenty-dollar gold piece?''

"That's mine alone for being the leader,'' Molly said with pride. "Oh, Ma.'' Molly suddenly yawned. "I'm that tired, I could drop. The fat man is safe at a party at the castle. I came home to give you me Christmas present. I'll just put me head down a minute before I go back.''

By the time Mrs. O'Brien found a safe hiding place for her treasure, Molly was fast asleep.

J.C. shut the door to his cubicle and, without removing his boots, flung himself on the bed. Running his hands through his hair destroyed its precise center part, but he was beyond caring about his appearance. Even Christmas Eve, with a servant's celebration in the offing, could not dispel his gloom. Pillowing his head in his hands, he stared at the whitewashed ceiling.

Each time he'd seen Jacqueline, who had developed a knack for avoiding him since their calamitous encounter on the backstairs, he had begged her forgiveness. He had assured her that he knew her to be a pure and undefiled sample of virtuous womanhood. She had thawed a trifle. Yet, somehow, her impenetrably polite toleration of his existence was worse than when she had hated him outright. She had not by so much as batting an eyelash acknowledged the receipt of his letter. The only bright spot was that she barely suffered Kinkade's presence either, except professionally.

J.C. smirked gleefully when reminded of Kinkade's comeuppance. Running hither and thither doing that young fop, Rodney's, bidding. Not at all the high-falutin valet to the master of the house he'd bragged about. Scuttlebutt had it that he'd have to serve Mr. Benjamin, too, when he recovered. Yessiree, Kinkade was dancing to a different tune these days. And then there was Fergus, who had made an astounding—nay the others were calling it miraculous—

recovery. The arrogance of the man amazed him. There they were, a whisper away from disaster, and he was vying for the affections of one Miss Isabella Humbolt. A very rich and beautiful young lady she was, rumored to have been Benjamin's darling. And the way he'd begun fawning over Rodney all of a sudden. But enough! He resolutely blocked his thoughts from any further exploration of Fergus's peccadillos.

At least Max was treating him like an equal, when they had some private moments. Hopeless case or no, Max had even helped him select a gift for Jacqueline.

Stirring, he recalled the haggard face of the gentle Stork. Remorse hit J.C. like a stone. Abject apologies in that quarter had earned him nothing but contempt. With a groan, he forced himself to roll off the bed, and ready himself for the festivities.

Sloshing some Pinaud's Brilliantine into the palm of one hand, he set the bottle down and rubbed both hands together before applying it to his hair. While peering into the small mirror over the dresser, he carefully restored his center part. His melancholy mood still upon him, he tossed the comb onto the dresser top, and slumped to the floor.

The heavy silver head of Rodney's cane did not make a large wound in J.C.'s head, but it was well placed. And fatal.

"Where have you been?" Abigail demanded. She was annoyed, and it showed.

Scandalously late for dressing Abigail for dinner, breathless from her recent unaccustomed running, but bursting with news, Jacqueline's English failed her. She stammered incoherently in a fractured French that Abigail refused to try and interpret.

"What are you blathering about?" Trying to calm her maid by being stern, Abigail imitated the imperious tone her father used to such good effect.

Gently placing Abigail's gown on the chaise, Jacqueline cupped her hand to her ear, and stooped as though at the

196

keyhole of a door. "His Lordship." She waved her free hand in the general direction of Frederick's rooms. "I listen." Standing straight, hands clasped in front of her as though lined up for inspection, she continued, "Stork tells Lord Hunterswell what he do—did."

"You are shameless, Jacqueline!" Abigail exclaimed, turning aside so that Jacqueline could not see the smile she could not control. Instantly regaining her composure, she feigned being shocked. "Why, you are little better than an adventuress!"

Eyes wide, Jacqueline blushed, unsure whether her mistress was teasing, or pleased.

"Well, don't just stand there, Jacqueline." Abigail sat at her dressing table. Gesturing toward the curling iron, she beckoned to her maid to get on with her toilette. "Tell me the particulars."

Now that her hands were busy, Jacqueline had no difficulty continuing, "Oh, Miss Danforth, you will never believe it."

"Believe what?" Abigail stifled her impatience.

"His Lordship laughed!"

"Did he now?" Abigail said, admiring Jacqueline's skill in the mirror. "And what was it that Stork had done?"

"Oh, Miss Danforth, I am so sorry. I could not hear it. Samuel comes and I hide. When I go to the door, I hear laughter, then his Lordship say he was *tout de suite*—how you say, to leave—"

"At once?"

"Yes, Miss. So I run before they find me."

"Curiouser and curiouser."

"I was so afraid his Lordship have so much anger that he give Stork the sack."

"I hope Stork was telling him the truth at last, and not just an amusing story." Abigail frowned. Obeying her father's instructions, she had ignored all of Frederick's overtures. It should not be too difficult to encourage him to seek her out, and thereby persuade him to tell the details of Stork's predicament. Although it no longer mattered as far as her future was concerned, she was not unpleased to discover that he had a sense of humor buried beneath his shy formality. "Come, come, Jacqueline." Impatience with being groomed for the fifth time in a day showed in her tone. "Let us hurry. Father said he wanted to see me before the guests arrived," she said, resolving to also create an opportunity to ask Frederick if he knew of Max and Fergus's early departure.

Jacqueline proceeded with all due speed, but her haste did not show in the result. Abigail was ravishing. Her gown, in six shades of blue, was the latest fashion from Paris. She had finished the requisite pirouetting to ensure that everything would stay in place, and had just reseated herself at the dressing table so that Jacqueline could effect a minor repair, when there was a knock on the door. Her father entered without waiting for her to respond.

Abigail started to rise to greet him.

"No, no, daughter." He held out his hand in a gesture for her to remain seated. In the other hand he carried a square, black velvet jewel case. "Don't get up." While not inured to the sight of his daughter, he had become more skilled at controlling his feelings.

Jacqueline started for the door.

"You need not leave, Jacqueline." Mr. Danforth's voice was gruff. Not a small part of his pleasure in the past had been in slyly watching his wife's maid. Her eyes would widen, impressed with his largesse, and the splendor of her mistress's new bauble. Casually, he held out the case to Abigail.

"For me?" Abigail glanced up at him through her lashes as she took it.

He nodded. "Go ahead." Waving his hand loftily, he said, "Open it."

She opened the box, and gasped with delight. Glittering in their black velvet nest lay a necklace of diamond-encircled sapphires set in a swirling design that could but flatter any feminine throat. "They are beautiful, Father!"

As he nodded in agreement, she removed the necklace and held it out to him.

Jacqueline sucked in her breath, her expression more than enough to satisfy Mr. Danforth's memory.

When the matching earrings were dangling majestically from her ears, she turned to him for approval. "Thank you so much, Father," she said. "They are beautiful."

"It is you who do them justice, Daughter," he beamed. "Just ring for Kinkade at the end of the evening. He knows to wait up for their return to the safe."

"But aren't they mine, sir?"

"Of course, they're yours," he said, huffily. "Once given, I'm unlikely to take them back. Jacqueline has not been in your service long enough to be trusted. Whereas Kinkade—" he stopped in mid-sentence, and paused thoughtfully before continuing, "Which reminds me. I'd like any suggestions you might have about him—"

"Beg pardon, Father," Abigail interrupted. "That is not what I mean. Is this necklace truly mine?" She stroked it with her gloved fingertips. "Could I sell it?"

"Of course you cannot sell them!" Andrew Danforth was horrified. "They belonged to your mother."

"Did they really belong to her? Or was she merely allowed to wear them?"

"Your meddlesome questions are beginning to annoy me, child," he said ominously. "That necklace and all your mother's jewels belonged to her. Now that you are coming of age, they will belong to you."

Turning away from him, she said softly, "I thought that unless a person had the right to dispose of something, to sell it and keep the money, it didn't really belong to them."

"What nonsense, Abigail! I gave these jewels to your mother. They were a gift." In a hoarse voice, he continued, "Your mother gave me this ring." He held out his right hand toward her. "I'd sooner sell my arm than part with it."

"It seems to me, Father," Abigail said quietly, "if you had said that these sapphires are mine to wear instead of mine to keep, it would have been more near the truth."

"I fail to see the difference, daughter," he replied. "I had quite forgotten how your mind could natter a question to bits. Come," he offered his arm. "Let us go before you spoil my good humor for the entire evening."

She decided to wait until after dinner to ask him about Fergus buying those train tickets.

In the music room, seated in the front row of gilded chairs that faced a concert grand, Fergus glanced at Max, fairly itching to clasp his hands over his ears to shut out the slightly off-key soprano of Miss Isabella Humbolt. Although he was certain he was not the only guest in the crowded music room who felt that way, social ruin awaited anyone committing such a rash act. Besides, the young lady was rich, and stared at him adoringly whenever the lyrics touched upon the delicate subject of love. Her male accompanist, Fergus had forgotten his name, looked daggers at him.

Crammed as it had been between a dozen other courses, the Christmas goose flambéed in red currant sauce had been memorable and the crested port after dinner superb. Fergus allowed himself to become drowsy, hoping that his sleepy-eyed look would be interpreted by Miss Humbolt as sensual. He was indifferent to what the pianist thought.

Abigail was amused to note that her father had not yet joined them from the dining room. There had been only twenty of their most intimate friends for dinner and—knowing full well that Miss Humbolt was to sing—he'd no doubt remained at table with some of the more astute gentlemen. Aware that Frederick had chosen to brave the racket in order to be near her, Abigail let it be known by some tactful fluttering of her fan that she'd welcome his company nearby. In due course, he was sitting in the chair behind her, leaning forward.

"I have just been placed in a most delicate position, Miss Danforth," he whispered into the privacy she created by extending her fan. "I wonder if I might seek your advice on the matter."

"With pleasure, your Lordship," turning slightly in her chair to hear him over Miss Humbolt's enthusiasm. If he did not volunteer that his friends were departing before her debut, she planned to ask him if he knew. "How may I help you?"

"It's about Stork."

Miss Humbolt finished her number. Frederick and Abigail clapped politely along with the others and, after a dewy-eyed curtsy in Fergus's direction, she plunged straightaway into another ditty.

Abigail watched with alarm as Ben left the room, looking worn out. Or did he still care for Miss Humbolt and was hurt by her attention to Frederick's companion? At their father's insistence, this had been his first venture into society and she feared he'd overdone. Fanning herself, she was distracted as she asked, "Stork? Is something the matter with Stork?"

"He told me that J.C. and Aref were blackmailing him." Frederick's voice was urgent.

"Is that so?" She feigned surprise.

"How do I proceed? How do I tell Max that his valet has been threatening my man? Or Abdulsamad?"

"Do you think either Mr. Driscoll or the Nawab knows what happened?"

"Unthinkable!"

"Then you must go to the source," her voice was firm. "If it is J.C. and Aref who've done Stork injury, then they must be confronted."

"But I do not deal directly with servants!" Frederick pulled back in horror.

"I fear you must on this matter, your Lordship, if Stork is to be avenged."

"How can I talk to a mute? I'd much prefer to thrash him," he said angrily. "Just look at him, so smug over there."

Indeed, across the room, the beautiful Aref did appear dreamily content, standing a pace behind the Nawab, who seemed to be enjoying the recital.

"Here comes Father," Abigail said, shielding Frederick from view with her fan. "You really must move on, your Lordship."

Unwilling to jeopardize his long-awaited, private interview with her father on the morrow, Frederick angled his chair closer to the black-gowned Miss Cunningham. When the clapping had died down after the pianist finished his solo, she thanked him prettily for the box of monogrammed chocolates that he'd presented to her for Christmas.

He was about to respond when one of the guests hovered nearby. "Miss Cunningham," the newcomer said, loud enough for all to hear. "Do you have any more of those jolly conundrums that you entertained us with at the Vandergilt's? Like the one about the white bear?"

Those of the other guests who had been at the Vandergilt's—and there were many, as the Danforth's circle was select, and closed—chuckled or guffawed at the memory. There was a general good-humored murmur of agreement and, "Put us to the test!" from Miss Humbolt's father.

No expression whatever betrayed whether Maude was pleased or annoyed by their importuning as she stationed herself by the concert grand. When she felt she had everyone's attention, including Andrew Danforth's, she began, "I am going to give you a sequence of letters of the alphabet. You are to supply the one letter which would naturally follow in the series." She paused for effect, then said, "There is only one correct answer."

Waiting until the approving murmur had quieted, she continued, "The letters are O, T, T, F, F, S, and then another S. What letter, naturally, comes next?"

Abigail stilled her fan. Not having been at the Vandergilt's, she was surprised at Maude's willingness to speak in public. Ben had no doubt missed her performance as well, for he'd made no mention of her talent. These puzzles were all the rage, and a source of a great deal of competition. Those who hadn't the faintest idea how to proceed, feigned boredom.

Unable to believe that the solution to this one was so simple, Abigail rose quietly and went to Maude. Shielding her remarks from the others with her fan, she told Maude the answer.

"That is correct," Maude said, with some surprise at

how swiftly Abigail had discovered the solution. "But you are the hostess. You mustn't tell. Give the others a chance."

Nodding her head in agreement, Abigail asked, "May I please be excused, to look after Ben?" She glanced at Miss Humbolt. "He looked dreadful when he left a moment ago."

Maude gave her permission with a nod.

Watching his daughter's leavetaking, Andrew Danforth immediately sought Lord Hunterswell's whereabouts. Satisfied that Frederick was engrossed in solving the riddle, he relaxed.

Abigail had crossed the master hallway and was so intent on reaching Ben, she was startled to hear Jacqueline's voice.

"Oh, Miss, come quick!" Jacqueline cried, racing toward her, hand on her heart. "He is dead! It is horrible!" Jacqueline reversed her direction as soon as she was certain that Abigail had heard her.

"Benjamin?" Abigail dashed to her side. "Has anything happened to Ben?"

"No, Miss," Jacqueline said as she led her mistress down the backstairs. "It is J.C."

Ashamed that she felt so relieved that it was not her beloved brother, Abigail asked, "J.C. is dead?" Skirts arustle, both women rushed along the hall to J.C.'s quarters.

"Oui," Jacqueline whispered. "Master Rodney hit him with his cane!"

"Rodney!" Abigail kept her voice low so that they would not attract anyone else's attention.

"Oui! I do not so soon forget the cane that hurt my chin." Standing in the doorway to J.C.'s room, Jacqueline pointed an accusing finger, "There it is on the bed."

Abigail paused in the doorway and steeled herself to look at yet another dead person. Taking a deep breath, she tiptoed toward the body on the floor and kneeled to examine it. Hair hid much of the actual wound, but not the indentation in the skull. "Well, he is indeed dead, and not just passed out as I'd hoped." She shuddered as she stood. "And you're right, Jacqueline. By the size of the wound, it was probably made by Rodney's cane.''

"Oh, the poor man,'' Jacqueline whispered, tears welling in her eyes. "Oh, Miss Danforth, what are you doing?''

Abigail had leaned across the bed and, without touching it, examined the silver head of the cane. "There is indeed black hair stuck here.'' She sniffed. "And I do believe I detect the odor of J.C.'s pomade.'' Standing straight, she peered at Jacqueline. "And how did you come to discover him? Why were you in the menservants' quarters?''

Withdrawing a slip of notepaper from her apron pocket, Jacqueline said, "It is Christmas, Miss. A time for the forgiveness. *Monsieur* J.C. has written me this, but I do not have it read to me until today.''

Abigail took the note and, after scanning it, looked at Jacqueline in astonishment. "It says that he wanted to marry you. That you'd be rich!''

"Yes, Miss,'' Jacqueline sobbed into her handkerchief.

"Do you suppose he had the Punjat's Ruby?''

"Oh, Miss Danforth, I don't know,'' Jacqueline wailed. "I cannot find him at the party, so I come here to tell him I have no love for him to marry with.''

Abigail frowned as she realized that there would be a need for only two tickets now.

"Miss Danforth?'' Jacqueline said timidly. When Abigail finally looked at her, she continued, "There is more you should know. Master Rodney was seen reading—''

"It's a lie!'' Rodney suddenly appeared in the doorway. "Whatever she's telling you, she's lying!''

Abigail motioned for Jacqueline to stand behind her, away from Rodney. "Have you come to retrieve your cane?'' she asked.

"My cane?'' His voice slurred. "What do you mean, my cane?''

"J.C. was killed with your cane, Rodney,'' she said. Noting his state of inebriation, she wondered if he could comprehend the import of her words.

"What?'' Rodney paled. "J.C. is dead?''

"Oui, Monsieur," Jacqueline cried. "And you were seen reading my *billet doux!"* She waved J.C.'s letter at him.

Striding to J.C.'s body, Rodney poked the limp form with his toe. "Ugh!" Pulling out a handkerchief, he covered his nose and mouth. "The man is dead."

Before Abigail could reply, Samuel appeared and stood aside as Andrew Danforth loomed in the doorway.

"What is all this commotion?" their father demanded. "Samuel here tells me that you smashed J.C. in the head with your cane, Rodney."

"But, sir—" Rodney stammered.

"Don't just stand there like a ninny, wiping your face like a girl!" Mr. Danforth roared. "Explain yourself!"

"Oh, Abigail, help me!" Rodney cried, flinging himself at the hem of her skirts. "I swear I didn't do it! I swear! Help me!"

Chapter Eight

Figures which can be made to coincide are equal or "congruent."

Euclid

"I absolutely forbid it!" Adamant, hands clasped behind his back, Andrew Danforth paced in front of the fire in his study, deaf to Abigail's entreaties. "I'll not have you play detective, and that is final. I don't care a fig if that fool brother of yours does believe you can clear him!"

Grateful that he had consented to see her alone, Abigail was careful not to sound quarrelsome as she asked, "What will happen to Rodney?"

It had taken no small amount of diplomacy to dismiss their guests without divulging that murder had been done in their midst. The police had come and gone, removing J.C.'s body. Max and Fergus had been properly distraught, however Abigail was now convinced that one of them, probably Fergus, had murdered J.C. Had they found the ruby as well? She had given both of them a wide berth, and had mentioned to no one that she knew of their plans for a premature departure. She knew full well that an untimely accusation with only her suspicions as evidence would be to no avail. She would have to somehow prove that he had done the dastardly deed. Time was short. But first she had to persuade her father to allow her to try. The household was quiet, except for father and daughter.

"After the holidays, the Inspector will assign someone to his case," her father replied.

"After the holidays!" Abigail exclaimed. "Must he languish in jail until after the holidays?"

"Nothing so vulgar as that, my child," he smiled. "I have oiled too many palms through the years. Shall we say that Rodney is under house arrest? He'll be permitted to attend your debut."

"But that is bribery!" Abigail exclaimed, forgetting her resolve to remain calm.

"Don't be naive, Abigail," he said testily. "That is how things are done in New York."

"I see," she said. Shocked to the core, she held back a quick retort. In an effort to calm herself, and before he could send her away too readily, skirts arustle, she strolled over to a Folion armchair—which sported carved lion's heads for arms and claws for feet—that reposed near his sculptured desk, and sat. "You intend to buy his freedom," she said as she arranged her skirts to fall as gracefully as possible. "Don't you care to find out if he is innocent, or whether the real culprit is caught?"

"What difference does it make if I care? It is unlikely that we will be able to find out the truth."

"And what if, pray, he were guilty?"

"It would be worth any price to keep a son of mine out of prison—even Rodney!" Hesitating, he strolled toward his desk. "Tell me," he went on without looking at her. "Do you think your brother is guilty?" He eased himself into the ornate chair behind his desk.

"If I may say, sir, I do believe Rodney is capable of murder," she replied. "But I do not know if he killed Mr. Driscoll's valet."

"Do you think he did it?" Sitting forward, he looked directly at her, his gaze piercing.

Unwilling to share her suspicions about the Messrs. Driscoll and Buchanan, she hedged, staring at her hands folded demurely in her lap. "Pray, sir, let me ask you," she said, glancing up at him from underneath her lashes. "What if he were not guilty?" Her grin was mischievous. "You are going to pay a great deal of money over the years for something you might not have had to pay for at all.''

''Hmmmmm.'' He sat back in his chair. ''True enough.''

''What if I were able to find him innocent?''

''You have a morbid thirst for the unusual, I must say, Daughter,'' he said. ''Do you actually believe you can?''

''I am certain of it, sir. If, that is, Gregory sees to it that your canes are polished every day.''

''Of course Gregory runs a proper house!'' he said, offended.

She looked directly at him. ''I cannot guarantee that it is not Rodney, but I know I can find out who did do it.''

''You astound me, child.''

''And if it should happen to be Rodney who is guilty,'' she smiled, ''at least you will be receiving that which you are paying for.''

Rubbing his chin thoughtfully, he said, ''You are correct in surmising that keeping your brother out of jail will be expensive.''

''And if I should discover that Rodney is not guilty, you wouldn't have to pay anything at all.''

''Now you remind me of myself!''

She laughed. ''If I were truly like you, sir, I'd have you pay me what you'd pay the politicians to keep him free. That is, if I discover that Rodney is not the culprit.''

His sigh was resigned. ''Can you find out who did it before the Inspector comes to call?''

''Before my debut,'' she assured him. ''But it is essential that we all see Mr. Gillette's play tomorrow, and attend his reception.''

''The man's just an actor, my dear, albeit the most famous in the country at the moment. I fail to see—''

''Trust me, sir.'' She stood, and once again her grin was mischievous. ''The money would be mine?''

On his feet in an instant, he stared at her for a long moment before holding out his hand. ''Done,'' he said, sealing their agreement with a handshake.

Before he could change his mind, Abigail went to the

door. Just as she reached for the doorknob, he called out, "Mistress Abigail!"

Bracing herself against his change of heart, she turned to face him. "Yes, Father?"

He cleared his throat. "Be careful," he said, and waved at her to be gone.

Abigail went straightaway to her rooms and penned a note to William Gillette, which Kinkade then delivered.

Like a seal at play, his Serene Highness Ahanti Khabir Abdulsamad slithered gracefully into his scented bath water in preparation for an evening at the theater. A blanket of bubbles covered him as he nestled into the fragrant warmth, content that the Punjat's Ruby would soon be his again. Aref had promised. He yawned mightily as a strange lassitude enveloped him.

Satisfied that the Nawab was unconscious, Aref stepped from behind the screen and, moving swiftly to the sunken tub, drained it. Toweling the inert form dry, Aref dressed him as though he were embarking upon a journey.

Perhaps if Abigail had not enjoyed *Sherlock Holmes* so much, Frederick might have enjoyed it more, although he did not admit to his motive, even to himself, when he voiced the single dissenting opinion. But it was the mystery of the Nawab's disappearance that had dominated the conversation as the party made their way to the Plaza and Gillette's reception.

Redolent with the scent of fresh-cut pine, the lobby was festooned with huge boughs of green and gilt, tied with thousands of crimson velvet ribbons. Mountains of brilliant red poinsettias were banked in every corner.

As a liveried servant bowed them into Gillette's suite, the gentlemen removed their gloves and, as punctilio demanded, placed them with their top hats and canes on small tables. Servants assisted the ladies with their wraps. The overly decorated room was obviously prepared for guests, but their host was not present.

Abigail and Maude had just settled themselves prettily on the sofa when the double doors flung wide. Cape swaying, pausing a moment for dramatic effect, William Gillette entered the room and strode directly to Abigail. "Ah, my dear Miss Danforth." With a conspiratorial wink that only she could see, he kissed her hand, which he continued to hold while he turned to the others and continued in his wondrous baritone, "Do forgive me for being late to my own reception. My horse threw a shoe and I had to get out of the cab and walk the rest of the way."

Maude fluttered her fan coquettishly.

Releasing Abigail's hand with obvious regret, Gillette greeted Miss Cunningham.

"I enjoyed your performance," Maude said. Much to Abigail's surprise, Maude blushed as she added, "Especially your new method of ending an act by dimming the lights instead of drawing a curtain."

"Yes," Andrew Danforth added after the obligatory pleasantries. "A deucedly clever innovation."

"Thank you, sir." Gillette smiled at Abigail. "You have an extraordinarily charming and persuasive daughter." With a sidelong glance at Frederick while still addressing Mr. Danforth, he added, "What a lucky man you are."

When it came his turn to be introduced, Frederick took an instant dislike to the actor. In person he seemed larger than life, as if he were still on a stage. In fact, Frederick decided, the drama the man created around himself was downright reprehensible. Beyond the scope of good manners. The stir he was producing at this very moment was example enough.

"How dreadful!" Gillette's voice boomed when introductions to Rodney, Max, and Fergus were formalized. "Have you had no refreshments?" He glared menacingly at the servants. "You must be famished!" He unbuttoned his cape and, with a flourish, shrugged it from his shoulders into the arms of the waiter. Seizing a platter, which was stacked with bite-sized honey-glazed morsels, he overplayed his host's role by passing it around personally. "You gentlemen must try these." Instead of proffering the tray properly, he thrust it upon them so that they had no choice but to take one. "I made them myself," he said as he continued to serve the men before the ladies. "They're my special Christmas rum balls."

It was impossible to refuse. Frederick got rid of his by putting it into his mouth at once. As did the others as Gillette passed the dish. Frederick had to admit it was delicious, but sticky. Before he could reach for his handkerchief, the servant had thrust a glass of champagne upon him. Fortunately, Gillette noticed something amiss, but, again, made too much fuss ordering napkins all around and replacing the glasses.

Abigail seemed to be enjoying the actor's performance. Smiling, she glanced in Frederick's direction as if to gauge his reaction. Smiling in return, Frederick swallowed his ire along with the champagne after Gillette's flowery toast, "To the belle of the Season." Since they'd arrived in New York, there had been little opportunity to be alone with her, even with Miss Cunningham as gooseberry. It would not do to appear too displeased in the face of her evident pleasure.

"I especially enjoyed the reality of the entire play, Mr. Gillette," Maude said.

"Ah, but Holmes smokes only a straight-stemmed clay or cherrywood pipe, not a meerschaum like the one I use on stage," Gillette replied as he signaled for Mr. Danforth's glass to be refilled. "But I discovered that I could not talk with one of those things between my teeth." Including his entire small audience in a sly glance, Gillette asked, "Would you like to hear a screaming joke on me?"

While Mr. Danforth encouraged him to continue and the others drew close, Rodney called for another glass of champagne.

"I hate to smoke!" Gillette said. "I don't even use tobacco. The prop man supplies me with some kind of weed that makes a lot of smoke for the effect only." While they commiserated with his situation, he removed his watch from his vest pocket. "Look at the time!" he exclaimed. "Here

I am enjoying myself so much, we'll be late for supper downstairs."

As the others filed into the corridor, Abigail tarried behind with Gillette. "How did I do?" he whispered, his eyes alight.

"You were superb, sir." She gazed up at him and winked. "I am forever in your debt."

"I shall work on charming your father at dinner," he said with a smile.

Trying not to watch them, Frederick broke away from Max and Fergus to reconfirm his long-awaited appointment with Mr. Danforth the next morning.

Tapping softly at Benjamin's door, Abigail let herself in. Moving slowly across the dark room, she approached the sound of his gentle snoring and upon reaching the bed, touched his shoulder lightly.

"Wha—?" he muttered, startled from his dreams. "Oh, it's you, Abby." Ben propped himself on an elbow. "How was the play? How was Gillette?"

"I'm sorry to wake you," she whispered, sitting on the edge of the bed. "It all went swimmingly, but I need your help."

"What can I do?" he yawned.

"I need you to chronicle my first adventure. I am about to unmask J.C.'s killer. And perhaps the killer of that unfortunate Miss Arrington as well."

"Oh, Abby," he sighed, resting his head on the pillow. "I don't know, love. I'm just too weary at the moment to answer. I'm not sure if it's because I've been awakened, or if my condition is permanent." His hand sought hers.

"I'm sorry, Ben. I should have waited until morning. I—"

"I'm flattered by your request more than I can say." He patted her hand. "May I let you know on the morrow?"

"Of course, Ben. Of course. Now go back to sleep."

Halfway to the door, she turned and called to him. When

212

he did not respond, she returned to his bedside. "Promise not to tell his Lordship I asked you?"

But Ben was breathing in that earnest manner which bespeaks slumber.

"Oh, Miss Danforth!" Jacqueline started guiltily. "You are back." Stiff from having dozed off over some sewing while awaiting her mistress's return, she stood slowly and, stifling a yawn, tried to stretch without appearing to do so. As she helped Abigail undress, she asked somberly, "When will the funeral be, Miss?"

"Arrangements are being made," Abigail said offhandedly, her thoughts still occupied with whether Benjamin would be able to help her. If for no other reason than to have Dr. Conan Doyle read of her success in solving the murder, and hopefully thereby recovering the ruby, she needed someone to chronicle her adventure. And clearly Frederick would not do. "I'll wear the mauve brocade dressing gown, if you please."

"I hope you will have the forgiveness for me," Jacqueline said as she fetched the requisite garment. "I do not mean to make the difficulties for Master Rodney."

"You cannot help seeing what you saw," Abigail said, slipping her arms into the dressing gown, which matched her heavily ruffled nightdress.

Watching with pride as Abigail tied the sash around her slim waist, she smiled. "The jewels of your mother have much beauty, Miss. Your father is most generous."

Sitting at her dressing table for the nightly hair-combing ritual, Abigail's dark eyes grew somber. "And so I seem to be upon the very brink of becoming that which I have so dreaded," she said to her reflection as much as to Jacqueline. "An object with no mind of her own, upon which expensive garments and furs are draped, decorated with gems, much like a Christmas tree." She sighed. "Brush faster, pray, and a single braid will do tonight."

Jacqueline was so astonished, she could no longer resist asking, "You do not wish to marry his Lordship?"

"Alas," Abigail responded dejectedly. "To marry seems to mean that I must give up any chance of being myself." She sighed once again. "Besides, Father will not allow it."

"But it is woman's nature to marry, Miss," Jacqueline said with a puzzled frown.

Abigail spoke to Jacqueline's reflection in the mirror. "You did not wish to marry J.C."

Jacqueline blushed.

"Now hurry!" Abigail said impatiently before she could respond. "I have much to do tonight."

Just as Jacqueline completed tying a ribbon on her finished braid, both women were surprised by a gentle knock on the door. "Who can that be at this hour?" Abigail frowned, as Jacqueline ran to answer it.

"*Monsieur* Stork!" Jacqueline exclaimed when she opened the door. "What do you want?"

"I must see Miss Danforth on a matter most urgent!"

"What is it, Stork?" Abigail called to him. "Shut the door, Jacqueline."

"May I see you alone, Miss Danforth?" He limped toward her.

"We are as good as alone, Stork." Abigail gestured to Jacqueline that she sit on the straight chair beside her bed. "Jacqueline will repeat nothing."

Seating herself, Jacqueline placed a finger to her lips in a vow of silence, while crossing her heart.

Abigail remained seated at her dressing table while Stork stood a few respectful paces away. "You needn't look any further, Miss Danforth," he said. "It was me that killed J.C."

Jacqueline gasped.

"And why would you do such a thing?" Abigail asked.

"He was blackmailing me, that's why!" Stork said. "I got that tired of it, I did him in."

"Is Aref next?" she asked, keeping her expression bland.

"Beg pardon, Miss?"

"If I recollect your situation properly, both J.C. and Aref were extortionists. If you've lost patience with one, I am

214

ready to assume that you will soon feel the same about the other.''

Stork's face reddened as he rubbed his ankle against his calf, unable to speak.

''While I shall most certainly take your confession into account when examining motives, Stork, I do believe I have a more scientific approach to use in detecting the criminal.'' She stood. ''You may go now.''

''But Miss—''

''That is all, Stork.''

''But Miss Danforth!'' Jacqueline said when she returned from letting Stork out. ''He makes the confession! You let him go?''

''After Stork told him about being blackmailed, Lord Hunterswell could have easily dispatched J.C. It seems to me that Stork was merely trying to protect his master.''

''His Lordship!'' Jacqueline gasped. ''But he is a nobleman. You cannot believe he would do such a thing! Can you?''

''I suspect everyone at this moment.''

''Kinkade, too?''

''He does not head my list.'' Abigail's gaze was piercing. ''Why would Kinkade kill J.C.?''

Jacqueline blushed and bowed her head.

''Well, bless my fanny feathers, if you haven't cut quite a swath, Jacqueline.'' Abigail laughed. ''Now fetch me Rodney's cane.''

''Yes, Miss.'' Jacqueline ran to the wardrobe. ''I hide it. You say it is important.''

''If Mr. Clemens's theory is correct,'' Abigail responded, ''that cane is going to help us catch a murderer.''

Jacqueline placed the wrapped parcel into Abigail's outstretched hands as gingerly as she would have passed her the Holy Grail.

''Now fetch me the box that was delivered from the Plaza Hotel,'' Abigail said as she went to her sitting room. Carefully unwrapping Rodney's cane, Abigail leaned it against her writing desk, lit the lamp, and seated herself by the time

215

Jacqueline returned carrying a large parcel wrapped in plain paper, tied with string.

Abigail studied her maid's face as she asked, "Are you positive no one saw you accept delivery?"

"Oh, no, Miss." Jacqueline crossed her heart and shook her head solemnly. "And no one sees me hide it too."

Too impatient to untie it, Abigail cut the string with scissors.

As Jacqueline stuffed the paper into a wastebasket, she could bear the suspense no longer. "What is in the box, Miss?" she asked. "A Christmas gift?"

"Better than that, Jacqueline," Abigail smiled, opening the box. "I am about to trap a murderer."

Jacqueline was dumbfounded as Abigail unfolded the tissue paper. "But that is just the glass for the champagne!"

"No, Jacqueline." Abigail handled the glass gingerly by the base. "These are extraordinary. See the tag tied to its stem?"

Jacqueline dutifully bent over to examine the square of cardboard, "What is written, Miss? Names?"

Abigail nodded. "Mr. Gillette staged a clever diversion when we visited him tonight, by personally offering a sticky sweet so that the gentlemen could not refuse to take one." Abigail giggled. "You should have seen his Lordship's expression."

"Miss?"

"Thus, each man's thumb and one or two fingers clung to these glasses for one precious moment."

Her frown deepened in puzzlement, Jacqueline shook her head. "Oh, Miss Danforth, I am so sorry. I do not see what the dirty glass has to do with catching the killer."

"You will soon," Abigail assured her. "Now fetch me some soot."

"Soot!" Jacqueline was horrified.

"Yes, some very fine soot, please. There's plenty in the grate."

"But I—"

"I don't need a lot." Knowing full well that she had

profoundly insulted her maid by asking her to touch the grate, which was the province of a lowly underhouse parlormaid, Abigail overrode her objections. "Here is an envelope," she said as sweetly as her increasing impatience would allow. "Just sweep a tiny bit into it."

By the time Jacqueline returned, Abigail had removed and unwrapped all four goblets. Magnifying glass in hand, she was peering intently at the stem of the cane in the light.

Her face a mask of disapproval, but unable to quell her curiosity, Jacqueline asked, "Please, Miss, what are you looking for?"

"Fingerprints, Jacqueline," Abigail said without looking up. "Fingerprints!"

Jacqueline was flabbergasted, "The print of a finger?" she asked, examining her fingertips.

"Yes, and it is going to be a long night."

With an air of injured dignity, Jacqueline asked as firmly as she dared, "Does Miss Danforth wish for me to ring for a maid to rekindle the fire?"

"No," Abigail responded, intent upon the magnifying glass. "Better to be chilly than alert the entire house. You might as well curl up on my chaise and try to get some sleep. I will need you to deliver some notes for me as soon as I am done."

From her vantage point across from the Plaza Hotel, Molly rubbed her eyes, blinked, and rubbed her eyes again. Glory be, if two baldheaded giants wrapped in yellow bedsheets didn't step out of a grand carriage. They wasn't from a circus, 'cause no swell place like the Plaza would of let 'em in, and in they had walked like they was some kind of high society. She'd watched real careful, expecting them soon out on an ear, but in they had stayed. Until now.

And didn't they have the Nawab between 'em? And him dragging his feet like he didn't want to come. She blinked again. "Holy Mother," she whispered to herself. "His Highness is fast asleep, he is."

Her whistle was shrill and startled more than one old nag as she rallied her crew to action.

Superbly mounted on one of Andrew Danforth's Morgans, Frederick indulged in a sprint upon reaching Central Park. Avoiding Max and Fergus after breakfast had been awkward, but the minor embarrassment had been worth it for this opportunity to see Miss Danforth alone. Her note had been brief, merely telling him when and where to meet her. He hoped that their tête à tête would pertain to her burgeoning feelings for him, but suspected that she more than likely wished to discuss that unpleasant business of J.C.'s demise. Could she have discovered so soon that her father had relented just this morning? Resuming the role of Dr. Watson could have its advantages he thought, as he maneuvered his mount so that he could survey the tree-lined terrain for her approach. It was unlike her to be tardy, but there was no one else about except a bewhiskered gentleman galloping toward him. On Crosspatches. When the gentleman reined in beside him, he cried, "Miss Danforth, is that you?"

Crestfallen that he had recognized her, Abigail asked, "How did you know it was me?"

"I didn't." Touching the tip of his top hat with his crop in greeting, he replied, "It was Crosspatches. He'd never let another ride him the way you do." As they kneed their mounts into a slow walk, he asked, "Why on earth are you dressed like that?"

"I had to talk to you alone. And that is impossible as you know—"

"I wish I could compromise you." Unable to keep his news a secret as Mr. Danforth had requested, he said impetuously, "Your father has granted his permission."

"I pray you, your Lordship," she responded. "I have something serious to discuss with you, and have gone to great lengths to be able to do so."

"What can be more important than how I feel for you? And now that we have your father's consent—"

"I know who murdered J.C."

218

"You do? How amazing!" he exclaimed. "I mean, how can you be so certain?"

"I found his fingerprints on the cane," she replied. "Or to be more accurate, the print of his thumb."

"Fingerprints?" Full of high spirits, merely teased by the sprint and eager for more, Frederick's horse was restive. Some of his attention was focused on controlling it.

"There is just one problem." Crosspatches began a high-stepping prance as if daring the Morgan to race. "Fingerprints are of no practical value in a courtroom." Holding Crosspatches in to a walk, she smiled, "That is why we must wrest a confession from the scoundrel."

"We?"

"Yes, if you please, your Lordship. I need your help. That is why I have asked you to meet me."

"And you shall have it!" He responded with alacrity. "Happy to oblige. Who did the dastardly deed?"

"I truly dislike telling you this." She paused until she had his full attention. "Your friend, Mr. Driscoll."

"Maximilian?" He wheeled his mount so sharply that he faced Abigail. "Are you trying to tell me that Maximilian killed his own valet?" he asked, incredulous.

She nodded.

"I don't believe you!"

"Fingerprints don't lie," she said calmly, drawing close beside him.

"Fingerprints? What twaddle!" His restless mount pawed the ground. "Every gentleman gets out of sorts with his valet from time to time, but not to the extent of killing him." He laughed. "Why I myself have more reason to kill J.C. than Max does!"

"I am not certain that all was as it appeared—"

"What do you mean!" He drew himself straight. "What are you implying!"

"Mr. Driscoll may not really be who he represents himself to be. Or for that matter, Mr. Buchanan."

"Mother had them checked," he said indignantly. "Max's grandfather—"

"Your Lordship." She paused as a pair of riders approached at a canter and glared at them for blocking the path as they passed. She continued, "I suspect that Mr. Driscoll not only knew about J.C.'s blackmailing Stork, I think he put him up to it! I believe they were all in cahoots with the Nawab to purloin the Punjat's Ruby."

"Miss Danforth, I most respectfully suggest that this silly detecting game of yours has gone far enough when you begin to slander the fine names of my best friends. Max saved my life."

Trying to soften the blow, she spoke gently, "That entire event was probably staged."

He glared at her coldly, as though she'd suddenly become his worst enemy.

"Did you know that Mr. Driscoll and Mr. Buchanan were leaving for Chicago this afternoon?"

"What?"

His surprised response confirmed everything she had suspected. Before he could ask her how she knew, she continued, "I sent an anonymous note to Mr. Driscoll, asking him to come here. It would not surprise me if Mr. Buchanan is not far behind."

Frederick reined the Morgan around, away from Abigail, searching the terrain. Frisky after remaining still for so long, his horse was at the gallop instantly when he spotted Max's mounted figure in the distance.

"Come back!" Abigail shouted after him. "He is dangerous!"

Racing straight toward Max, Frederick paid no heed.

Max waved in greeting as Frederick drew close.

Slowing his horse as he drew near, Frederick leapt from the saddle, grabbed Max around the shoulders, unhorsing him. Losing his grip on Max when they struck the ground, Frederick slid to the base of a tree.

Rolling with the momentum of his fall, Max landed on his knees nearby and struggled to his feet. He'd lost his hat in the fall and leaves were tangled in his blond curls. "What's the matter with you, old boy?" His grin was puzzled and his tone jocular as he dusted himself while stumbling toward Frederick. Standing over him, Max offered his hand.

With a growl deep in his throat, Frederick reared up and grabbed Max around the waist, shoving him a few feet backwards before pinning him to the ground. His face was contorted with anguish. "Why?" he gasped. "Why?"

"Why what, old man?" Max laughed, knowing full well what Frederick meant. His only hope of escape lay in his pretending to believe that Frederick was having a bit of fun at his expense. "Have you gone bonkers?"

"Stop your lying, Maximilian!" Frederick straddled Max's chest, pressing his arms to the ground. "I know you for the treacherous cad you are now!"

"Hey, I saved your life," Max said without resistance. "Have you forgotten? At great risk to my own." He feigned being insulted. "And you call me a liar?"

"You staged the entire incident." Frederick released Max's arms and kneeled back. "And you killed J.C."

As she rode closer to the two men on the ground with their horses in tow, Abigail was mystified by the masculine need to settle disagreements with fisticuffs. She was certain that Max would never talk under duress and was amazed to hear Max say, "Well, what of it?" He shoved Frederick away and regained his feet. "What if I did kill him? You'll never prove it."

"Oh, yes I will," Frederick said triumphantly. As he stood, he glanced at Abigail. "Your fingerprints are on the cane!"

Paying no attention to the stranger holding his mount, Max laughed heartily. "Has Miss Danforth been playing detective again?"

"Why, Max? Why?" Frederick brushed at the dirt on his knees.

"It was all J.C.'s idea," Max sighed, his expression ingenuous. "I told you I was broke. That's not news to you." Max paused. "That's my real crime, isn't it?" He looked directly at Frederick. "It's not done to be down and out, is it?"

"But you used me," Frederick said. "Why did you have

221

to pretend a friendship? Why couldn't you have just—'' arms wide, he gestured to the entire landscape of the park, ''taken my money? Robbed me? Why did you have to make me like you? And Fergus?''

''You used us, too,'' Max said. ''We did as much good for you as you did me. Isn't that what friends are for—to use one another? You're on the brink of winning the girl you want because of me!''

''Why did you kill J.C.?''

Max took a deep breath and, glancing at Frederick with a sly smile, he said softly. ''Because of you.''

Frederick just stared at him.

''He was threatening to tell you lies about me, your Lordship. The scoundrel was blackmailing me, too.'' Max watched Frederick closely for his reaction. ''We argued. It was an accident!''

Wanting desperately to believe him, Frederick turned away and strolled the few paces to the tree.

Max followed. ''I was going to tell you, honest I was,'' he said, his voice smooth. ''I was going to explain everything and prevail upon you to help me. But when it looked as though Rodney had done it, I hoped you need never know.''

''You deliberately used his cane?'' Frederick asked, back still turned.

''Mr. Danforth will pay his way clear,'' Max said. ''No one will be hurt.''

His thoughts in turmoil, Frederick leaned against the tree.

Stealthily, Max picked up a large stone and crept closer.

''Watch out, your Lordship!'' Abigail shouted. Dropping the reins to their horses, she spurred Crosspatches to the gallop. Charging behind Max, she struck him on the head with the stock of her riding crop. Wheeling Crosspatches around, she tumbled off, ran to his unconscious form and, bending over him, whipped off his cravat.

Mouth agape, Frederick watched her, too stunned to move.

Rolling Max over onto his stomach, she bound his hands behind his back.

"What are you doing?" Frederick protested at last. "Have you gone mad?"

Stepping away from Max to face Frederick, she brushed her hands. "He was trying to kill you," she said, breathless from her exertions.

"I don't believe you!" He was rigid with shock and disbelief.

Abigail began to lose patience. "He was about to bash you over the head with a stone!"

Shaking his head vehemently, Frederick shouted, "That's not true!"

"There is the very stone!" she shouted back, pointing to a large rock lying within Max's reach.

With great care, Frederick picked it up and, turning it over in his hand, stared at it uncomprehendingly.

"Why is it so difficult for you to see the perfidy of this man?" she cried.

His gaze was bleak. "Max and Fergus are my best friends."

"They were never your friends," she said firmly.

Frederick stooped and tenderly turned Max over.

Max groaned and opened his eyes.

"Max?" Frederick whispered, kneeling over him. "Tell me it isn't so."

Max felt as though his throbbing head might split asunder. Discovering that his hands were bound so that he could not rub at the pain, he lost control and twisted himself up to one elbow. "Oh, poor Lord Hunterswell!" His cultured accent disappeared. "Sliding out of your mother's womb onto a satin pillow! How bloody tragic!"

His face desolate, Frederick regained his feet.

"Not permitted to want for anything!" Max's voice was venomous. "Every whim satisfied! Oh, poor deprived bastard! My heart is supposed to bleed for you? You make me sick!" Straining against his bonds, he sat upright. "Who would want to be friends with the self-pitying likes of you? You are a crashing bore." Struggling to a kneeling position, he continued, "All you have is money!"

"Enough!" Abigail commanded.

"Who is that?" Max shook his head in an effort to clear it as he stood.

Before Frederick could reply, Abigail interrupted in a deep voice, "A good Samaritan."

Max bowed low, his refined accent returned. "Does the good Samaritan ride about the park bashing people on the head for amusement?"

Bowing in return, Abigail touched the brim of her hat with her riding crop.

"Most undignified my standing about bare-headed, don't you think?" Max continued affably. "Would the good Samaritan be kind enough to fetch me my hat." Turning to Frederick, he said, "Ridiculous being tied like this, old boy." His friendly manner was restored as though his outburst had never happened. "Untie me, will you?"

Frederick hesitated.

"Oh, come on," Max wheedled seductively, turning so that Frederick could reach his bonds more easily. "I promise I'll not try to escape." He winked.

"I think not," Frederick said.

With a growl, Max lunged, trying to butt Frederick off his feet.

Frederick sidestepped him easily.

Max staggered a few feet beyond him, but could not maintain his balance. Breaking his fall by twisting to land on his shoulder, his momentum carried him back to a standing position.

Frederick turned to face him.

Max crouched like a bull about to charge.

"It is over, Maximilian." Frederick stood still, trying to subdue his grief as the good Samaritan returned with their hats.

Max sauntered toward Frederick, "I suppose now you're going to marry Miss Danforth and play her Dr. Watson?"

Taking his hat from Abigail with a significant glance, Frederick said, "If she will have me."

Ignoring his remark, Abigail whispered, "Ask him about Miss Arrington and Mr. Buchanan's valet."

"I say, Max," Frederick cleared his throat. "Miss Arrington. Was that an accident?"

"You'll have to ask Fergie about that, old chap."

"And the accident at the Hunterswell's stables. Fergus's valet—?"

"The bastard was getting restive, old boy." Max said. "He was about to give the whole game away with his—" Max stopped himself.

"You killed him, too?" Frederick asked, when Abigail nudged him. "Or did Fergus?"

"I'm not going to say another word, your Lordship." Max glanced at the good Samaritan.

Positioning herself so that Max could not overhear, Abigail addressed Frederick, "Pray take Mr. Driscoll to the police station. I must return home before I am missed. Father can deal with Mr. Buchanan, if he has not already escaped. That he would desert Mr. Driscoll in his time of need should reveal the true nature of his character to you."

Frederick collected the reins to Max's horse and his own. "Seems that I owe my life to *you* now."

Concerned with getting home before her father discovered her absence, Abigail had reached the edge of the park before the questions began. Drawing Crosspatches to a halt, she wondered why Frederick had not braced Max about the missing ruby just now. Had he been too upset by the man's treachery? And when had he learned to speak French?

But then the answer struck her. *It was Stork, not his master, who held the missing clue.* Fuming at herself for not having asked him the vital question when she'd had the opportunity, she set her top hat securely and spurred Crosspatches into a dangerously fast race home.

Fergus did not bother to pack. When he could not find Max in his rooms after breakfast, he knew that the bastard had skipped, leaving him to take the rap. As he urged the cabby to a faster gallop, he did not notice the one-eyed urchin following close behind on a bicycle.

* * *

225

Bundled in dressing gown and lap robe, Ben reclined on his chaise by the fire. He placed the book he'd been reading across his lap when he heard the knock at the door. "Greetings, Rodney," he called out. "How nice of you to come."

"Bah, humbug." Rodney replied, remaining in the doorway. "You sent for me?"

"Did I?" Ben replied blandly. "I just thought it might be nice to talk. I didn't realize it would sound like a summons."

Closing the door behind him, Rodney swaggered into the room. "Father ask you to pry into my latest escapade?"

"I don't have the strength to spar with you, Rodney," Ben replied patiently. "Father gave me no instructions. I heard what happened Christmas Eve after I retired. I thought—"

"Oh, well, seeing as I'm confined to quarters, I might as well have a visit with my sickly older brother." From his spats to his neckcloth, Rodney was elegantly attired, but his petulant expression spoiled his appearance. "I've been busy since I've been home." Standing over Ben, he held out a bottle. "Want some?"

"What is it?"

"A little holiday cheer," he replied, handing the bottle to Ben while fishing into the inside pocket of his frock coat for a glass.

Raising his eyebrows, Ben whistled, "Father's best claret? No, thank you." He returned the bottle to Rodney. "Too early in the day for me."

"Suit yourself." Dragging the wicker armchair closer, Rodney slumped into it and spread his legs toward the fire. Pouring himself a generous dollop, he took but a moment to admire the wine's color before swallowing half of it. "Sometimes I wish I were a woman," he sighed.

"You cannot be serious!" Ben exclaimed.

"Never more." He filled the glass and deposited the bottle on the floor. "All they have to do in this world is look pretty."

Ben stared at him, aghast, unable to respond.

"Think about it, Ben." Rodney laughed, then drained his glass in a gulp before continuing, "All they need do is tinkle a tune or two on the piano, sing off-key, or embroider a trifle, and everyone thinks them a splendid sample of virtuous womanhood. And what did they do to deserve such praise?"

Ben shrugged.

Pretending to flutter a fan, Rodney forced his voice into a falsetto, "Nothing."

"You asked for Abigail's help soon enough!"

"Ahhhhh," Rodney growled, disgusted. "She can't prove anything. Father will pay."

Trying not to insult him, Ben asked as kindly as he could, "Did you do it?"

"No, brother dear. Which merely means that father will be paying a huge sum of money to bail out his second son for nothing." He filled his glass again. "Would that I were getting the money he's spending on me for something I didn't do." Rodney's laugh was ugly. "Just because he can't believe I am innocent."

"Wait a minute, Rodney," Ben said. "You can't blame father for wanting to protect you. If he hadn't paid, you'd be languishing in a jail cell right this minute, instead of swilling his priceless claret with me!"

"There you go defending him again." Rodney stood. "Don't you understand that he paid because he believes the worst of me!" he cried. "He thinks I killed a man!" Rodney stalked about the room, wine sloshing from the glass. "And you think I could have, too." He whirled and pointed his finger at Ben. "Well, I didn't!" With a sly smile he added reasonably, "Why should I want to kill my golden goose? He was going to lead me to the Punjat's Ruby. Or so I thought." With an evil chuckle, he drained the glass and held it high. "Oh, but I have had a jolly time leading Abigail a merry chase."

Ben stared at his brother with distaste. "How can you have nerve enough to ask her to help you after you deliberately set out to have her ridiculed?"

"Easy, brother, easy." Bending down to retrieve the bottle, Rodney refilled his glass, holding the bottle upside down to drain the last drop. "Because if anybody can find the real murderer, she can." Satisfied that he could not get another drop, he stood and tossed the empty into the wastebasket by the chaise. "But then dear father came along and put up the cash." His smile was bitter. "That's what really matters, you know. Money! Much more important than right or wrong. Who cares whether I did it or not?"

"I care, Rodney," Ben said quickly.

"Sure you do." Rodney finished the glass in one long swallow and smacked his lips. "You can say that. Words are cheap. But I know you doan like me and you doan care a fig if I'm innocent." He belched and wiped his mouth on the back of his sleeve. "Even if Abigail does find the killer, it won't make any difference. Father has already paid, rendering her useless. That's what I wanna be. Useless. Like a woman. Then nobody'd expect me to be anything, and father wouldn't be disappointed in me all the time."

Disgusted by his brother's rapid descent into maudlin drunkenness, Ben could not keep his feelings from his voice, "Yours is a most difficult disposition, Rodney," he said. "No one can please you. You're always so dissatisfied."

Bending over him, Rodney breathed wine in his face, "You would be, too, if you weren't fortunate enough to be the firstborn!" He turned away and, drawing a bead on the door, stalked stiff-leggedly out of the room, slamming the door loudly behind him.

With a luxurious stretch and yawn, Ben reached for his book. Since childhood, every encounter with his twin had ended with Rodney's being angry at him for being the firstborn. He had suffered torments, wishing he could make it up to him somehow. In the darkest hours of his illness, when death would have been a welcome release, he had finally realized that Rodney would actually have been pleased had he quit fighting and died. He then discovered that he was unwilling to satisfy his brother. With that decision had come the knowledge that there was nothing he would ever be able to say or do to assuage Rodney's jealousy. Knowing the truth had given him peace at last. A slight smile played at the corners of his mouth as he began to read.

Molly skillfully blended herself into the scenery in the alley near the Danforth's carriage house and stables to wait. Much to her dismay, by the time she had recognized Abigail leaving on horseback in her gentleman's disguise, she had been too late to stop her. Determined to see her before the morning passed, she kept a sharp eye out for her return. When, at long last, Molly saw Abigail return, she whistled their secret signal.

Stabling Crosspatches, Abigail hurried to their prearranged meeting place. Swiftly, Molly told her what she'd seen, personally, at the Plaza Hotel.

"Did you follow the Nawab and the two yellow-sheeted giants?" Abigail asked.

"Oh, yes, ma'am. Uh, sir. Uh, ma'am," Molly replied. "Me and One-eyed Jack, we followed 'em to the docks and saw 'em all climb into a row boat that was like to dump clean over, what with them all being so big. Jack came that close to gettin' himself caught at lifting a dinghy, so we couldn't row after 'em. They got real far out like they wasn't comin' back, but 'twas hard to tell, it being so dark and all."

"Aref was with them?"

"Oh, yes, ma'am, sir." Molly pursed her lips in thought. "If you don't mind, ma'am, sir. What with all he was toatin' and haulin', I'd swear that li'l Aref fella was helpin' them two nab the fat man."

"Who are you?" Ben demanded. "What are you doing in my rooms!" Standing, he reached for the intercom to call for help.

"Shhhh! Don't, Ben," the bewhiskered gentleman said.

"It is I, Abigail." She shut the door and tiptoed toward him.

"Abby?" Astonished, Ben slowly eased himself back on the chaise, peering at the figure approaching him. "Is that really you?"

"Yes," she said, pleased at the effect she was having upon him. "Lord Hunterswell—is on his way to the precinct with Mr. Driscoll. I must change and alert Father to apprehend Mr. Buchanan, if he has not already escaped. I know who has the Punjat's Ruby. I need you to chronicle my first success."

"Whoa, dearest Abby," Ben sighed. "Slow down." He frowned. "I have given your flattering request a great deal of thought."

"Oh, Ben," she said when he did not immediately continue. "You're not going to say no, are you?"

"I fear I must, my dear. I scarcely have strength to read. Writing, especially when I'd need to keep up with your adventures, is beyond me."

Trying not to let her disappointment show, Abigail shrugged, "I'll not press you, Ben. You know best."

"I am sorry," he said as they shook hands. "What am I doing?" he laughed as he released his grip and turned her hand so that he could kiss it.

"So am I," she said, withdrawing her hand. "So am I." Backing away, she started for the door. "Please forgive me. I have much to do. I must run."

Her hopes dashed by Ben's refusal, Abigail was distraught as she stealthily descended the stairs to her quarters. What good did it do to solve a mystery if she had no one to write about it? She had just turned into the corridor that led to her rooms, when she heard the unmistakable timbre of her father's voice—issuing orders to a servant—coming toward her. There was no time to reach her own rooms beyond Maude's door, which Maude kept locked when she was out. Heart pounding, she held her breath and prayed that Maude was in, preferring to risk her chaperon's reaction to her disguise than suffer her father's. To her vast relief, the door opened when she turned the knob, and she slipped into the room, without knocking.

Chapter Nine

I have seen too much not to know that the impression
of a woman may be more valuable than the conclusion
of an analytical reasoner.

> Dr. Arthur Conan Doyle
> *The Man with the Twisted Lip*

"Who is there?" Maude called out sharply. Appearing
from behind a door that concealed an alcove in her sitting
room, she looked Abigail over as if examining a horse. "And
who might you be?"

For one wild moment, Abigail was tempted to bluff her
way out, but removing her top hat, she whispered, "It is I,
Abigail. Father is in the hall. He mustn't see me dressed
like this!"

"I should say not!" Maude responded instantly. "Hurry!
You can hide in here." She indicated the door to her alcove.

Astonished by the contents of Maude's sanctuary, Abigail
momentarily forgot her difficulties. Bereft of feminine frills,
one wall was lined with filled bookcases and more books
were stacked on the window ledge and floor. One straight-
backed chair was pulled away from a plain desk. Even the
lamp shade was unadorned. Underneath the subtle fragrance of lavender there was a hint of tobacco smoke.

"Don't worry," Maude said. "No one is allowed in here.
Not even the servants. I have the only key."

"Thank you, Miss Cunningham," Abigail said fervently, removing her gloves.

"What have you been up to, dressed like that?" Maude asked casually. "I must say you had me fooled."

"Catching a murderer," Abigail responded with a smile. "Mr. Driscoll killed J.C."

"For that, you dressed as a man?"

"Pray, ring for Jacqueline, Miss Cunningham." Abigail ignored her question. "She can bring me my clothes. I can change in here, with your permission. Then if I am seen leaving your rooms, it would merely appear as though we'd been discussing my debut."

Without further ado, Maude left to use the intercom in her bedchamber. Abigail had spotted a small table set against the far wall that held two crystal decanters. She suspected that they held liquor, but that Maude would keep whiskey in her rooms was unthinkable! Shocked upon having identified bourbon, she was sniffing the cork to the second, when Maude returned.

"Would you care for a drop?" Maude asked, leaving the door to the alcove open so they could hear Jacqueline when she arrived. "You have had a busy morning."

"No, thank you," Abigail said nonchalantly, replacing the top as though she were in the habit of drinking hard spirits, but just did not care for any at the moment.

"You may sit in my chair if you like," Maude gestured toward the chair at her desk. When Abigail declined, she sat in it herself. "Why the costume?" Maude seemed on the verge of smiling.

"Dr. Conan Doyle frequently has his detective wear disguises," Abigail replied defensively.

"Tosh!" Maude exclaimed contemptuously. "Just being a woman is disguise enough."

"I cannot agree with you," Abigail said. "There are some things I simply cannot do as a woman."

"Drivel!" Maude replied. "You just need to learn how to make being a woman work for you," she said, watching Abigail remove her moustache and wig. "I had always scorned women who had the vapors. But when I was truly ill, I discovered how convenient female weakness could be.''

''Weakness, a convenience?'' Abigail was appalled.

Maude nodded. ''Something odious to be done? You do not want to do it? Just sigh that you're coming down with one of your sick headaches and retire to your rooms. Someone will come along and do it for you. And give you sympathy to boot!''

''But that is deception!'' Abigail cried.

''Look at yourself!'' Maude exclaimed. ''What do you call that?''

Abigail glanced down at herself, *''Touché.''* She laughed.

''I have been meaning to congratulate you on the way you've been handling your father,'' Maude said, her eyes revealing more warmth than Abigail had seen in them before. ''You have him eating from your hand. Flattery will get you anything, you know. Especially from a Leo.''

''A Leo?'' Abigail examined the bookshelves as she asked, ''What is that?''

''Your father's birth sign. I dabble a bit in astrology. But let us not go into that subject now. Your father is a perfect example of what I am talking about.''

''I am not insincere,'' Abigail said, insulted.

''He is really quite blind, you know,'' Maude watched Abigail with a speculative eye. ''Sees just what he wants to. He has made up his mind about me. And he'll not re-examine his opinion. He'll not check to see if I have changed. Or if he has. All I need do is sigh and start telling him details, which I know bore him, and he leaves me alone in disgust. Can you imagine how we'd get along if I challenged him? As a weak helpless woman, I am as good as invisible. I can do as I please.''

''Confined to your rooms?'' Abigail was not impressed.

''I hardly feel constrained when I am doing exactly what I wish to be doing.''

''And what might that be?''

''I write.'' Maude gestured at her cluttered desk. ''I've had two treatises published in one of the more esoteric journals on botany, which I daresay would interest you not a whit. At present, I am working on my second romantic novel, my first is making the rounds of the publishers as we speak.''

"How thrilling!" Abigail exclaimed. "I wish you luck."

Maude shrugged modestly.

"What a pity you must confine yourself to this cubbyhole," Abigail sighed heavily as she stacked some books near the small table to make a stool for herself. "Why can't we be more honest?"

"Being underestimated by others is the best disguise of all, Miss Danforth," Maude said quietly. "It can give you an inestimable advantage."

Seating herself gingerly on the pile of books, Abigail said, "Wouldn't it be easier all around if we were considered equal to men? Then there'd be none of this sparring for position."

"And take all the fun away?"

Abigail shrugged.

"You instinctively chose the best way to humor your father. Your tact in pretending to agree—"

"But I wasn't pretending!"

"Then why the clothes?"

Abigail had no reply.

"Tell me," Maude said more kindly. "Do you intend to marry this Earl of Hunterswell?"

"Oh, I don't know," Abigail sighed. "I just found out this morning that Father has granted his permission, but it seems that to love a man is to lose any chance of doing what I want to do. I'm not sure I am ready to give myself so completely."

"You're such a child," Maude said in a disparaging tone.

"I am seventeen!"

"I am not referring to your age, Miss Danforth." She looked at Abigail directly. "The love of a man and returning his love can be life's most rewarding gift."

Abigail stared at her, speechless, wondering what a thick-waisted spinster, with her hair pulled back so unfashionably, could possibly know about love.

"Mr. Tennyson said it better than my poor pen ever could." Maude's voice grew hoarse as she recited:

> 'O love! O fire! Once he drew
> With one long kiss my whole soul through
> My lips, as sunlight drinkest dew.' "

Emotions that she did not know she possessed, nor could she give them a name, stirred in Abigail's throat, sending shivers through her.

"Until you have known the physical love of a man, and returned it with your own passion, you have not yet come of age." Hugging herself, she smiled.

Awed by the radiance of the first smile she had ever seen Maude bestow, Abigail gulped and wished her to continue, too moved to say a word.

With a deep-throated chuckle, Maude said, "Oh, how he could make me moan in bed." She glanced at Abigail with a look that, again, sent shivers all through her. "I must tell you, I soon learned how to make him cry out as well."

Both women were startled by the knock on the hall door. Maude called out, "Who is it?"

They could barely hear Jacqueline's muffled voice.

When Jacqueline had been dismissed, with instructions to return with Abigail's clothes for lunch, Abigail rejoined Maude and said casually, "I didn't know you had been married."

"We weren't," Maude stated as she turned her head and smiled at Abigail.

Unable to take her gaze from Maude's transformed face, Abigail crossed the room to sit on the stack of books. The sight of Maude's sparkling eyes and dimpled grin was infinitely more shocking than the news of her lack of virtue.

"We were in our own fantasy world in San Francisco," Maude said. Suddenly her eyes went dead and her smile vanished. In a tone so flat that no feeling escaped, she said, "Charlie was killed on the way to the church. Murdered."

Abigail gasped, "How horrible for you!" She could feel the books begin to slide underneath her as she watched Maude open a box on the desk and remove a hand-rolled cigarette. She had to stand before she fell off her precarious perch when Maude lit it.

"The worst was losing the baby," Maude continued in the same monotone, a swirl of smoke enveloping her head. "It was said that I was delicate, that I'd grieved overmuch and lost him. I don't believe it. I was meant to have many babies. I was corseted too tightly. I have never worn one since."

"Does father know?" Abigail whispered.

"Of course not! Do you think he'd give me house room, if he knew I were a fallen woman?"

"You trust me not to tell him?"

"Isn't that obvious?" Maude's eyes were friendly, but the smile did not return. "You trusted me. Considering my own disguise, you took quite a chance on bursting in here dressed like that."

This time, Jacqueline entered without knocking. Aghast at the sight of Maude smoking, she remained in the sitting-room doorway, waiting for Abigail to join her in Maude's bedchamber.

Abigail paid no attention to her maid's disapproval as Jacqueline swiftly completed her toilette and departed; she was too busy chastising herself for having allowed her brother and father to mold her opinion of Maude.

"How pretty!" Maude exclaimed, looking up from the project on her desk when Abigail at last stood beside her, gowned in an elaborately beribboned afternoon frock.

"I thank you, Miss Cunningham," she said, wanting to apologize for not having made an effort to get to know her better sooner, but at a loss for words that would not embarrass them both.

"Lord Hunterswell loves you passionately, you know that don't you, Miss Danforth?" Maude said, apparently unaware of Abigail's hesitation.

"Yes, I know." Abigail sighed, the moment for apology lost. "Furthermore, after hearing you talk, I believe I could return those feelings." She blushed. "However, there is a singular lack of consistency which bespeaks deception, if I may paraphrase Conan Doyle. I wonder if I might further impose upon you and ask you to do a great favor for me, Miss Cunningham."

"Of course, Miss Danforth. Is it your father's sudden change of heart that troubles you?"

"No, that is secondary, my dear Miss Cunningham. Secondary."

"What then?"

"Would you please summon Stork? It is of vital importance that I discover the nature of the payment that J.C. extorted from him."

Ben stood and stretched. He had dismissed the servant who had carried off the remains of his tea, and was contemplating whether to lounge on the chaise or indulge in a full nap on the bed when his father entered. "An honor to see you," Ben smiled.

With a fresh rosebud for a boutonniere, Andrew Danforth looked dapper and seemed in splendid humor. "Quite a morning, I must say!" he exclaimed.

"Abigail told me about Max and Fergus. Rotten business for Lord Hunterswell." Ben indicated the wicker chair by the fire. "Did you find Fergus?" he asked as his father settled himself.

"The constable and I apprehended the varmint just as he was boarding the train for Chicago. He'll cool his heels in jail for what he did to his Lordship. I've seen to that."

"Wasn't Abigail clever to discover Mr. Driscoll's fingerprints on Rodney's cane?"

"Fingerprints? Balderdash! Mere toys, son. It took his Lordship's confronting the vile fellow to make him confess. Fingerprints are less use than my motor car. That contraption will never take the place of horseflesh. How could it? There are no decent roads to drive it on." Warming to his subject, he stroked his moustache, "Remember the fuss when bicycles first became so popular? All that costly road-paving just so people could ride a few miles? Can you imagine cobblestoning distances great enough to make the auto car worthwhile?"

Ben shrugged his agreement with his father's unassailable logic.

"Fingerprints fall in the same category." He pounded his knee for emphasis. "No court of law will ever take them seriously."

Ben sighed. "The city would be cleaner if the motor car did catch on. At least they don't pollute the streets."

"Fact of life, son! Won't ever be rid of horse droppings. And as for fingerprints," he snorted, "if a girl can figure out how to use them, they must be too simpleminded to be of any real value."

Ben nodded his head in agreement.

"Even so," his father continued magnanimously, "I've approximated what it would have cost to keep Rodney free for one year and have added it to her dowry."

"Her *dot?*" Ben replied. "Why not give it to her outright? She earned it."

"What use has Abigail for money?" he responded in a huff. "I provide all her needs. And generously, I might add."

"That is true enough, sir," Ben replied quickly.

"Besides," Mr. Danforth continued expansively, "I thought I'd let you know that I have relented and will allow Abigail to marry Lord Hunterswell. She shall have the wedding of the century!"

"Oh, that is jolly good, father!" Ben exclaimed, smiling. "What changed your mind?"

"Finally had a powwow with the gentleman and realized what a suitable match he'd be for Abigail," he said somewhat sheepishly.

His father's humble demeanor puzzled Ben, but he dismissed it, realizing how difficult it must have been for him to have changed his mind.

"Titled. Rich," his father continued. "And he promised that they would live at least six months of every year in New York!"

"Abigail must be thrilled." Unwilling to ask his father how he had resolved his concern over Abigail's ability to bear children, he said, "I am surprised she hasn't been in to tell me the good news herself."

"I haven't told her yet. His Lordship and I want to surprise her just before the guests arrive tonight."

"I won't say a word," Ben vowed. "Rodney must be pleased with our sister?"

"Laughed like a lunatic when I told him," his father replied, annoyed. "Accused me of believing he was a murderer!" he sighed heavily and stood.

Ben attempted to stand also, but his father motioned for him to sit while he poked at the fire, "I am past trying to understand that boy. It is difficult for me to realize that you two are brothers, never mind twins. If only he could be more like you. I no longer know what to do with him." He replaced the poker in its cradle.

"Perhaps if you liked him more?" Ben ventured.

"I find it difficult to like him." His father reseated himself and looked at Ben with a pained expression. "Now that's a hard thing to say about your own flesh, but how can you like someone who is always so dissatisfied? No matter what I do for him, he finds something wrong. I send him to London and he returns complaining about how troublesome Abigail was to chaperon. Imagine! Abigail causing trouble! She is the most docile and obedient daughter a father could wish for. A model of virtuous young womanhood."

Once again, Ben agreed with a nod of his head.

"I might send Rodney to North Carolina for a while. Do him good to learn the tobacco business." Mr. Danforth smiled. "Send Kinkade with him."

"I'd like it if Kinkade could stay with me. My health is on the mend, and I'll soon need someone full-time again."

"He'd serve me better watching over Rodney."

"Shouldn't Kinkade have something to say?" Ben asked.

"Why? He's just a servant," his father said. "I pay him very well to do what he is told!" Clearing his throat, he cast a sly glance at Ben. "Not still interested in that Miss Humbolt, are you, son? She didn't show such good judgment, chasing after those false friends of your future brother-in-law.''

"Actually, father," Ben smiled, "the lady did me a favor. I got to see just how fickle she is. And her voice! Did she always sing that flat? Or was I blind? Or deaf?" He laughed.

With an embarrassed guffaw, his father said, "Good! Looks like I'll only be losing two of my children, Benjamin, and though I'll be glad to see the backside of Rodney, I'm glad you don't have any plans to depart. Couldn't stand living in this house alone with that lifeless Miss Cunningham.''

"I'm feeling stronger every day, sir." Ben smothered a yawn. "All I want to do is be healthy enough to join you in your endeavors.''

"Thank you for that, son." Mr. Danforth stood and patted him on the shoulder. "Now you get some rest," he said, striding to the door. "I want you to feel like celebrating your sister's engagement tonight.''

During the fortnight he had been in the Danforth's household, Stork had never tired of using the wondrous servants' bath. The extraordinary luxury of a hot shower, which eased the ache in his ankle, made him feel of noble birth, instead of born to serve nobility. Refreshed by his daily indulgence, he had all but forgotten the horror on board ship, and his eyes were aglow with contentment as, standing at the mirror in his private cubicle, he whistled while adjusting his tie.

J.C.'s blackmail had been a hoax. His Lordship had told him of Mr. Driscoll's full confession. The young girl had not only not been pregnant, she'd been a dollymop, hired to seduce him. Stork's relief at the news far outweighed his embarrassment at having thus been taken in.

His admiration for Miss Danforth knew no bounds and he fervently hoped that she'd accept his Lordship's troth this evening. Hearing a knock on the door, and expecting Kinkade, he sang out, "Come in."

"What are you so happy about?" Kinkade's sonorous voice filled the tiny room as he closed the door.

Stork restrained himself from hugging the man, but pumped his hand vigorously while thanking him profusely for his good advice and regaling him with his Lordship's discoveries.

"Congratulations, old boy!" Kinkade's joy was unfeigned.

"I want to make you a proposition, Mr. Kinkade," Stork said seriously, his hand on Kinkade's shoulder as he looked him in the eye. "Come back to England with his Lordship and me. You're getting a rum deal here. I'm that sure I could get you a place. Probably even with a duke."

"I might just take you up on that," Kinkade replied, shaking Stork's hand enthusiastically in turn. "If things don't improve around here, I just, by golly, might do that."

Awaiting Abigail's presence in his study, Mr. Danforth was seated behind his sculptured desk. Frederick fidgeted in the Folion chair. Each covertly admired the other's white-tie perfection. The silence had become awkward by the time her welcome knock was heard.

Both men stood at once when Abigail entered, and extravagantly praised her pale blue gown, which was shot through with silver threads that shimmered when she moved. With a handle of filigreed silver, her fan of egret feathers was dyed the blue of her dress. Her mother's sapphires sparkled at her throat and ears.

His pock-marked face transformed by happiness, Frederick seated her at a chair pulled close to the front of her father's desk before taking his seat.

Mr. Danforth cleared his throat pretentiously. "I have some happy news for you, Daughter."

"Sir?" She gazed at him, her fan at rest in her lap.

"The Earl of Hunterswell has asked for your hand and I have agreed. I think he will make you a splendid husband."

Abigail showed no response whatever, but calmly turned her gaze to Frederick.

Mr. Danforth blinked with surprise at her cool reception of his glad tidings.

Unable to contain his excitement, Frederick stood. "You will make me the happiest man on earth if you will accept, Miss Danforth."

"I see." She smiled at him, pointing with her fan to an unopened box of his monogrammed chocolates on the desk. "You were waiting for my consent before you handed it over?"

"Whatever do you mean?" Lord Hunterswell asked, all color drained from his face.

Ignoring Frederick, she turned her attention once again to her father. "Will you still allow me to marry his Lordship when I tell you that he no longer possesses the Punjat's Ruby to trade me for?"

Reaching across the desk, Frederick grabbed the box of candy and tore it open.

"It is no longer in there, your Lordship," she said coolly.

"What have you done, Miss Danforth?" Frederick cried, thrusting the opened box toward her.

"What is going on here?" Mr. Danforth sputtered.

"The ruby is no longer in Lord Hunterswell's possession, father."

"Explain yourself, Mistress Abigail!" her father thundered.

"I removed it from its hiding place," she responded, waving her fan ever so slightly.

Collapsing into his chair, Frederick looked at her in utter amazement. "How did you guess?"

"I do not *guess,* your Lordship." Indignation crept into her tone, which she belied with a coquettish flutter of her fan. "While you were quarreling with Mr. Driscoll, I thought it odd that you never once asked him about the missing ruby. I was prepared to ask him many questions about his connection with the Nawab Abdulsamad. When you did not do the obvious yourself, I became intrigued by your silence."

"I could have told you that Mr. Driscoll had stolen it, and you'd never have been the wiser," he groaned. "Certainly, your father would never tell."

"Not quite." She stood.

Both gentlemen rose to their feet instantly.

Abigail wandered to the fire and, turning to face them, she continued, "Jacqueline just happened to overhear Stork telling you of his having been blackmailed. After your extraordinary reaction of laughter, she thought she heard you say you must go somewhere *tout de suite*—in a hurry. So she left. Even before the incident with Mr. Driscoll, I had begun to wonder why you had suddenly spoken French. Or for that matter, what had been so funny. After all, blackmail is serious business. The one thing I could deduce that would be that amusing is if you, your Lordship, had stolen the Punjat's Ruby yourself, before Stork'd had a chance to take the box."

"You don't think that I—" Frederick began.

Holding out her hand to stop him, her voice was firm as she said, "And that you were not going anywhere *tout de suite,* but were telling Stork that you had hidden the Punjat's Ruby in a box of *sweets!*"

" 'Pon my word, Mistress Abigail!" Mr. Danforth exclaimed.

"What have you done with it?" Frederick asked, fearing her answer.

"Oh, it is quite safe," she replied. "On its way to London."

"You are clever indeed, Miss Danforth," Frederick said, concealing his despair. "I suppose you have also figured out how it was done?"

"Once I knew Stork's role in the matter, solving how you did it became simple," she replied, strolling back to her chair and sitting once more. "It depended on some very careful timing. Correct me if I'm wrong, your Lordship. Your father knows nothing of this?"

Frederick shook his head in amazement as he sat. "You are uncanny," he said.

Mr. Danforth lowered himself into his chair, spellbound.

"When I reviewed all of the events in my mind, once more," Abigail continued, "I kept returning to the incident in my cabin wherein the marchioness fainted. The marquess's reaction gave me the clue."

"How?" Frederick asked.

"Your father's first reaction was to ring for help. He would not have remained in the cabin had I not produced the smelling salts. Therefore, I concluded that when she had fainted upon discovering that the ruby was missing, your father had probably left your mother quite alone while he sought help. You must have given her a copy of the key that would reveal the idol in the box and, while he was out of the room, she used it, and hid the ruby in her gown. When your father returned to his bedchamber to retrieve the case, she gave the idol to you."

Frederick shook his head, speechless.

"You don't say!" Mr. Danforth exclaimed. "The marchioness herself!"

"It was cunning of her to ask me to recover it." Abigail smiled, her eyes warm with pleasure. "Threw me off the scent for some time."

"Mother won't like this," Frederick moaned. "Oh, she'll keep her word and pay you," he hastened to assure her. "She'll admire you all the more, Miss Danforth. It is not often that my mother is bested."

"I am in her debt, your Lordship," Abigail responded.

Frederick turned to Mr. Danforth, "This does not mean that our betrothal is off, sir, does it?"

"Under the circumstances," Mr. Danforth stood, "I do not see how I can permit the match."

"What are your feelings, Miss Danforth?" Frederick asked urgently.

"I shall obey my father," she replied demurely.

"But Mr. Danforth—" Frederick stumbled to his feet, distraught.

"There is no more to say, your Lordship," Mr. Danforth said in his most overbearing manner. "Our business is at an end!"

"Not quite, if you please, Father," Abigail said.

"What else could there be?" Mr. Danforth asked. "I forbid you to marry Lord Hunterswell. Like the dutiful daughter you are, you have agreed."

"If you will permit me, sir, you have forgotten one small detail," she replied softly.

"And what might that be?" he asked.

"The terms of our wager, sir. About Rodney?"

"You cannot mean that you want to collect?" Mr. Danforth said huffily. "Whatever for? You have no need for your dowry now."

"With your kind permission, Father, I would rather fancy a long trip," she sighed unhappily.

"Oh, my poor dear child, of course. Of course!" He glared at Frederick disapprovingly. "How thoughtless of me," he said, going to her side to pat her hand sympathetically. "You must be dreadfully disappointed at this wretched turn of events. A world tour will set things right." Not in the least wishing to accompany her, yet trying not to let his reluctance show, he added, "Where shall we go?"

"Oh, sir, I would not dream of disturbing your busy schedule to ask you to come with me." Abigail gazed up at him appealingly. "Could Miss Cunningham act as my chaperon?"

"Why, Miss Abigail, do you mean to say you prefer the company of that dried-up old maid?" Mr. Danforth said in a jocular manner, trying to conceal his relief that she did not require his presence.

Frederick cleared his throat, "Mr. Danforth, may I please have your permission to speak with Miss Danforth alone, sir?"

With eyebrows raised questioningly, Mr. Danforth looked at Abigail.

"I beseech you, sir," Frederick continued when Abigail did not readily respond. "If I am to say good-bye to your daughter forever, I cannot just walk out of the room like this. I promise not to press you. Or her. Just one last word of farewell."

"Abigail?" Mr. Danforth said, his expression making it clear that she could do as she desired.

When she did not make a move to join him, Mr. Danforth shrugged. "I'll see to our guests." He turned to go. "The door must remain open," he said gruffly as he left.

The moment her father was gone, Frederick hurried to Abigail's side and fell to one knee. "Oh, Miss Danforth," he cried, reaching for her hand. "I do not understand. I love you. I want you. If you want me in return, why did you take the Punjat's Ruby? Why didn't you talk to me before you sent it away?"

Her body taut with anger, Abigail pulled away. Striding to the hearth, she whirled to face him. "You tried to buy me, like a . . . a . . . a *horse!*" she exploded.

"Buy you!" he exclaimed. "Oh, Miss Danforth, no!" He regained his feet. "It was not like that at all. I did not know how to woo you. I went about it the only way I know." Hands apart, imploring, he rushed to her side. "I fail to see what I did that was wrong."

"Did it not ever occur to you to be direct with me?"

"Men have always given beautiful gifts to the women they love," he said, completely bewildered by her fury. "And they also attempt to do great deeds to capture their affections."

"How dare you make fun of me!"

"What?"

Swiftly, Abigail moved away from him to stand behind her father's desk. "How you must have laughed at me, all the while you pretended to be Dr. Watson while I searched that ship. And all the time, you had the ruby!"

"Oh, Miss Danforth! That was Rodney's idea. So I could be near you. I swear I never laughed at you!"

"How can I believe you? Even I know how amusing I must have seemed!"

"But I couldn't tell you. Mother didn't want you implicated."

"Because of the games you and your mother invented, an innocent girl and two men are dead. Two others are in jail!"

"They would have come to a bad end in any case!" He

247

faced her across the desk. "They were deceiving me. This is different."

"How is this different? You were deceiving me!"

"But I did it for you, Miss Danforth!"

"And in the process you have made me feel like one of your trophies!" Even though she realized that her attempts to make him understand were futile, Abigail persisted. "Were you going to hang me on the wall with the tigers in the game room?"

Appalled, he gasped. "How can you think that of me?"

"What must you think of me?" she replied, her voice deep with anger. "I am a person. Not some ornament you can purchase. I have ideas of my own."

"That is why I admire you so."

Utterly frustrated, Abigail glared at him.

Hands planted in the middle of the desk, Frederick leaned forward, almost touching her. He whispered, "I do love you so very much, Miss Danforth."

Abigail's anger dissolved. "Oh, dear Lord Hunterswell," her voice betrayed her sadness, "I know you are not a beast. Nor did you intend to hurt me. And yet I feel mortally offended by your actions. Perhaps we are just caught in something I am too young to comprehend that drives us apart."

"But mother thought—"

Abigail shook her head. "You must tell the marchioness that I cannot be bought," she said softly. "I'll wager that will surprise the dear lady."

As she spoke, Frederick had been slowly edging himself around the desk and was standing quite close.

Sensing his presence, Abigail shivered, struck with the irrelevant question of what his arms would feel like were he to hold her, what his lips would feel like upon hers.

His voice husky with passion, Frederick asked, "Can you, will you, forgive me?"

"There is nothing to forgive, your Lordship." Her knees trembled, her voice was faint.

"Please, I beg you." Taking her hand gingerly, he asked, "May I kiss you good-bye?" His gaze wandered hungrily to her mouth. "Just one small kiss." His lips grazed her hand. "One small kiss to last me a lifetime."

Like a brush fire, a tingling swept through Abigail, setting a pulse pounding in her throat. Completely unnerved, she snatched her hand away and fled.

Too stunned to call after her or give chase, Frederick stared at the open door. Slowly, he turned and stumbled to the fire and stared into it, sightless. Tears that began as a trickle soon ran in a flood, "Oh, Miss Danforth," he sobbed, "what have I done?" Pounding the mantelpiece with his fist, he sobbed, "What have I done? What have I done?" He gasped for breath. "Oh, Miss Danforth," he cried. "I have lost you!"

Eager to see his daughter in the new ermine cape he'd bought for her debut, Mr. Danforth was delighted with the chill in the air on New Year's Day as he waited for Abigail in the foyer. Glowing with pride, he watched her descend the stairs in her ravishing gown of white. As she drew near, he asked, "You are not too unhappy that the Earl of Hunterswell is not here tonight, are you, my dear?"

"How can I be sad when you have been so generous, Father?" Her smile was radiant as a servant draped the fur wrap around her shoulders.

"He won't be the last man in your life, Mistress Abigail," he reassured her. "They'll be lined up at the ball tonight to take you away from me."

"Now, Father, you know I am only interested in my forthcoming journey with Miss Cunningham."

Mr. Danforth looked at her appraisingly. "It is a pity you weren't born a man," he said with an intensity that startled her.

"I do not understand your meaning, sir."

Proffering his arm, he said, "Why you might have become a great detective!"

Epilogue

"The whole is greater than the part."
Euclid

Gentle Reader,

I beg your indulgence for my haste in penning these last few words. Preparations for our impending journey have consumed much of my time and I have scarcely had a moment to complete this manuscript. The Humbolts have lent us their private varnish for our journey to San Francisco Tuesday next. I have an old score to settle there and Miss Danforth has promised me her assistance.

Kinkade will accompany us, make travel arrangements, attend the luggage, and act chauffeur. I daresay we will be traveling more than he anticipates. Unbeknownst to her father, Miss Danforth received a generous check from the marchioness. Good sport, that one.

Jacqueline is going to have her tiny hands full, but she has energy enough, and more, to go the distance. I only wish that she and Kinkade would quarrel less.

The Nawab Abdulsamad and the beautiful Aref have vanished. Their whereabouts is our only remaining mystery. At Miss Danforth's behest, Molly and her crew will receive money for a decent education. Benjamin, who is on the mend, will attend to details. Rodney has not drawn a sober breath since learning of his father's plans to pack him off to Durham. Perhaps they will be able to dry him out.

Dr. Conan Doyle cabled his congratulations to Miss Danforth. He received the Punjat's Ruby in good condition, and will see to it that the marchioness returns it to the Prince of Wales, with the utmost discretion, of course.

Although I feel confident that everyone answered my conundrum (which letter follows O, T, T, F, F, S, and S), I do dislike loose ends. For those of you who might not have figured it out for yourselves, the answer is E (for eight).

Maude Cunningham
New York City
January 1900

ESPIONAGE FICTION BY WARREN MURPHY
AND MOLLY COCHRAN

GRANDMASTER (17-101, $4.50)

There are only two true powers in the world. One is goodness. One is evil. And one man knows them both. He knows the uses of pleasure, the secrets of pain. He understands the deadly forces that grip the world in treachery. He moves like a shadow, a promise of danger, from Moscow to Washington—from Havana to Tibet. In a game that may never be over, he is the grandmaster.

THE HAND OF LAZARUS (17-100, $4.50)

A grim spectre of death looms over the tiny County Kerry village of Ardath. The savage plague of urban violence has begun to weave its insidious way into the peaceful fabric of Irish country life. The IRA's most mysterious, elusive, and bloodthirsty murderer has chosen Ardath as his hunting ground, the site that will rock the world and plunge the beleaguered island nation into irreversible chaos: the brutal assassination of the Pope.

Available wherever paperbacks are sold, or order direct from the Publisher. Send cover price plus 50¢ per copy for mailing and handling to Pinnacle Books, Dept. 17-338, 475 Park Avenue South, New York, N.Y. 10016. Residents of New York, New Jersey and Pennsylvania must include sales tax. DO NOT SEND CASH.